FOR Elise

OTHER BOOKS AND AUDIO BOOKS

BY SARAH M. EDEN

Courting Miss Lancaster

The Kiss of a Stranger

Seeking Persephone

Friends and Foes

An Unlikely Match

Drops of Gold

Glimmer of Hope

As You Are

FOR Elise

A Regency Romance by

Sarah M. Eden

Covenant Communications, Inc.

Cover image © Dave Curtis, courtesy Trevillion Images
Cover design copyright © 2014 by Covenant Communications, Inc.
Author photo © 2014 Claire Waite Photography

Published by Covenant Communications, Inc.
American Fork, Utah

Printed in the United States of America
First Printing: September 2014

20 19 18 17 16 15 14   10 9 8 7 6 5 4 3 2 1

ISBN-13: 978-1-62108-787-8

To Zelda, queen of pliers, and Bob, king of citrus,
for a lifetime of love, support, and encouragement.

Chapter One

May 1815
Cheshire, England

MILES LINWOOD'S ENTHUSIASM FOR LACE was decidedly lacking. Fortunately for his sister, his patience was not.

"What do you think of this particular pattern?" Beth held up a corner of white lace. It looked precisely like every other length of white lace he'd ever seen, including the dozen or so she'd asked his opinion of that day alone.

Still, a brother had to indulge his sister or risk earning her lace-fueled wrath. "It is very nice, Beth."

"Nice?" she scoffed. "Have you no greater compliment than 'nice'?"

"I did say *very* nice."

Beth was clearly dissatisfied.

Miles smiled. "Forgive my ignorance of lace and its finer qualities. I am certain your Langley would not have proven such a disappointment. But you know your bumbling brother too well to expect anything but woeful ignorance out of me."

"Yes, my Langley is rather wonderful." Beth summoned the same besotted smile she'd first produced the day she'd been introduced to the gentleman she would later marry. The passage of seven years obviously hadn't lessened their attachment to one another. "And you, dearest brother, are the bumblingest marquess in the entire kingdom."

Her teasing barb brought a smile to his face. "Perhaps I ought to distribute apologetic leaflets throughout England, reminding everyone that I am also the *newest* marquess in the entire kingdom."

"Toss in the fact that you are also unwed, and the ladies, at least, will forgive you almost anything."

"Are ye nearly ready?" The shop proprietress unceremoniously spoke across their conversation, eyeing them both impatiently. "I've other work to see to."

Miles couldn't manage an immediate response. The impatient interruption was so unexpected from a shop owner toward a customer.

Beth, however, pulled her dignity about her like a battle cloak and gave the woman a rather freezing look. "By all means, return to your other work. If I require your assistance, I will inform you."

The woman seemed to realize she'd been rude and quickly curtsied before scurrying back behind the counter.

"I don't remember your being so formidable, dearest sister," Miles observed under his breath after they were alone once more in the corner of the shop. "You are absolutely terrifying. I feel an overwhelming need to pull out a pen and parchment and write out 'I will not be rude to Beth Langley' one hundred times using my finest penmanship."

Beth shook her head in amusement. "I have missed your teasing these past years, Miles. The West Indies are so very far away."

He had missed her as well. He had missed everything about England. "I am here now, though, enjoying my favorite activity—indeed, every gentleman's favorite pastime."

"Dare I ask what that is?" Beth raised an eyebrow.

"Why, admiring lace, of course. This one, for example" —he fingered a length of white lace— "is simply divine. Such artistry. Such fine loopingness."

"*Loopingness?*"

"That is the term true connoisseurs use," Miles insisted. "Surely you knew that."

She swatted at him playfully. Miles wandered to the shop windows. They hadn't intended to stop in this tiny town, but a broken wheel on Langley's traveling carriage necessitated it. The town was too small for any diversions other than standing about in the draper's pretending to be enamored of laces and ribbons.

"Ye'll have to wait," the proprietress hissed at someone. "I've got payin' customers in the shop now."

The proprietress, red in the face, shooed away a very humbly dressed woman and her little girl. The two, clearly poverty stricken, slipped quietly into the far corner of the large shop.

As if feeling Miles's gaze, the child, likely no more than three years old, looked over her shoulder and directly at him. Her gaze dropped, but only for a moment before she raised her eyes to him again. He could hardly make out her features, hidden as they were behind an oversized bonnet, but he knew she was looking at him.

Miles smiled at her. She tipped her head a bit to the side, still watching him closely from across the room. He waved, but she didn't return the gesture. She held tightly to her mother's hand without looking away from him for even a moment. What was it that had captured her attention so entirely?

"Is this not the oddest pattern you have ever seen on a muslin?" Beth said from somewhere beside him.

"Yes. Odd," he answered without really seeing it.

Beth moved away again, continuing her perusal. The little girl still watched Miles. Near-black curls hung about her shoulders. He smiled again. Was she smiling under the shadow of her bonnet?

He leaned against the wall near the window, keeping his attention on the child and her mother. Only the little girl faced him. He couldn't see anything beyond her mother's back.

"Well, I have seen about all I care to see in here." Beth rejoined Miles at the window. "Shall we rejoin Langley on the hope that a working carriage is awaiting us?"

Miles nodded.

"Are ye leavin'?" the proprietress called after them.

"Indeed," Beth replied before gliding through the door Miles held open for her.

Before Miles let the door close, he glanced back in time to see the shopkeeper turn to the mother and child in the corner and bark out, "Might as well come dig through the scraps now. Jus' lost me most promisin' customers."

Dig through the scraps. Poor little thing.

"Where shall we go now, Miles?" Beth linked her arm with his. "Perhaps there is a milliners. Or a haberdashery."

"Perhaps," Miles muttered.

Dig through the scraps. The idea sat like lead on his heart. Somehow, he couldn't bear the thought of that little girl living in such want. If he put his mind to it, he could devise a way to discreetly discover her name and her most pressing needs. His newly acquired wealth ought to be put to some good.

"What has you so solemn, Miles?" Beth asked. "That last muslin was rather horrifying, but this seems an overreaction."

He attempted to smile at the jest, but even after four years of separation, she knew him too well to be fooled.

"The little girl in the shop?"

Miles hadn't realized Beth had even noticed.

"They both looked so frail and ragged," Beth said. "And the little one was so intent upon studying you."

"I find myself unable to rid my mind of her," he said.

"And now you are wondering what must be done to help the poor child. Sometimes, Miles, there is nothing you can do."

He knew all too well how true that was. "I wish I could though."

Beth squeezed his arm. "You never could resist a girl with dark curls."

A girl with dark curls. For him, that description would only ever bring to mind one person. "Sweet Elise," he whispered.

His heart would never stop breaking for her. His dear, young friend he'd lost at such a tender age. How he missed her and mourned her and wondered what might have become of her after all these years.

"Do you remember the time we decided to sell hot chestnuts to the neighborhood children?" Beth asked as they began walking toward the smithy.

Miles remembered well. "We burnt at least half of our inventory. So we attempted to sell the remainder at twice our original asking price."

"And Thomas Hatfield accused us of extortion and who knows what else because our prices were so ridiculously high." Beth took up the retelling. "Then Elise gave you her two pence, probably all the pin money she had, and said she wanted to buy a chestnut. But you, softhearted little boy that you were, couldn't bring yourself to sell her one at such an unfair price, and the whole scheme came down around us."

"She ruined more of my mischievous plans than Mother, Father, and Eton combined." Miles couldn't look back on those years without sadness mixing with the laughter. "She either made me feel guilty as the devil or got herself into a scrape before I had a chance to get myself into one, and then she begged me to save her from whatever she'd done."

"And you couldn't resist her hopeful smile."

Miles's smile disappeared, as did the light banter between the two of them. "She still haunts me."

"I know." Beth leaned her head against his arm. "I think of her often."

"I think of her every day. Every single day."

The three of them had grown up practically as siblings. Miles had taught Elise to swim. In return, Elise had taught him to crochet, quite against his will. He'd spent the harrowing days of his mother's final illness with Elise at Furlong House. She was his most faithful correspondent while he was at Eton. They had been the very best of friends.

But when she was fifteen, Elise had disappeared. All efforts to find her had proven fruitless. She'd simply vanished.

"Miles," Beth urgently whispered. "Look. Just there." She motioned with her head.

A few paces ahead, down a narrow side street they'd only just reached, was the girl he'd seen at the drapers. She was watching him again. Miles offered a little wave. The girl and her mother stopped at one of the many doors along the small street. While her mother unlocked the door, the little girl continued to look at him from beneath her raggedy bonnet. Then, hesitantly but with an air of desperation, she reached out toward him as if begging him to come help her.

Miles's heart cracked. Such need and weight for so tiny a child.

"I mean to see if I can do anything for them," he told Beth.

"They might not be willing to accept it," Beth warned him. "Pride is a difficult thing. And men of position are generally viewed with suspicion amongst the lower class."

"I have to at least try," he said.

"Of course you do." She squeezed his arm. "The inn is just at the end of this road. You do what you can. I'll wait for you there."

Miles waited until he saw Beth enter the inn before turning back to the humble door the little girl had gone through. He could hear low voices inside. An unexpected surge of nervousness clutched him. How would he be received? The effort might be futile.

But that little girl, who reminded him so very much of his long-lost Elise, needed him. He felt in his bones that she did. He couldn't turn his back on her.

He summoned his resolve and knocked firmly. He'd simply appeal to the girl's parents to allow him to help. Surely they would set their pride aside for the sake of their own child.

The hinges protested as the door slowly opened. Miles arranged his features in as unthreatening a look of friendliness as he could manage. The girl's mother peeked around the door.

"Good afternoon," he said. "Is—"

He choked on the words when she looked up fully into his face. She was likely no more than twenty, with thick, dark-brown curls and blue eyes. No freckles spattered the bridge of her nose, and her hair was pulled up instead of hanging about her shoulders, but Miles knew her in an instant. His heart stopped even as his mind spun violently. All color fled from her face. She took a step backward, staring at him as though she'd seen a ghost. In a very real way, *he* actually had.

His lips moved silently as he searched for words. Any words. In the end, all he could whisper was her name. "Elise."

Chapter Two

He reached out, desperate to be certain she was real. But she moved out of his reach.

"Do you not recognize me?" Miles couldn't countenance that she wouldn't. Other than the usual differences between a nineteen-year-old and a barely twenty-four-year-old, he hadn't changed much since they'd last seen each other.

Her mouth tightened. She didn't look away, but neither did her expression change from bone-deep apprehension. *Apprehension?* Was she not at all happy to see him?

"Bring the young man in, Ella," a quavering voice instructed from inside.

The door opened wider, and "Ella" stepped aside to allow him room to pass. He doffed his hat and stooped as he crossed the threshold. After a moment, his eyes adjusted to the relative dimness of the damp interior. The space was small and sparsely furnished.

An older woman sat bundled in shawls in a rocker by the fire, studying him. Miles offered an inclination of his head and an uneasy smile. His gaze returned quickly to Elise. He could hardly believe she stood so near, that he'd found her after so many years. Other than a fleeting look of alarm when their eyes had first met, Elise had still given no indication that she knew him at all.

"Well, child," the older woman said. "Do you mean to introduce me, or will you be standing there like you don't remember your manners?"

Elise stepped forward but didn't immediately speak. She looked like a cornered fox, poised for flight but afraid the slightest movement would bring the hounds down on her. Her eyes locked with the silver-haired woman, who nodded.

"This here's Mama Jones." She motioned to the seated woman.

Miles tried not to gape. Elise sounded so different. Her cultured and refined accent had entirely disappeared. She spoke like a tenant, like a lower servant. She'd made a completely inept introduction, not at all what he knew her governess had taught her. And yet, she absolutely had to be Elise. The resemblance was too great.

Miles remembered his own manners and bowed to the older woman. "A pleasure to meet you, ma'am," he said, hoping his confusion wasn't too obvious.

"And you, sir," she answered, studying him closer before turning her eyes back to Elise.

The young woman was Elise, wasn't she? He felt suddenly unsure.

"Ella?" the older woman pressed.

Ella took a heavy and shaky breath. Why did she not look even remotely pleased to see him? This could not be his Elise.

"Forgive me. I—" he began but was cut off.

"No need apologizin'," Mama Jones—that was the only name he had for her—told him.

"But I wonder if perhaps I've been mistaken." He looked more closely at Ella. How could she not be Elise Furlong? He'd have sworn to her identity.

Then, suddenly, she spoke again. "This is Miles Linwood."

The words came out so rushed Miles almost didn't put together what she'd said. *This is Miles Linwood.* She knew him.

"Elise! It *is* you." He reached for her again.

She backed away from him, eyeing him almost contemptuously. When had she ever looked at him with contempt? Miles couldn't reconcile the Elise who stood in front of him with the sweet, dear friend he'd once known. Without fail, she'd tossed herself into his embrace every time he'd returned from school. She'd sneaked into his room when he was nine because a sore throat had kept them apart for a week and she'd missed him too much to stay away. And now, four years of separation and she didn't seem the least interested in being reunited. She almost seemed angry that he was there.

"You do remember me, don't you?" he asked, perplexed.

"I know who it is you are." Again that strange accent. What had happened to her? Why was she shying away from him? And why was there an edge of hostility in her tone?

"Haven't you even a smile for me?" Miles could do little more than watch her in bewilderment. "*Pon rep*, Elise. We've known each other all our lives, and I haven't seen you in more than four years. Are you not at all happy to see me?"

She didn't answer.

"At least tell me how you came to be here, so far from home."

"This *is* me home."

Miles looked over at Mama Jones. "I . . . I don't understand." He held his hands out in frustration.

"She is m' daughter-in-law," Mama Jones said. "Married to me poor Jim. He was a soldier."

Elise is married? Was *married?* In his mind, she was still the fifteen-year-old girl she'd been the last time he'd seen her.

"*Was* married?" Miles asked, trying to piece the story together.

"Jim was cut down by them Frenchies in some foreign place. Now I just have Ella an' the girl."

"Why do you call her Ella?" She was Elise. He knew that for certain, and yet so many doubts spun about in his mind.

Elise, who had shared all of the most important moments of his life before her disappearance, clearly didn't want him there asking questions. Something had happened. Something had changed her.

"Go get the girl, Ella," Mama Jones instructed gently.

"No," Elise answered emphatically. It was the first spark of feeling he'd seen in her.

"He'll wish to meet her."

"I do not wish for him to meet her. An' I'll thank you not to drop more of m' troubles in his ears."

"Ella." The single word came out as a command.

The moment Elise disappeared into a back room, Mama Jones spoke. "I am glad you've come, Miles Linwood. Ella's been hidin' for too long."

Chapter Three

ELISE SLID TO THE FLOOR beside the closed bedchamber door and buried her face in her hands. Miles was in her home. Miles. The person she'd once treasured more than any other on earth, who had once cared so much for her.

The person who had snuffed out the last flicker of light she'd had left inside.

He had found her and, in the instant he'd appeared in her doorway, had torn open her unhealed and unseen wounds. She'd spent four years trying to piece together a life after his coldness had ripped her away from all she'd known and loved. And now he was back.

I can't go through this again. I cannot.

She didn't cry as she sat there hunched over by the door. She never cried. Not anymore. But she shook, aching inside, fear mingling with unforgotten pain.

Perhaps if she refused to come back out, Miles would leave. It would be as if she'd never seen him. She could go on as she had before. If he left, he couldn't hurt her again.

Tiny hands touched her face, pulling her gaze up. Her sweet little girl, her Anne, stood watching her with such a perplexed look in her eyes. Anne had lived so much of her life in hiding, tucked away from the world for her own safety. But a threat Elise hadn't anticipated had simply walked right into their home.

She pulled Anne into her embrace and held fast to her.

Oh, Anne. What are we to do?

Anxiety shook through her. Miles was not a physical threat, she knew that well enough. But he could deal a blow to a trusting heart from which it would never recover. He, who had once been a rock amidst the storm-driven waves, had left her to the cruelty of the world. She would shield Anne from that pain using whatever means possible.

"Don't dawdle, Ella. You're keeping the gentleman waiting," Mama Jones called out from the parlor.

Mama Jones knew enough of Elise's history to understand perfectly well why she wasn't rushing back into Miles's presence. Elise adored her mother-in-law, but the woman was set in her ways. Once her mind was made up, it was made up for good. If she intended to force this reunion, it would happen whether Elise wished it to or not. Her only source of comfort, though a small one, was that Mama Jones cared for her a great deal too much to insist on something if she didn't think it best.

She could indulge her mother-in-law in this. A quick moment of introduction, a word or two, and she could send Miles on his way. Mama Jones could not expect more of her than that.

Elise forced an aura of calm, though it did not sink very deep. She could pretend for Anne's sake. She rose slowly to her feet, Anne firmly in her arms, and turned to face the doorway. She slowly, quietly opened it, needing a moment to watch Miles in preparation for this encounter but without his realizing she was studying him.

He stood looking out the window. Time had darkened his hair from a bright, fiery red to a deep auburn. His shoulders were broader. He held himself with more authority than he had before. She'd seen the earliest hints of that change during the last few weeks she'd lived at home. The whimsical, lighthearted playmate of her childhood had begun to turn gruff and dismissive.

Anne leaned more heavily against her as she too studied Miles. Her brows pulled in, and her dark eyes clouded with uncertainty.

My feelings exactly, dearest.

She needed only to endure his company for a moment, then Miles would leave. She could go on as she had before.

"Ah, you've returned," Mama Jones said.

Miles spun around. Elise held ever tighter to Anne. Her pulse pounded in her head. She kept to the far side of the room, out of reach. She'd not come any closer if she could at all help it.

"Good heavens, Elise." Miles all but stared at Anne. "She's the very image of you as a child."

Anne's eyes darted from Miles to Elise, then back to Miles, where they then stayed. Anne watched Miles with palpable interest, something she never did. Miles was pulling at her.

"Aren't you goin' to introduce 'em?" Mama Jones prodded.

There was no avoiding it, really. "This is Anne."

"I am pleased to meet you, Miss Jones." Miles gave Anne the tender smile Elise remembered from her earliest years. If Elise wasn't careful, Anne would fall under Miles's spell, thinking she was safe and cared for.

"She's not called anythin' but Anne," Elise said.

"And you are called Ella," Miles said. "Why is that?"

"Ella's a fine name," Mama Jones observed, rocking calmly in her chair.

"But her name is Elise." Miles sounded increasingly frustrated. He turned away, pacing again and rubbing his face with his hand.

Elise took a small step backward. Frustration had been his defining emotion during the terrible last few weeks she'd spent with him. She didn't at all like seeing that look in his face again.

"You've seen me, and you've met Anne. Now you can just go on your way." Elise spoke as firmly as she could manage. Seeing him again was undermining every bit of peace she'd found in the last four years.

He looked at her once more. "Beth is here in town."

Beth. The name brought an unexpected moment of longing. Beth had been both older sister and surrogate mother to her. But no. No. She couldn't face even more memories.

"Will you come to the inn to see her?" Miles asked.

"No."

"Might I bring her here?"

"No." Would he not leave her be? Had he not hurt her enough already? "Just go, Miles. You aren't welcome here."

"How long do you plan to be in Stanton?" Mama Jones asked before Miles could speak a single word.

"How—? Uh—" After fumbling a moment, Miles pulled himself together. "Only through this afternoon, actually. We are having a carriage wheel repaired and should be on the road again very soon. Immediately, I would imagine. But . . . now . . . I could not leave now."

"You must," Mama Jones replied with a firm nod of her head.

Relief swept through Elise.

"And you must take Ella and Anne with you," Mama Jones added.

"What?" The word ripped out of Elise. *Take them with him?* Was Mama Jones mad?

"Of course," Miles answered, a sudden air of eagerness in his tone. "They must come. We are traveling to my home. There is more than enough room there. She is like family and—"

"Mama Jones *is* m' family." Elise cut over him, stepping closer to the woman in the rocker. "And *this* is my home. I'm not goin' anywhere."

"Child." Mama Jones looked up into Elise's face. "You must go."

"I'll not leave you."

"Sweet child." Mama Jones patted Elise's hand.

"Ma'am." Miles crossed to the rocking chair.

Elise immediately moved farther away. She set Anne on the floor, placing herself between Miles and her daughter.

He knelt in front of the rocking chair. "I would be most pleased if you would also agree to come to my home. I could not ask Elise and Miss Anne to leave behind any member of their family."

"I'm of a mind to accept your offer. Ella can go with you today," Mama Jones said authoritatively. "And Anne, o' course."

This was insanity. "Mama—"

"If Miles Linwood'll arrange for a cart, I'll see that our things are brought to his home, myself along with 'em." Mama Jones pierced Miles with a stare. "Know this, Miles Linwood. If you take my Ella from here, you're responsible for her. She cannot come back."

"This is not his decision." Elise tried to make her objections but wasn't permitted to.

"I assure you, Mama Jones," Miles said. "You will, all three of you, be looked after. I promise you that."

An empty promise if Elise had ever heard one. "I am not leaving."

Mama Jones turned her gaze to Elise. There was a firmness in her expression that couldn't be ignored. Mama Jones had made up her mind.

But Elise would never agree to this lunacy. "I will not leave. Not with him."

Her very personal objection brought shock to Miles's expression.

"Miles Linwood," Mama Jones said. "Go see if you can find something interesting out the window to keep you busy a moment while I have a talk with m' daughter."

Miles obliged but with several glances back at them.

"What is this madness, Ella?"

"*I* am acting mad?" Elise lowered her voice to a whisper. "You know what he did and why I can't go with him now."

Mama Jones's expression softened. "I know you were hurt, and I know you're afraid now. But you are tossing away an opportunity you will never have again."

"I'd not call this an opportunity."

Her mother-in-law clearly didn't agree. "You'd be leaving behind poverty, Ella. Miles Linwood'd never let you go hungry."

"I'll not sell Anne's safety and mine for a mess of porridge."

Mama Jones took Elise's hand in hers. "You've reason to be afraid; I'll grant you that. Laws, I'd be surprised if you weren't terrified."

"I am." Elise could hardly find her voice.

"You must be strong enough and brave enough for this, my darling Ella." Mama Jones patted her hand. "Though the path has its risks, walking it will offer Anne a life she'd not have otherwise. She'd not be pushed aside by an entire world that sees her as nothing but a poor child hardly worth acknowledging."

"She would still be a poor widow's daughter no matter where we go," Elise pointed out.

"But a poor widow's daughter who'd have a doctor when she needed it." Mama Jones held firmly to Elise's hand. "I cannot promise you everything will be easy or that you won't be hurt again. But Anne deserves better than this dark, damp corner of nowhere."

Elise glanced at Miles across the room. The very sight of him made her heart pound out a dread-filled rhythm. "I can't do this, Mama. I can't."

"It is often those things we think we can't do that we need to do most."

Elise knew then that she was beat. Mama Jones had made this a matter of walking the hard road to help Anne. Elise couldn't argue with that. She would have to go, but she didn't have to let herself be hurt by him. She held tightly to Anne's hand as she walked back toward the room they shared. Anne looked over her shoulder, no doubt at Miles.

He'll break your heart, dearest. He'll break it clear to pieces.

"You'll pack quicker if you leave Anne with us," Mama Jones called after her.

"I'm not leaving her with *him*. Not ever." She shut the door firmly behind her, not knowing whether to rage or weep. The quiet stillness of her life was evaporating before her eyes.

Nothing she did would undo the upheaval of the last hour. But she would do the one thing in her power. She would never let Miles get close enough to hurt her again.

Chapter Four

ANNE BOLEYN HAD LIKELY LOOKED more pleased during the march to her own execution than Elise did walking at Miles's side to the inn.

One did not generally expect to be met with simmering rage whilst rescuing one's dearest friend from deprivation and poverty and returning her to the bosom of her loved ones. It wasn't entirely unreasonable to think a person might get a smile at the very least. But Elise's stoic aura of displeasure could be only one of two things: either she was afraid, or she was angry. Miles didn't at all like either possibility.

Those blue eyes of their childhood that had always been full of joyful exuberance were guarded and snapping now. Her mouth, which had once perpetually smiled, remained tight and unyielding.

When she was four, only a little older than Anne appeared to be, she'd begged him to tie a parchment of scribbles to a bird so it could fly a letter to heaven for her mother to read. Tears had filled her eyes when he'd told her that birds could not carry messages to heaven. Elise had cried and Miles, not more than eight years old himself, had simply sat beside her in the meadow behind Epsworth, holding her hand. She had turned to him then for comfort but certainly didn't want it now.

What did I do wrong? She had shielded Anne from him, clearly seeing him as a threat. And she'd expected him to leave them both behind.

I will not leave. Not with him. Those words echoed in his mind, growing more confusing with each repetition.

He ushered Elise and Anne into the inn. The innkeeper's gaze slid quickly to Elise. Miles didn't at all like the curiosity in the man's expression or the almost smug smile he gave Miles. The innkeeper had clearly jumped to an unflattering conclusion of Miles's intentions and Elise's morals.

"Point me in the direction of Mr. and Mrs. Langley." Miles summoned the aristocratic demeanor the Duke of Hartley and Miles's cousin Lady Marion Jonquil had recently helped him perfect. It worked almost magically.

The innkeeper made a deferential bow, no longer eyeing Elise with such blatant denunciation. "Mr. and Mrs. Langley are in the front parlor."

"These bags are to be placed in our carriage," Miles said.

He received a silent acknowledgment.

Miles placed his hand lightly on Elise's back to usher her inside. She flinched. *Flinched!*

Every rejection cut deeper than the last. He hung back until she'd stepped inside the parlor. Beth stood near a window beside Langley, watching with wide eyes the woman who had preceded Miles into the parlor.

"Allow me to take your cloak," Miles said quietly to Elise when she neither spoke nor moved. She hadn't even looked in Beth's direction.

She unfastened her cloak and slipped it off her shoulders, handing it to Miles without looking up at him. Miles had almost forgotten about Anne. She was Elise's very copy in appearance, yet she was so quiet and still, entirely unlike Elise at that age.

Elise bent down, apparently saying something to Anne and pointing toward the small fire across the room. The little girl made her way there without a sound.

Beth's eyes locked with Miles's. "Elise?" she silently asked.

Miles managed a half smile and nodded. His sister fought for composure as she stepped closer. She would be so disappointed at Elise's lukewarm reception. Beth had been devastated when Elise had disappeared. How could he possibly prepare her for an Elise who did not seem at all pleased to be with them again?

Miles looked to Langley, hoping to convey the silent message that his support might be necessary. Langley moved smoothly to his wife's side just as she reached Elise's.

Elise had removed her bonnet, and Miles could tell Beth was staring at her thick curls. Her eyes would be the other indisputable clue; they had not changed physically, though they bore a different look than before.

"Elise?" Beth asked, her voice quiet and uncertain.

At the nearly whispered question, Elise turned and looked at Beth, her face full profile to Miles. She still had the tiny dot of a nose he'd once teased her about and the adorably small mouth that had pouted so sweetly when she was a child.

This *was* his Elise. Even Beth hadn't been his companion as often as Elise had. And something, he knew after all this time, was terribly wrong with her.

Elise tensed, though her gaze never wavered. "Beth," she whispered, her words tight, as if she held others back.

Beth clasped her arms around Elise fiercely and held their childhood friend, tears running down her cheeks. Elise allowed herself to be embraced but did not return the gesture.

At least she didn't flinch.

Miles moved toward the fireplace, feeling chilled and uneasy. Anne looked up as he approached, her brown eyes watching him closely. What would it take to make the child smile? Every child ought to smile. "Hello, Anne," he said quietly.

She watched his face as he spoke, seemingly mesmerized, but offered no return greeting.

What made these two so solemn? Elise had already pulled back from Beth, who was attempting to dry her eyes and cheeks but finding the effort futile. No emotion registered on Elise's face except the wariness that never seemed to fade.

"Is this your daughter?" Beth asked, motioning toward Anne. "Well, it must be. The resemblance is remarkable. What is her name?"

Miles looked down at the girl, wondering how she felt hearing herself spoken about. But Anne was still watching him, not taking note of anyone else in the room.

"Anne," Elise said.

Beth glanced from Anne to Elise. Langley watched his wife and Elise. Miles kept an eye on all of them.

"That is a very beautiful name," Beth said.

There was still no reaction from Anne. Perhaps the girl was timid? But her continued study of Miles made him doubt that.

"Excuse me, my lord," a voice interrupted from the doorway.

Miles felt Elise's gaze on him and, as he turned to look in the direction of the voice, allowed his own eyes to meet hers. He saw a momentary flash of surprise and confusion. It only made sense. When they'd last been together, Miles had been merely Mr. Linwood, but now he was the Marquess of Grenton.

"Your carriage is rigged 'n ready, your lordship." The man at the door bowed as he spoke.

"Thank you. We shall be there directly."

Miles saw Beth squeeze Elise's hand. But he also saw a certain hardening in Elise's expression, and the tiny ember of emotion that had crept into her eyes after being reunited with Beth seemed to be extinguished.

"Elise will be completing our journey with us," Miles informed Beth and Langley.

"Of course she will be." Beth replied as if the idea of Elise not coming was utterly preposterous. Then she began looking about the floor. "Has she no bags, no trunks?"

"I ordered her bags placed in the carriage when we first arrived," Miles answered.

Beth offered an apologetic smile at her doubt in him. "Forgive me. I am simply so overwhelmed. I ordered the kitchens to pack a basket. I will ask that they add more to it, for Elise and sweet little Anne." Beth lowered her voice. "Is anyone else expected?" The question dangled, another inquiry left unspoken.

"Elise is a widow," Miles answered in a whisper.

Sadness and understanding simultaneously flooded Beth's face.

"We can leave instructions for the kitchen as we head to the carriage, dear." Langley stepped to the women, offering Beth his arm. "I for one would very much like to reach the Wren and Hound before nightfall."

Elise's eyes turned to Langley then. "Mr. Langley," she said with a brief curtsy.

Langley smiled at her. "Forgive me for not greeting you before, Miss . . . er . . ."

"Mrs. Jones," Elise answered quietly.

"Mrs. Jones," Langley continued. "I did not realize you remembered me, and I did not wish to take away from Beth's reunion with a dear friend."

"I most certainly do remember you, though I were little more than a child last I saw you."

Beth stared. It was the first sentence Elise had uttered that was long enough for her lowered accent and word choice to be truly obvious. Langley wisely pulled Beth away before she could pester Elise with questions.

Elise, to Miles's surprise, made her way to where he stood. Perhaps seeing Beth had eased her nerves enough for her to warm to him again. Miles smiled at her approach, but she moved past him and directly to Anne. She touched the girl on the shoulder, and for the first time since Miles had moved to the fireplace, Anne looked away from him.

Elise motioned toward the door. Anne nodded and slipped her hand into her mother's. The two walked away from him without a word or a look. Elise acted as though he didn't even exist. Why was she so cold and distant? How could she possibly be so devoid of emotions when his own were reeling?

She stopped at the doorway, however, and turned back toward him. Miles held his breath. Would she smile? Offer some word of kindness?

"They called you m' lord.'"

That was all she meant to say? Nothing remotely personal? No expression of happiness at being reunited? Frustration boiled over. "You are not the only one who has had a name change, *Ella*," he answered.

Her spine stiffened at his chiding tone, her expression grew even more closed, and Miles instantly regretted his outburst. Before he could offer an apology, Elise turned and walked from the room, picking up the home-sewn cloak as she left.

Anne gave him one last penetrating glance as Elise pulled her through the open door. The pleading in her expression pulled at him as surely as if she'd tugged at a thread sewn to his heart.

I'm not about to give up, little Anne. I promise you that.

Chapter Five

Only by sheer force of will did Elise climb inside the traveling carriage. If not for the steady rainfall, she'd have insisted on riding up with the driver. But she wouldn't subject Anne to the weather or allow the girl to ride inside without her.

They'd been on the road for two hours. Two agonizing hours. Elise tapped her feet over and over, faster and faster. She pushed through each fast, shallow breath, watching the road intensely. Anne had fallen asleep on the seat between Elise and Beth. Mr. Langley sat across from them beside Miles.

Miles. No, he was Lord Something-or-other now. How had that happened? She hadn't known he was in line for a title. Had Miles known? If so, he'd never told her.

The carriage hit a rut. Elise held her breath. Her heart raced. Anne stirred, leaning against her. Elise stroked Anne's hair, settling her back into sleep even as she herself struggled for calm.

"Elise?" Beth whispered from beside her. "Are you unwell?"

Elise shook her head but said nothing, keeping her eyes fixed out the window. She had to get out of the carriage. Soon. She shut her eyes for a moment, fisting her hands and trying to slow her desperate breathing. But images and sensations, unbidden and unwanted, rushed in from the recesses of her memory.

A rumbling carriage. The dark of night. A sudden shift followed by a jarring stop. Angry voices.

"Elise."

Elise opened her eyes on the instant, the memories still too vivid in her mind. "We have to stop," she insisted, recognizing the first vestiges of panic in her voice. "We have to—"

"We *have* stopped," Beth said.

"Why? Why 'ave we stopped?" She could hardly form the words, so fast was panic setting in. "Is somethin' wrong? Has—"

"We've reached the inn."

Elise heard the confusion and concern in Beth's voice but didn't turn to look at her. Elise reached for the handle of the carriage door even as she slid off her seat. She had to get out of the carriage. She had to be outside, away from the memories and the panic.

She flung the door open, but before she could step out, a hand took gentle hold of her arm.

"The step isn't down, Elise," Miles said.

She jerked her arm free of his grasp.

"It will only be—" Miles stopped short as a liveried servant came to the side of the carriage and, without comment, let down the step.

Elise didn't wait for assistance but flew down the step, clutching Anne to her. She took great gulps of air, moving quickly away from the carriage, uncaring that the rain continued to fall. Only when she reached a bench just outside the entrance under a protective awning did she stop. Anne had understandably awoken. She watched Elise with surprise. All Elise could do was hold her and try to breathe.

She hadn't expected the ride to be as bad as it was. She'd anticipated some discomfort but not the panic. Too many memories. Too much pain.

"Elise?"

She couldn't endure Miles's company just then. She hadn't the strength to keep herself calm and in control.

"What's wrong, Elise? Can I do anything for you?"

"No."

"But you—"

"I didn't ask you to drag me away from my home, so you can just leave me alone now that you've forced me into it." She turned enough to shield Anne from the mist of rain making its way under the overhang.

"The rain has stopped a great many travelers, Grenton," Mr. Langley said to Miles. *Grenton? Miles's new title?* "There are only the two rooms we reserved earlier."

Elise pulled Anne to her. They had no place to sleep, it seemed. She would think of a solution. She had learned self-sufficiency very quickly not many years back.

"Perhaps Beth could share with Elise and Anne. You and I could use the other room," Miles suggested.

Mr. Langley nodded his approval. "The rooms *are* adjacent to one another," Mr. Langley said, though Elise wasn't sure whom he was trying to reassure. "There should be no concern over anyone's safety."

"Anne needs to rest," Elise said to the others in general. "If you'd show us to our room, I'd be appreciative."

They were quickly deposited in a snug room with a bed and a trundle. Beth's maid laid out their meager clothes, a luxury Elise had been long without. A sudden surge of emotion accompanied the realization that someone was looking out for her again. She clamped the emotion down as she always did. She simply could not let herself be lulled by long-forgotten familiarity or pleasant luxuries.

The others would most likely expect her at dinner, but Elise couldn't bring herself to go. She was tired and overwhelmed and plagued by flashes of memory. She missed Mama Jones, the only friend she'd had for years.

Elise laid Anne on the trundle, then lay down beside her, knowing she'd probably never sleep.

The enormity of all that had happened settled on her like a crushing weight. She was back in Miles's sphere again, where he held so much sway. He'd had the power before to sever every lifeline she'd had. Now he was a titled member of the aristocracy. She hadn't warranted his consideration before. Their circumstances were now horribly disparate. She could no longer expect to be extended the kindness she had once taken for granted. He hadn't thought her worthy of it even before she'd sunk so low, so he certainly wouldn't now.

Elise stroked Anne's hair. Her breaths had already grown deep and slow, a sure sign the child slept. Did Anne realize the magnitude of their change in situation? Elise hoped at the very least Anne wasn't afraid. Elise was afraid enough for the both of them.

Oh, my sweet girl, I fear I may be in deeper than I can stand.

She was returning to Epsworth, Miles's home, a place she'd dreamed of and dreaded for years. She'd known some of the most wonderful days of her life there but had passed the worst in those halls as well. Being there again would put her within walking distance of Furlong House, though she had no idea who lived there now.

She could see all of it so clearly in her mind. The meadow so large that both estates had claim to part of it. The apple trees they'd climbed as children. The rambling garden, where they'd often played. The bower in front of Epsworth, where Elise had tried to buy roasted chestnuts from Miles and Beth. The nursery where she'd found Miles after his mother's death. They'd sat there for hours, neither one talking but both understanding his pain. But clearer than all the rest was the Epsworth library and the bitter, hateful words that had ended her time there.

She would be there again. Facing it all.

"I am afraid," she whispered into the dark room. "I am so very afraid."

She focused on Anne. The girl disliked the dark—she felt lost without light. Elise pulled Anne close to her, tucking the blanket around them both. Anne curled into a ball with Elise's arms wrapped around her. She was so tiny, not a baby but not fully a child yet either. Elise settled Anne's head beneath her chin. She closed her eyes and hoped she would quickly fall asleep. Only in the oblivion of slumber did the pain leave her.

* * *

Little was spoken of at dinner. Miles knew he was poor company, his mind occupied every minute of the evening with thoughts of the past.

It slid over him in alarming detail, as if he were living it anew.

"Upon your father's death, all of his responsibilities, financial and otherwise, fell to you, Mr. Linwood." Mr. Cane, the family solicitor, had set a stack of papers on the desk in the Epsworth library. "Of course you will need time to sort out all of these."

Miles had nodded mechanically, fingering the black band around his arm. Father had been gone only forty-eight hours. It was still too surreal for comprehension. His mind struggled to wrap around his loss, let alone his new responsibilities.

"I would not burden you with these"—Mr. Cane indicated the stack— "if not for two pressing matters which require your immediate attention."

Miles took a deep breath. He was only nineteen years old. He ought to have been preparing to return to Oxford, not mourning his father and taking over the management of their estate. "What are these pressing obligations?"

"Your father left behind some debts."

Miles nodded a little impatiently. His father had not been irresponsible. The debts would be insignificant.

"And there is also the welfare of your late father's ward."

"His ward?" Miles had never heard of his father having been someone's guardian.

"Your ward now," Mr. Cane said. "I understand it has been determined that Mr. Furlong predeceased your late father."

Miles nodded.

"Your father was named in Mr. Furlong's will as guardian to his daughter," Mr. Cane said. "Upon Mr. Furlong's death, guardianship passed to your father and, upon his death, passed to you."

"Elise? I am Elise's guardian?"

"It seems so." Mr. Cane gave him a significant look. "I do not believe she has any family and cannot be expected, at sixteen—"

"Fifteen," Miles corrected.

"At fifteen," Mr. Cane amended, "to live alone or manage her own affairs."

"She will always have a home with me," Miles assured the man. He would no sooner abandon Elise than he would Beth.

"You are now responsible for all of her concerns," Mr. Cane said. "The late Mr. Furlong did not leave his affairs in a favorable way."

"In what way are they unfavorable?" It seemed he was to have trouble heaped on top of trouble.

"The bulk of the difficulty lies with the Furlong finances. You will find a brief overview in the papers provided."

One of the advantages of both Mr. Furlong and Miles's father having used the same solicitor was how the connection would simplify Miles's sudden load of responsibilities. Still, he let out a tense breath. What he wouldn't give for the freedom to go for a long, bruising ride and simply leave his obligations behind.

"I should go speak with Elise." Miles wondered how she was holding up. Elise had said very little since coming to stay at Epsworth a few short hours after their fathers' deaths.

"I have not said anything of this to Miss Furlong," Mr. Cane said. "I felt that was best left to you."

Miles nodded his agreement and rose, leaving the room to search out Elise, though he was fairly certain he knew where to find her.

A particularly large tree grew very nearly in the center of the meadow their estates shared. He and Elise had spent most every summer afternoon under that tree when they were young and still wandered there to talk and laugh. It was often the center of the croquet field they constructed every September to celebrate the coming of autumn.

Miles stepped over several croquet arches still up after two months of spirited games and made his way to the tree. Elise sat under it. She looked up as he approached. The raw pain he saw in her eyes deepened his own very real suffering.

"I have something diverting to share with you," Miles said, attempting a lightness he knew he didn't achieve.

"I believe I would like to hear something diverting."

Miles lowered himself beside her on the blanket and took her hand as he had done ever since they were small children. "It seems, my dear friend, that by some quirk of fate, I have been appointed your legal guardian."

She looked up at him once more, surprise evident in her eyes. "You?"

Miles raised his eyebrows ironically.

"You have been charged with keeping me out of scrapes and mischief?" She actually smiled. Miles realized, seeing it, that it was the first real smile he'd had from her in days.

What a horrible burden she had to be bearing. He was determined to ease her pain, if only for a moment.

"And I will be tight-fisted with your pin money like any good guardian would be."

Elise's smile, though shaky, remained.

"And, of course, I will be highly responsible and the perfect example of good behavior."

Elise looked doubtful.

"And in a few years' time, I will have the great pleasure of petrifying any and all of your suitors and threatening your future husband should he neglect your welfare."

The shaky smile slipped all together. "Papa used to say that too," Elise whispered as the tears began falling. She leaned heavily against him.

"Do not cry, Elise," Miles pleaded, wrapping his arms around his friend. "I will take care of you."

"Do you promise, Miles?" Sobs broke her words. "Do you promise you'll never leave me?"

"I swear to you, my dearest Elise. I will never leave you."

Six weeks after he'd made that promise, Elise had vanished.

But she was with him once more. He intended to keep that long-ago promise. He would see to it that she had more than a tiny dark cottage to live in, that she needn't beg for scraps from the local merchants. More importantly, he would find out what had happened to her, why she'd left home, where she'd been since then. And somehow, he would find again the bright-eyed, smiling girl he'd adored since his childhood.

Chapter Six

Elise didn't speak to any of them the next morning. Dark smudges marred the skin beneath her eyes, and she was paler and dragging. She'd barely touched the breakfast laid out for all of them in the inn's private parlor.

Miles was worried. Was she ill or simply ill at ease? He stepped up beside her as she fastened her cloak around her shoulders. "Elise?"

She startled at his sudden words. She stepped back, her gaze as guarded as it had been the night before.

For a moment, Miles stood silently mourning the loss of openness that had once existed between them. "You do not appear to have slept well."

She looked over at Anne, who stared out the window to where the carriage was being loaded with their trunks and bags. "I'm fine."

"Yesterday you were quite distraught in the carriage," Miles added.

"I do not like carriages." She offered no further explanation than that.

"I don't remember that about you." He searched her face for some kind of emotion.

"People change," she answered before crossing to Anne. She didn't look back, didn't speak to him again. A moment later, she was in the inn yard.

"People don't change that much," Miles said to the empty room. Elise was still there, somewhere; he was certain of it. He simply had to find her and draw her out.

She hadn't entered the coach by the time Miles reached it. She looked paler still, though it hardly seemed possible. What was it, precisely, about being in the carriage that unnerved her so? "We will take the journey in short stages," Miles said. "And we will reach our final destination some time tonight." He reached out to offer reassurance, but she didn't permit it.

"I've asked you to leave me be, Miles," she said. "I'd appreciate if you did."

She handed Anne up into the carriage and, with a look of determination, climbed into the carriage herself. Miles tried again to reconcile the change in her. Even having seen it these past twenty-four hours, he couldn't at all make sense of it.

They were soon all seated, and the carriage rolled along the road toward their destination. Elise looked every bit as uncomfortable as she had the day before. Something about the carriage ride upset her. Something about *him* upset her. He couldn't explain either.

"Beth?"

Elise's voice captured Miles's attention immediately. Though she wasn't speaking to him, she was speaking.

"Yes, Elise?"

"How is it we're to reach Epsworth by tonight? The journey oughtta take several days."

Epsworth? Elise thought they were headed to Epsworth?

"We are not going to Epsworth," Beth answered.

"But—" She shook her head. "I was told we were goin' home."

She didn't know. Good heavens! She didn't know.

"Epsworth is no longer my home, Elise." The admission proved more difficult than he could have anticipated. "My father's debts were too great. I had to sell Epsworth four years ago."

Elise grew perfectly still, her eyes not focused on any of them. The surprise frozen in her expression held the tiniest hint of sadness. Did she mourn the loss of Epsworth, empathize with him, even the smallest bit, for having to part with his family home? It was the first sign of anything other than anger that he'd seen in her.

She gave a tiny nod. "You were afraid you'd 'ave to sell."

"I held out as long as I could." For some reason, it was important that she understood he hadn't simply given up.

She made no response.

"Beth," Langley said. "Come sit with me, love."

If Beth was surprised by the request, it didn't show. Miles took the opportunity he very much suspected Langley had purposely provided and swapped seats with his sister, finding himself beside Elise. She immediately turned her gaze to the window.

"I'm sorry about Epsworth, Elise. I did try. The last thing I wanted was to sell our home. Especially with—" *With you still missing.* But he wasn't ready to discuss that yet. "I'm sorry."

A moment passed. No one spoke. Miles wasn't sure anyone even breathed. Somehow, he had to breach the wall she'd erected between them. He took one of her hands in his as he'd once done almost daily. She yanked her hand free and scooted as far into the corner of the carriage as she could get, slipping Anne onto her lap. His hand hovered a moment as his mind attempted to wrap around her rejection. He took a breath and laid his hand back on his lap.

Miles looked to Beth, wondering what her impression was. Beth shrugged and shook her head. Langley seemed equally perplexed. Anne watched Miles without her gaze wavering.

Well, little one, what do I do now? Your mother detests me, and I don't know why.

"Where do you live?" Elise asked quietly after a moment had passed.

"At Tafford, in Derbyshire." If only she would let him hold her hand. Before, it had made whatever either of them had been dealing with that much easier to face. There had been many times in the last four years he'd longed for his friend, even closed his eyes and pretended she was with him. He'd needed her presence. "I inherited it from a cousin of my father's almost a year ago."

She looked up at him, and for a split second, she looked more intrigued than provoked. It wasn't exactly an invitation to be her friend again, but it was a step in the right direction.

"You said y' sold Epsworth four years ago."

He understood her question even though she hadn't asked it. "I have been in the West Indies. Father left me a property there, the only Linwood property I did not have to sell to pay his debts."

Elise nodded. She seemed to sigh, though she made no noise and hardly moved. "Your father an' mine left behind an enormous mess."

That was one of many things that had bothered him after their deaths. Neither his father nor Mr. Furlong were spendthrifts or risk takers. They hadn't seemed so, at least. Their estates had appeared solvent. Yet there were debts and bad investments dating back several years in both men's accounts. Miles couldn't deny his father's signature and very recognizable hand on the paperwork. The debts had been both legitimate and devastating.

The carriage shifted precariously beneath them as it traversed the rutted and muddy road. A tiny intake of breath was the only audible sign of distress, but Elise's fists were tightly balled on her lap once more. What little he could make out of her face from around the wide brim of her very serviceable bonnet showed barely restrained panic. A second shifting of the wheels seemed to force Elise's eyes closed, as if she couldn't bear the sight of the carriage interior any longer.

Anne sensed her mother's distress. She turned and looked up into Elise's face with concern before leaning against her and putting her tiny arms around Elise's neck. With a shaky breath, Elise embraced her daughter, though she still looked entirely unsettled.

Miles thought of how their two families had often traveled together to local dinners and entertainments, even to church on Sundays. She'd never been uneasy in a carriage then. But there was no mistaking her strain as she sat beside him, traveling the ill-maintained road south into Derbyshire.

"Do we need to stop?" he asked quietly, concerned for her.

Elise shook her head. "I'd rather it be over and done with." She closed her eyes tightly.

"Several hours yet remain before we will stop for lunch," Miles gently warned.

Elise only nodded.

Miles rubbed his mouth and chin, feeling completely at a loss. For a moment, he'd seen a tiny glimmer of Elise as she'd once been. It wasn't joy or laughter or even grief he'd glimpsed in her, but longing. She missed her home. She had treated him with astounding coldness, but that fleeting moment of warmth gave him hope.

Miles glanced in her direction. She wasn't looking at him, but Anne was. Anne tentatively lifted her hand and stretched it out toward him. He gently wrapped his fingers around her tiny hand. She didn't smile, but neither did she pull away. Every moment of connection between them felt like a plea. She needed something from him but was too young to tell him what. Perhaps she didn't even know herself.

Every jolt of the well-sprung carriage brought the slightest, briefest tensing of Elise's frame. She didn't turn her face away from the window to look at any of them. She likely didn't even know her daughter had reached out to him. Miles held Anne's hand as the minutes passed. Her eyelids grew heavy, though she didn't sleep.

He hazarded a look at Beth, who sat opposite him. She watched Anne and Elise with a worry that matched his own. This was a family in such need, in such pain, and as long as Elise continued locking him out of her life, he was helpless to do anything about it.

* * *

Elise managed to survive the first leg of their trip without succumbing to her sense of panic, though it had been a harder battle to keep herself from crumbling at the news that Epsworth had been lost. Epsworth had been a second home to her. It seemed there was nothing left of the life she'd once lived.

Their midday meal eaten and all the necessities seen to, the group gathered at the front door of a small inn, awaiting the calling up of their carriage. Elise had strengthened her resolve once more, fortified herself against both the coming carriage ride and the emotions she struggled to keep under control.

"Mail comes through 'bout now," a groom told Miles. "Any minute now, 'spect. We'll bring up yer coach soon as it passes by. Mail don't slow easy and don't stop for no one's pleasure."

Miles nodded his understanding.

Elise remembered with heart-thumping awe how fast a mail coach moved, all but flying. Anne would enjoy the spectacle.

Where was Anne? It was not like her to wander off. Ever since the girl had begun walking, however, Elise had worried that she would do just that.

A rumble of wheels and thundering of hooves sounded from just out of sight of the inn yard. The mail, no doubt, was moments from arriving, and Anne was nowhere to be found. A horn announced the arrival of the mail just as Elise spied her daughter walking toward the inn's front gate, which stood open in anticipation of the imminent arrival of the enormous mail coach.

"Oh, merciful Father, help me," Elise pled in a strangled whisper as she began a frantic dash toward Anne, running as swiftly as her legs and skirts would allow. The rumbling approach of the coach that stopped for "no one's pleasure" positively shook the ground, and for the first time, Anne seemed aware of its arrival. She turned and stared in wide-eyed curiosity.

Elise reached the tiny girl just as the mail coach crossed through the gates. She spun around, running from the oncoming vehicle. Her heart thudded painfully in her chest.

A powerful arm snaked around her waist and pulled both of them away in one swift, smooth motion. The air around her swished wildly as the coach flew past. Elise held Anne in a grip likely tighter than necessary, and she shook uncontrollably, her breath coming in gasps. *We're safe. We're safe.*

"Are you hurt?" Miles's deep, rumbling voice asked.

Miles. Of course it was Miles.

"You're shaking." Miles's arms closed more tightly around them.

"Anne was nearly run down by the mail coach. I'll admit that's shaken me a bit." Elise slowly got to her feet. Her legs weren't entirely steady. She kept Anne in her arms but stepped out of Miles's.

He didn't seem offended by the distance she put between them. Perhaps he'd begun to realize she wasn't the vulnerable girl she'd once been. That would be safer in the long run.

"Anne, are you hurt?" Miles pressed.

Did he not realize?

"Anne? Is she hurt? Why won't she answer?"

"She can't hear you, Miles," Elise whispered, hoping no one else had overheard. Anne's condition had caused no end of difficulties with those not inclined toward compassion.

"She is deaf?" Miles asked, his voice equally as low.

"Not entirely. She can hear but not very well."

Most of the population of Stanton had seen Anne's near deafness as a sign that she was somehow less than a person.

"We should be goin'," Elise muttered, walking away. She shook from deep inside. The near miss with the mail and her forced admission of Anne's situation were taking a toll. Her emotions were in turmoil.

For just a moment, she'd found a degree of comfort in Miles's arms that she hadn't known in years. The little girl she'd once been cried out for that, wanted to believe he could be trusted, but she knew the harm he was capable of, and it terrified her.

Chapter Seven

SCARLET FEVER, MILES THOUGHT TO himself as the carriage rumbled southward. He thought he'd heard that scarlet fever could cause hearing loss. Other illnesses were often associated with deafness as well.

He looked across at Elise and Anne, both sleeping. They'd sat tense and quiet for the first hour after resuming the trip to Tafford, as had Miles. Seeing them nearly run down by the mail coach had rattled him. Elise may have changed during their separation; she may have become distant and unwelcoming, but underneath it all, she was still his very best friend. And she, along with Anne, could have been killed.

His heart had finally ceased its racing, and his mind had settled once more on the question of Anne. He'd noticed Elise speaking to her, but Anne didn't seem to comprehend everything she was being told. Her low hearing explained her constant silence and, perhaps, her tendency to stare at him. On the other hand, Anne didn't stare at Langley or Beth the way she did at him. Miles rubbed the back of his neck, shifting on the carriage seat.

Elise had obviously had little or no money these past years. Had Anne ever seen a doctor, an apothecary, even? Was there perhaps something that could be done?

"How fortunate that Elise is able to sleep," Beth whispered loudly enough to be heard from the opposite corner of the carriage. "She was so panicked during the ride this morning I had my doubts she would be able to endure this afternoon."

"Do you remember her being so unnerved by a carriage ride?" Miles asked, looking once more at Elise.

Her face was noticeably softer in her sleep, younger even. For the first time since he had found her the day before, she looked her age. She was barely twenty; he knew that for a fact. But her solemnity aged her far beyond that.

"Do you not?" Beth asked, obvious surprise in her voice. "It was never as pronounced as it seems to be now, but during those last few weeks before she disappeared, Elise was very much afraid—no, *uneasy* would be a better word—of being inside a closed carriage."

"I do not remember that."

"It was a very difficult time, Miles. You were struggling with burdens beyond your years, not to mention our father's death and her father's. I daresay there is a lot about those weeks that you do not remember very clearly."

"On the contrary, there are things about those weeks I remember far too clearly."

"Then try to extract this from your memory." Beth offered a small, sad smile. "The first Sunday after Father died, you and I and Langley were to drive Elise to church. Do you remember?"

"I seem to recall that she didn't want to go."

"She wanted to go," Beth corrected. "But not in the carriage."

"That's right. She was so quiet and uneasy during the drive to and from." Miles watched Elise as she slept with Anne under her arm.

"Even I was nervous about traveling after . . ." Beth let the sentence dangle unfinished. They hadn't discussed Father's death above a dozen times.

"I hadn't thought of that," Miles muttered. He'd spent a lot of time trying *not* to think about Father and Mr. Furlong and Elise traveling the road leading to Epsworth late at night. He worked hard not to remember that he was supposed to have gone with them to the Gibsons' dinner party but had stayed at Epsworth. The carriage had never arrived home. Miles had missed the last night of his father's life.

* * *

Elise awoke with a start. It was dark, and the carriage she rode in was coming to a stop.

"We've arrived," Beth whispered beside her.

"At Tafford?" Elise pulled Anne closer to her.

"You, Anne, and Miles were all sleeping, so Langley thought it would be best to simply push on." Beth smiled at her husband across the carriage. "We sent word ahead when we last changed horses. Dinner should be ready for us."

Elise nodded. She was famished. She'd skipped dinner the night before and had hardly touched breakfast. Lunch was the only meal of significance she'd had in more than twenty-four hours. But the thought of Tafford, the grand estate of a peer, overwhelmed her. She'd lived as a member of the lower class for years. She had no place in a magnificent home.

Mr. Langley stepped out of the carriage first. He turned back and handed Beth out. Miles followed, turning to assist Anne, who stared at him as she always did. Elise hadn't yet decided why that was. Anne was far too young to be fascinated by a handsome face, though Miles had certainly grown into a fine-looking man. The girl was usually quite shy, but she watched Miles unabashedly.

"Elise?" Miles held his hand out to her.

She took a breath. Was she ready for this? The estate wasn't Epsworth, something she found both comforting and disappointing.

She laid her hand in Miles's and found the contact even more uncomfortable than the last time. When they were children, he'd held her hand regularly. It had simply been their way. But she couldn't let it be that way now. Elise carefully took the carriage steps, determinedly keeping her eyes lowered. She very much feared if she glanced up at Tafford, which she felt certain was magnificent beyond anything she'd ever seen, she would falter and stumble.

Feet firmly on the ground, she turned back and reached for Anne. A question pulled at Anne's brow. "Ma?"

Miles appeared completely flummoxed by her speech. The odd timbre of her voice grated on most people.

"She *can* hear a little," Elise reminded him.

"And speak a little too, it seems." Miles watched Anne.

Elise turned her full attention to her daughter, kneeling in front of Anne with her back to Miles. Anne balled her right hand into a fist and rubbed a circle against her belly. That was her way of indicating she was hungry.

"We will eat in a moment," Elise told her as she nodded and made the motion of spooning food into her mouth.

Anne looked over Elise's shoulder, no doubt at Miles. It hadn't taken the girl long to realize where their meals were now coming from.

"Let us get you settled," Miles said.

Elise stood and took a deep breath, releasing what tension she could. Anne took firm hold of Elise's skirts, and they stepped forward.

For the first time, Elise glanced up at Miles's home. Her mind remained full of visions of Epsworth and its Tudor facade. Tafford was quite different: a mishmash of styles and eras, no doubt the result of generations of extensions and improvements. The house was enormous, but its haphazard assembly was oddly inviting, as if it were a friendly mutt completely unaware of its dubious appearance.

"This is your home?" Elise didn't know why she was whispering.

"This is Tafford, the home of the Marquess of Grenton for some three hundred years," Miles answered.

That stopped Elise in her tracks. "You're a *marquess?*" This was more than a mere rise in standing. Other than dukes and the royal family, Miles now outranked the entire kingdom.

Miles raised an auburn eyebrow as if he found the situation quite ironic. It *was* ironic in an awful way. They'd been separated for more than four years. They'd both lost their fathers, their homes, and their fortunes. Miles had inherited an old and prestigious title, fortune beyond anything they could have hoped for in their previous situations, and a fine home. Elise, on the other hand, had more than once gone a full day without food, had clothed her daughter in dresses made from remnants begged from the draper's, and had no home or money to her name.

What am I even doing here? I am as far beneath him now as the dirt under our feet.

"Humphrey," Miles greeted an austere individual who absolutely had to be the butler. His expression was far too starchy to be anyone else.

Elise instinctively pulled back. The top-lofty butler would not approve of a widow of obviously straitened circumstances entering the house of a peer to whom she was not related. Would he assume the worst of her?

"Courage, Elise." Miles smiled at her. "Humphrey is more of a puppy than a bloodhound."

At that pronouncement, Humphrey's chest puffed, and his chin and nose lifted in obvious disapproval of his master's description.

"I trust Mrs. Langley's letter arrived."

"It did, my lord," Humphrey answered quite correctly. "And might I say that the household is quite pleased that you and Mrs. Langley have been reunited with a friend of such long standing."

Elise blinked a few times. Had the stuffy butler just bestowed his approval? And why, she demanded of herself, did that realization threaten to break her composure?

"Thank you, Humphrey," Miles said. "We are, indeed, most pleased to have found Mrs. Jones. Mrs. Humphrey, I am certain, has prepared a chamber for her."

"Yes, my lord," Humphrey answered, walking with them into the entrance hall, where he proceeded to take Miles's hat and coat.

A maid was on hand to relieve Elise and Anne of their outer coverings. Elise stumbled only a moment with the now-unfamiliar service before allowing her coat, bonnet, and extensively mended gloves to be taken. Anne took a little more coaxing.

Elise used the minute or so required to hand over her outer things to look surreptitiously at her surroundings. The exterior of Tafford gave the impression of uneven cobbling together, but the inside, or the entry hall, at least, was anything but haphazard. The floor was smooth tile set in an intricate pattern of black and white. The walls were painted a light blue, landscapes and portraits hanging at pleasing intervals. Entry tables bore vases of freshly cut blooms. A majestic stairway led to the upper floors from which a landing overlooked the entry below. The space exuded taste and wealth.

"Mrs. Humphrey has chosen a room for you near the nursery," Miles told Elise, coming to stand directly beside her and speaking in a low whisper.

She didn't like the close proximity or the familiarity of the position. With Anne pressed to her side, she placed more distance between them and Miles.

He hesitated only a moment before continuing. "Does that meet with your approval?"

"My approval wasn't needed to begin this journey. Why should it be required now?"

"Mama Jones did run a little roughshod over you, I admit, but—"

"Mama Jones wasn't the only one," Elise muttered. She took another long look at the finery around her. This wasn't her world any longer. She almost couldn't bear to even stand in the entryway. "Where will Mama Jones be placed? I'd much rather be near her, whether it's in the attics or a tenant cottage or somethin' like 'at."

"She is to come as a guest, Elise. Not as a servant."

"She would feel . . . uncomfortable as a guest in a house like this, Miles." She shook her head. "*I* feel uncomfortable as a guest here."

Miles stopped on the step and looked at her, that same look of hurt he'd borne earlier. "Don't say that, Elise," he said. "I know this isn't Epsworth, but this is my home. I want you to be comfortable here. I want you to feel like it is your home, the way our homes were interchangeable for us as children."

"We none of us belong in a place like this." Elise shook her head as she looked around at the grandeur. "Not Anne. Not Mama Jones. Certainly not me."

Miles continued climbing the stairs but didn't speak. Elise felt him stiffen and sensed she'd upset him, but she'd spoken no less than the truth. Their lives were not the same as they'd once been. They were no longer equals. She realized that even if he didn't yet.

Chapter Eight

SOMETHING MOVED IN MILES'S PERIPHERAL vision. He turned away from the fireplace in the library to look toward the door. Elise stood there pale faced but otherwise emotionless. She looked directly at him.

"I came for a book," she explained quietly.

He all but jumped to his feet. "You're welcome to any book you'd like."

Elise didn't immediately accept his offer. She watched him with a look of intense concentration that echoed the expression her daughter always wore when watching him.

He crossed to the door, smiling at her. She did not return the gesture. He hadn't expected her to. Being patient was difficult, but the closer he looked, the more pain he saw. She might have been lashing out with anger, but he felt certain the root of it was a deep misery.

"What type of book are you looking for?" he asked, careful to keep his tone casual.

"I'm not sure." He heard uncertainty in her voice, perhaps a hint of embarrassment. "I've not read a book since . . ." Her voice trailed off, but Miles knew what she'd been speaking of. She hadn't read a book in all the years she'd been gone.

"Come, now." Miles motioned her farther inside but kept his distance. "I have perused this vast collection a bit since my arrival at Christmastime. There are books on gardening, astronomy, mythology." Miles allowed a teasing smile to touch his lips as he looked down at her once more. "I do believe I even saw a few selections from the Minerva Press."

"I do not think Gothic novels would be the best way to return to the world of literature." More lightness touched her tone than he'd yet heard, and now that he thought on it, her accent had improved a bit as well.

When had that changed? That was a good omen, was it not?

Slow and steady, he reminded himself. "I seem to remember you had a fondness for *Robin Hood*," Miles said.

"Yes." Her tone remained extremely guarded.

"There is a very fine edition of that tale in this library." He crossed to where the book sat. "My cousin, whose father was the late Marquess of Grenton, is named Marion. I believe the Robin Hood legend was a favorite of that branch of the Linwood family."

"She, no doubt, was actually permitted to *be* Maid Marion during her childhood." Did he hear the slightest hint of a smile in her tone? "I, on the other hand, was never given that role."

Miles remembered those episodes well. Robin Hood had been one of their favorite games as children, though Beth had insisted she be the ever-suffering Marion. "You made an admirable Little John though."

"That I did." Had she actually just laughed, even the tiniest bit? How he hoped so! "I doubt there was a finer Little John in all of England," she said.

"Although I doubt the original Little John ever tied Maid Marion to a tree stump."

"It was *my* turn," Elise said. "Beth promised I could be Maid Marion and then wouldn't let me. I really had no choice."

Miles felt the need to tiptoe through this conversation. Elise was less hostile, but he wasn't foolish enough to think that couldn't change in an instant. "And we wondered why Beth quit playing with us." Miles pretended to be confused.

"We were a couple of savages, weren't we?" A look of longing crossed Elise's face. Longing was decidedly a step in the right direction.

"And now I am a marquess. Makes me wonder if the peerage is doomed." His jovial quip seemed to miss its mark.

Before his eyes, she pulled back into herself. She was unreachable again. Her expression was nearly blank, her gaze lowered.

Miles realized in that moment why her now-characteristic stance—drawn expression, lowered head, quiet, respectful tone—struck him as oddly familiar. Elise could not possibly have looked more like the countless women scattered throughout England who were weighed down by the struggle to feed their families, to earn their bread, to simply survive.

He crossed to where Elise stood and held the illustrated *Robin Hood* out to her. "Anne will enjoy the pictures, I daresay." He studied her with growing concern. The moment of camaraderie had disappeared too quickly. Like a flash of lightning, it had existed for only a moment before leaving them in the dark once more.

He'd let himself hope Elise would return to herself once their journey was complete and she was no longer confined to the carriage. He'd thought to see more of her old personality emerge. But the Elise he remembered had yet to make an appearance.

"Anne will be entranced," Elise said. "She has never seen a picture book."

"Is she sleeping?"

Elise nodded. "But if she wakes and I am gone, she will be upset."

"Has she seen a doctor about her hearing?" Miles knew the instant the words left his mouth that he'd been too blunt.

Elise's mouth pulled tight. "I could not always afford to feed her. Doctors were out of my reach." She spun on the spot and began a stiff-spined march from the room.

There was a glimpse of his Elise! She had always been sweet-tempered and kind to a fault, but—lands!—she had been proud at times. It wasn't the side of Elise he'd expected to see first, but it was oddly encouraging.

"Are you going to push me out of a tree now?" Miles called after her.

That stopped her on the spot. She looked back over her shoulder, confused.

"Once, when I upset you, you pushed me out of a tree." Miles raised an eyebrow. He waited for the flash of memory, for a hint of shared humor. But it seemed the atmosphere was too strained and tense.

She didn't smile at the memory, didn't give him an ironic look. If anything, her expression grew more pensive, her eyes boring into him.

Miles pushed out a breath. "I'm sorry." Nothing he did seemed to work. He only wanted to have his friend back again.

"You broke your wrist," she said quietly, her voice suddenly thick with what sounded like emotion.

"Oh, Elise," he whispered and crossed to her. To his shock, she didn't glare or turn away. Her sad eyes simply held his gaze.

"You never even scolded me for that," she said. Why had that memory brought about this rare moment of openness?

"You were five years old," Miles said. "And you cried about my wrist more than I did."

"I was convinced you hated me." She sniffled. "I was absolutely certain you would abandon me."

"But I didn't," Miles pointed out.

"Not then," she whispered.

"Not—?"

Elise abruptly pulled away. "I should go back to Anne."

"Elise—"

"Good night, Miles." She was all the way to the door already.

"Elise."

But she was gone.

Not then. The words repeated in his mind over and over. *Not then.* What the devil did she mean by that?

* * *

Elise sank onto her bed, the volume of *Robin Hood* on the night table. She took a shaky breath. A hot tear escaped the corner of her eye. She closed her eyes tightly, not allowing room for another tear to follow the first.

Miles had conjured up so many memories. And though she did regret the day he'd broken his wrist, the times she'd reflected on while standing there in the library had been happy ones. For a fleeting moment, she'd wanted to simply melt into his reassuring embrace just as she had on the most horrible night of her life. He'd held her in front of him as they'd ridden in silence back to Epsworth, Elise shaking with cold and fear and pain. He had held her so many times in the weeks that followed.

How easy it would be to lean on him again when her heart was so heavy. So very easy, but so very dangerous.

"Help me," Elise said into the darkness. "I cannot bear to be hurt again."

Chapter Nine

AFTER A MORNING OF WRITING letters, Miles was desperate to be out of doors. He'd contacted his solicitor, as well as Mr. Cane, the solicitor who had once handled his father's affairs; he had also acted as liaison with the man of business who had handled the account Miles created in Elise's name before leaving for the West Indies. Miles had then written to the current occupants of Furlong House, now known as Hampton House, to request the few items belonging to the Furlong family that the Hamptons had agreed to store in the house's attics. No doubt, word of Elise's reemergence would be all over the neighborhood where they'd once lived in a matter of days.

A cool, humid breeze rushed past as Miles made his way determinedly onto the back grounds of Tafford. He'd decided within hours of inspecting his new home that the meadow was his favorite place on the estate. It even had a tree, though it was not in the middle as the one in Warwickshire had been. It was a magnificent tree, an oak, the leaves of which he imagined were a sight in the autumn. They would turn a brilliant gold, he'd wager.

Miles pushed his way past the formal garden and into the open expanse of the Tafford meadow. It would rain by nightfall; he could feel it in the air. A good brisk walk to the banks of the Trent would help relieve his tension. In the West Indies, he'd spent nearly all day, nearly every day out of doors, walking among his workers and all over the estate.

Today, there were no obstacles, nothing Miles needed to concentrate on as he walked, so he allowed his mind to wander. The first thought that bombarded his overworked brain was Elise's visit to the library the night before. They'd shared happy memories, a welcome change from the heavy, stilted conversations they'd shared thus far. She'd seemed lighter, if not happy.

"You have a meadow."

Miles actually jumped at the sudden sound of Elise's voice. She stood not twenty feet ahead of him, her expression as guarded as it had been nearly every minute since he'd found her. The lightness he'd seen briefly the night before was gone.

But she was speaking of meadows, something they had often spoken of. They'd shared a meadow all their lives. It was a fragile connection but a connection just the same.

"Yes, I do." Miles was seized by a sudden and unexpected urge to pull her into his arms and simply hold her to him. He knew better; she would only grow more distant if he did something so foolish. But the desire was there, and he couldn't seem to shake it.

"I have always been fond of meadows," Elise said.

"I know." He glanced about. "Where is Anne?"

"Sleeping. I needed to escape the house for a moment. She'll nap a while longer, but I can't be away long."

The silence that followed proved awkward. Elise didn't look directly at him but kept her gaze roaming the meadow around them, her mouth compressed into an unreadable line. Her hair was pulled into a prim bun at the nape of her neck, such a contrast to the way she'd always looked before.

She had begun putting her hair up that last year, though it was never terribly neat. She'd spent too much time running and spinning and riding her mare at top speed for her grown-up coiffure to remain in place. Standing there in the meadow at Tafford, Elise was neat and almost unnaturally put together. Miles felt the oddest impulse to reach out and pull a tendril of her hair loose just to see her looking more like the girl he'd once known.

"Have you seen the tree?" Miles asked, breaking into the silence.

Elise's eyes rose to his once more. Her blue eyes contrasted with the deep brown of her hair. No one else's eyes had ever been quite that shade of blue.

"The tree by the river?" she asked.

Miles had been contemplating her coloring with far too much of his concentration and, for a moment, wasn't sure what she was talking about. "The tree . . ." Then he remembered. "Yes. By the river."

"I saw it from a distance," Elise answered warily.

Why did even a simple conversation about a tree make her so deucedly nervous? Did she dislike him that much? Or simply distrust him? What could he possibly have done to lose her trust so entirely?

"I seem to remember you were fond of trees as well as meadows," Miles said.

Elise's eyes darted away from him. Her expression reminded him forcibly of the night before and the conversation they'd had in the library. It was almost as if she was desperately holding something back: a word, a gesture, *something*.

"Are you happy here, Elise?" Miles asked abruptly, knowing his frustration was evident in his tone but unable to prevent it from creeping in. Nothing he did pierced the distrust and anger she constantly put between them. Frustration seemed unavoidable.

"I . . ." Elise finished the sentence with nothing more than a shaky breath.

Miles turned away. What could he possibly say to that? It was an obvious "no." She wasn't happy. He had always imagined that if he could just find Elise and bring her home, everything would be fine. She would be happy. He would have his dearest friend back. All would be well again.

But that hadn't happened. She was there and miserable, and she felt nearly as far away as she had been the past four years.

"Miles." Elise's quiet voice carried to him several paces away from her.

He stopped but didn't turn back. He couldn't bear to see her solemn and unhappy expression. Despite the anger so often in her eyes, it was the pain that hovered just beneath the surface that sliced through him every time he saw her.

"I do like trees," Elise said.

He nodded but kept his back turned.

"And unlike some people, I have never fallen out of one."

"I was pushed," Miles corrected.

"I said I was sorry," Elise answered and sounded very much like she'd rolled her eyes, though Miles doubted she actually had.

He glanced over his shoulder. Elise allowed a fleeting upward twitch of her lips. Almost a smile. Almost.

Her gaze shifted to the tree ahead of them. "How many hours do you suppose we spent sitting under our tree?"

"Most of our childhood, I would say," Miles answered.

"I have needed a meadow, Miles." She seemed troubled. Deeply troubled. He closed the distance between them. "And a tree where I could sit and think through my problems."

Miles forced himself not to take her hand. She had pulled away from that gesture too many times.

"It is a very good tree," he said. She hadn't looked away from it yet. "A decent substitute for our old friend."

Elise looked up at him. There was suddenly so much worry and uncertainty in her eyes. *What have you been through?*

"Will you introduce me?" Elise asked quietly, almost hopefully.

"To the tree?" It was the sort of request Elise would have made when they were younger: playful, imaginative, but this time without the enthusiasm that had been so much a part of her character. "I would be delighted." He hoped his smile was encouraging.

He walked at her side as they crossed the meadow. She didn't put further distance between them. But what was she thinking? She was impossible to read.

"It is an oak," Elise said. "Our tree was also an oak." Elise studied the tree they now stood underneath. "Have you sat under it often?"

"It has only just become warm enough to do so. And I have been away for several weeks, in Nottinghamshire, then Lancashire."

"And Stanton," Elise added.

"That was an unexpected stop," Miles said. "But a fortuitous one."

She looked at him again as if uncertain he was sincere. "You are glad you found me, then?"

How could she doubt it? "Are you glad you were found?"

Her brow furrowed. "I don't know yet," she whispered.

It was a confusing answer. "Perhaps this tree will tip the scales in my favor."

"It is a very fine tree." Elise looked at him, a question in her eyes. But she just as quickly looked away.

She began circling the trunk of the tree, her fingertips sliding along the bark as her eyes studied the branches above her. She used to do precisely the same thing when she was very young, except she used to sing as she'd circle, skipping and hopping.

Miles watched her fingers as they rubbed along the trunk. She always said she liked the feel of the bark beneath her fingers.

"You won't mind if I come sit here now and then?" Elise continued her perusal.

"You may sit here whenever you like." He leaned one shoulder against the tree trunk, bringing Elise to a halt.

"I don't know where the picnic blankets are kept," she said, fingers still on the tree trunk. "And I would rather not sit on the damp ground without one."

"That can be remedied, Elise." It was such a paltry difficulty.

"I don't wish to put anyone out."

"You won't inconvenience a soul."

"Thank you for introducing me to your tree, Miles." Elise smiled at him, the first smile he'd seen from her that looked almost happy.

His heart swelled in his chest. He had made a difference. He'd offered her his tree and had received, in return, a smile.

"You have as much claim to it as I do. We shared ownership of the tree at Epsworth—"

"At *Furlong House*," Elise corrected, her smile growing a bit.

He loved hearing her tease him over a memory from their childhood. They'd often pretended to fight over which of the estates the tree actually sat on.

"So I believe we can manage to share this tree."

"I'm glad. I do love trees." Elise looked up into the branches once more. "I should . . . Anne will be up soon."

"Has she settled in?" Miles asked.

Elise shook her head. She had turned a bit away from him. Her hand dropped from the tree. She clasped her fingers in front of her. She was retreating again.

"What is it?" Miles asked, though he was certain she wouldn't give him an answer.

She only shook her head again.

"I don't want you to be unhappy."

"I have been unhappy for a long time, Miles." She stepped away.

"But what can I do about it?" Miles followed her retreating footsteps. "How can I help?"

"I fix my own problems," Elise insisted, returning to her somber countenance and detached stance.

Whether she wished it or not, he would find the source of her pain and put things right. He owed that much to her father and his and to himself. And to Elise.

Chapter Ten

"I WANT TO DO SOMETHING for her," Miles told Beth the next day. "Something to help her feel more at home here. I think that is what weighs on her. She has been away from all of us for four years and has only known for a handful of days that this very unfamiliar place is home now. That is a great deal to take in."

"So you mean to find ways of making Tafford feel like home to her?" Beth asked.

"Exactly. I have been trying to think of her favorite things from our childhood." Miles paced across the rug in the library. "Obviously, climbing trees and dressing up in Mother's gowns won't do the trick now that she's grown. But I do remember she always enjoyed bread pudding. I've asked Mrs. Humphrey to make certain Cook serves that more often. Elise enjoyed spending time in the meadow yesterday. She found a picture book in the library that she meant to share with Anne."

"Elise was always fond of stories," Beth acknowledged. She seemed to be warming to the idea. "And when Mama Jones arrives, you should ask her which things have brought Elise the most comfort the past four years. If we can surround her with the familiar—"

"She might smile again," Miles finished on a whisper.

"I had a feeling that was bothering you more than you let on," Beth said.

"I want her to feel at home. If she can have that, she'll be happy here."

"I think this difficulty goes beyond the unfamiliar," Langley said, sitting beside Beth on the sofa. "Admittedly, I do not know her as well as you do, but from what I remember of her at Epsworth before her disappearance, something was bothering Elise *then*, even while she was surrounded by the familiar."

"Of course something was bothering her," Miles grumbled, feeling frustrated at his continued inability to bring a smile to Elise's face. "Her father had just been murdered. That was bothering me as well."

"You were unfortunate enough to have come upon their bodies," Langley acknowledged. "Elise, however, saw them killed." He gave Miles a pointed look. "She was little more than a child. She became unusually quiet. She picked at her food, didn't speak much. Any hint of lightness in her countenance vanished. You worry that she is not smiling now, but, Grenton, she stopped smiling *then*."

"I don't remember her being that grieved," Beth said. "I do recall she was upset, but—"

"You were deeply grieving, love," Langley reassured his wife, even kissing her hand. "As was your brother. And"—he returned his attention to Miles—"you were dealing with the desperate nature of your family's finances. I don't imagine any of you noticed much beyond those immediate worries."

"I would have noticed if Elise was—"

"Grenton," Langley interrupted, an unusual moment of incivility for the characteristically polite gentleman. "As the weeks passed, you became less aware of everything beyond the burden you'd been given."

Miles shook his head. He hadn't been that self-absorbed. He was certain he hadn't.

"Do you remember that Beth turned her ankle about a month after your father's death?" Langley pressed.

Miles shot a look at his sister. He didn't remember that. "Did you?"

Beth sighed and nodded. "You didn't seem to remember that even at the time."

"It was one of the reasons we were so hesitant to leave, even though we were anxious to reach Lancashire before winter made travel impossible," Langley said. "Not Beth's ankle, which healed quickly, but you and your distraction. And the knowledge that Epsworth hung in the balance also weighed on our minds."

"I honestly do not remember Elise wasting away." Miles paced in front of the fireplace, searching his inconveniently blank memory. "She seemed to be doing well. She was mourning and shaken by all that had occurred, but that was to be expected."

"She grew worse with time," Langley said. "I debated saying something, but I didn't because I wasn't sure she would appreciate me, a virtual stranger, sticking my nose in where it probably didn't belong. Then she disappeared, and I wondered if, perhaps, her grief had overcome her judgment."

"You think she ran away?" Miles felt suddenly defensive. He'd told himself all these years that, while running was a possibility, he would have known if Elise was so miserable as to take such a desperate step. He would have known, and she would have come to him for help before fleeing her home and friends.

"I think it is a possibility but not the only one."

Miles made another circuit past the fireplace. "You think she may have been abducted?" It was the explanation that had frightened him the most.

"She was the sole surviving witness to a triple murder, Grenton. If anyone could identify the murderer, it would be Elise."

Miles dropped into a chair, closing his eyes and rubbing his face with his hands. Those had been dark times, days and weeks he tried hard to forget. But the memory came anyway.

"Are you certain there was only one man?" the Bow Street Runner, up from London to investigate, had asked for the second time.

Elise had nodded, her face paler than it had been only moments before. "On a horse. A black horse."

"What did he look like? Short or tall?"

Elise blinked and seemed to twitch involuntarily. "Taller than Papa," she said, her eyes unfocused.

Miles clenched and unclenched his fists. His father and hers had been dead only a few days. He wanted answers, wanted to find the man who'd killed them, but the interrogation bothered him. Elise wasn't holding up well under the forced resurgence of memories.

"What type of weapon did he use?" the runner asked.

"Gun." Elise spoke in that same empty voice she'd used to answer all of his questions.

"What type of gun?"

Elise gave him a confused look, obviously not understanding that there were some very specific types of firearms.

"Did he hold it in one hand or did it require both?" the runner pressed.

"One in each hand."

Miles looked anxiously between the runner and Langley, who had offered his support throughout the ordeal. One gun—pistols, if Miles wasn't mistaken—in each hand.

"Did this man say anything?" the runner continued.

"He told us to get out of the carriage. It had turned over."

"Was anyone injured by the carriage tipping?"

Elise nodded. "But not like . . ." She shook her head and sank into silence, her brow creased.

"Did he do anything? Before telling you to get out of the carriage?"

"He said he'd shoot me if we didn't get out immediately."

"He said he'd shoot you in particular?" Miles stared at her. Elise didn't acknowledge the question but continued looking blankly ahead. The runner gave Miles a look that warned him not to interrupt again.

"And after you left the carriage?" the runner asked.

"He made us walk a little away from the carriage." Elise spoke mechanically. "The horses were struggling. Injured. The driver was"—she seemed to swallow with difficulty—"already dead." She breathed heavily. Miles found his own breathing just as labored. "Mr. Linwood said that if the man wanted our valuables, he could have them but only to leave us be."

"Did the man seem as though he wished to rob the three of you?"

Elise didn't immediately reply. Her lips were slightly parted, her eyes staring unseeingly ahead, her color dropping steadily.

"Did he accept Mr. Linwood's offer of the valuables?"

"He shot Papa." The words emerged shaky and nearly incoherent.

"Quick as that? No provocation?"

"Mr. Linwood said he could have the valuables. The man raised his gun. I thought he was only showing it to us, trying to scare us. But then he shot Papa in the head." A single tear dripped from her staring eyes. Her mouth closed tightly as if barely holding back a rush of bile. "Mr. Linwood told me to run. But the man pointed another gun at me. He told Mr. Linwood to go where he told him. We had to go around the trees. Mr. Linwood asked him to let me go. He asked why he was . . . why he was doing—" Elise shook her head and didn't complete the sentence.

Miles crossed to the sofa where Elise sat alone and took a seat beside her, pulling her hand into his. Lands, she was shaking.

"The man shot him." Elise tapped her chest right above the heart. Another tear trickled along the path of the first. "And he . . . he . . . The man laughed. He laughed." She breathed rapidly, her breaths alarmingly shallow. No color remained in her face.

"And then he shot you?" the runner pressed.

Miles squeezed her hand. She would not hold up much longer.

Elise nodded, touching her left shoulder. Her arm hung in a sling.

"I need you to describe him to me," the runner said.

"Black horse. Black coat."

"His face?"

"He wore a mask."

"Voice?"

"I don't know."

"Anything identifiable?"

Elise's brows had been drawn, even her lips had had no color. She'd turned and looked up at Miles, her blue eyes swimming in tears. "He laughed."

It had been one of the most heartrending episodes he'd endured. Elise never was able to say more than that. The murderer had carried two weapons, had ridden a black horse, and had worn a black coat. A mask disguised his face. The one thing she repeated in the days that followed that interrogation was that he had laughed.

It hadn't been enough information, and after a week of fruitless effort, the runner had returned to London, warning Miles that the murders would likely never be solved.

"Miles?"

He'd been lost in his thoughts and had completely forgotten Beth and Langley were in the room. "Forgive me."

"Think on what I said," Langley suggested with emphasis. "Elise was young, but she was not foolish. She must have had a reason to leave her home and her closest friend and confidante. I think you need to find out what that reason was."

Beth and Langley didn't stay in the library for very long after that. *She must have had a reason.* That insight echoed in his mind. There had to have been a reason. But what?

He couldn't simply ask her. The Elise he'd grown up with wouldn't have required asking. She would have bared her soul the moment she'd seen him. He'd known all her secrets up until the day she'd disappeared from Epsworth.

"Miles?"

He nearly jumped out of his seat. Elise used to bound into rooms, her exuberance announcing her presence. Now she sneaked about, appearing suddenly, without warning.

"Do you have any other picture books?"

Miles watched for some indication of her feelings, but her guard was firmly in place. "Anne enjoyed *Robin Hood*, did she?"

Elise nodded. "She is mesmerized. Anne stares at those pictures. I would love for her to have more books to look at."

"Are there not any in the nursery?"

"I'm not sure," Elise said. "I haven't . . . Anne is still in my room. We haven't ventured to the nursery."

"Why ever not?"

She seemed to flinch at the exasperation in his tone. "This is your home, Miles. Not mine. I did not wish to presume upon your kindness." Elise stepped back as if to leave.

"When has my home ever not been yours?"

She stopped. Their eyes met, and for the briefest moment, a rush of emotion swept through Elise's eyes. She clamped it down so quickly, so fiercely Miles wondered if he'd imagined it.

"Where is Anne?" Miles asked, careful to keep his tone light and gentle.

"In my room with one of the chambermaids."

"Let's take her to the nursery. That is to be her domain, after all."

"You don't have to—"

"After more or less commandeering your nursery when we were children, I believe I owe you a nursery," Miles insisted. "And it isn't as though anyone is being evicted. It is a marvelous nursery, almost like a fairy tale, Elise. And it is waiting for a child. It *needs* a child."

"A fairy tale?"

He'd piqued her curiosity. Miles felt a grin spread across his face. "You have to see it to believe it. I *have* seen it, and I almost don't."

She seemed to debate for a moment. Her eyes darted to Miles's face. He could see the interest there, though she obviously tried to hide it.

Please, Elise. Please give me a little hope.

"It isn't as though she'd be pushing another child out," Elise said tentatively.

That was enough for him. "Let's go get Anne."

"Let's," she answered. There was no mistaking the eagerness in her tone, as miniscule as it was.

He kept himself from shouting in triumph. If there wasn't a picture book in the nursery, he would buy every one he could get his hands on.

* * *

"Oh, Miles." Elise hadn't intended to sound so breathless, but the nursery was absolutely marvelous. She turned around one more time, amazed. "If I'd had a nursery like this one, I don't think I would have ever wanted to grow up."

"It's rather ingenious, isn't it? The trees painted on the walls are so lifelike. I half expect a breeze to blow through and rustle the leaves."

Anne was, at that moment, touching her fingers to the painted branches of a bush in the full-room mural of a forest. She looked up at Elise, making the motion with her hands she used to indicate a tree.

Elise nodded. "A painting," she further explained, matching her own hand motions to the words.

Anne pressed her palm flat against the tree bark, rubbing her fingers back and forth.

"Anne likes to draw," Elise told Miles. "And for so young a child, her drawings are actually rather good. She'll not be invited to display at the Royal Academy or any such thing, but one can easily tell what she's drawn, which is a feat for a three-year-old."

"A talent she clearly inherited from her mother," Miles said. "You were forever sketching and painting. Your mother was a talented artist. I don't know if you remember that."

She hadn't, actually. Mother had died when she was not much older than Anne. Elise had very few memories of her.

Anne rushed to the child-sized table, clearly in awe of the magical room, and dropped to her knees and crawled beneath it, looking up at its underside. The table was made to look like a tree stump. The chairs were painted to resemble toadstools and flowers. The floor was painted to look like grass, the ceiling like a sunny day, complete with wispy, white clouds.

"I know precisely which bedchamber Anne must have." Miles motioned Elise across the room and held a door open for her.

Inside was a room to capture any little girl's heart. The windows were draped in flowing pink crepe. A matching canopy hung over the bed. The walls were painted with butterflies and flowers.

"I may never see Anne again." Elise stood in awe.

"Do you think she will be happy here?" Miles asked quite seriously.

Elise nodded. "She will be infinitely happy here."

The thought of Anne happy very nearly undid her. She fought back a sudden surge of tears. Yes, Anne would be happy here for however long they were permitted to stay.

Chapter Eleven

"Miles Linwood's lost his mind, he has," Mama Jones muttered, looking around the bedchamber selected for her very near Elise's. "As if I be needin' something as fine as this."

"He wishes you to be comfortable and have all of the luxuries he assumes you wish for. I tried to explain to him that not even I, who once lived in this world, am at ease in these opulent settings." Elise fidgeted with the edge of her shawl, one she'd knitted the winter after Anne's birth.

"You're talking more like you did when you first came to me." Mama Jones pierced her with a searching gaze.

Elise felt herself redden. Jim had spent so many hours with her, practicing the accent they both knew she had to adopt to avoid pointed and uncomfortable questions. It had been part of her disguise for years.

"Now, child." Mama Jones pulled Elise to the four-poster bed and sat the two of them down on the mattress. "Laws!" she exclaimed in momentary distraction. "Never felt a thing that soft before." Mama Jones bounced a little on the mattress.

Elise smiled, pleased at the unexpected pleasure she'd given the woman who had done so much for her. "The linens are soft. And your maid will bring you a cup of hot chocolate every morning. To drink, Mama. Chocolate *every day* that you can drink."

Mama Jones's eyes popped wide at the thought. They had splurged each Christmas on a small piece of chocolate for each of them. To have the delicacy every morning, and as a warming beverage besides, was a luxury almost beyond comprehension. "This is the life y' were born to," Mama Jones said, a statement filled with both awe and sadness for the years of difficulty Elise had spent in Cheshire. "Do not think you're bein' ungrateful to be finding yourself again. My Jim always wanted you to find your family again."

"But you—"

"Aye. We're your family as well." Mama Jones seemed to understand. "But it weren't me nor Jim you longed for when Anne was born so sickly and you were so afraid for her. 'Twasn't our comfort you ached to have."

Elise studied her fingers. They had never discussed that time. Jim had been dead for several months when Anne was born. She was small and frail, and Elise had feared for her daughter's life. Mama Jones had been with her through the ordeal, but it was Miles she'd wished for. He'd seen her through so many of life's troubles. He'd comforted her again and again throughout the years. They'd once known each other so well that words weren't always necessary between them.

It was him and that deep connection they'd shared that she had needed in those days of distress. She had never spoken of it after the fact, too confused at her need for her friend after all that had happened between them and too humiliated to have shown such weakness and preference in front her mother-in-law.

"I have the picture you drew of my Jim, but it was your sketch of Miles Linwood that *you* kept." Mama Jones patted her hand. "Jim would want you to be home again—your real home."

"My home was sold—"

Mama Jones cut her off. "Your home is with these people. Always has been."

"But I need you with me too." Elise squeezed Mama Jones's beloved fingers in her own. "These past days have been awful. Well, not entirely awful. There have been some nice moments. But . . . Oh, I don't even know what I'm trying to say."

"I believe you're tellin' me you've been a touch confused since I last saw you." Mama Jones watched Elise with such patience and understanding. "You are happy to see your friends again, but you are afraid."

Elise's shoulders slumped as Mama Jones, true to form, hit directly at the heart of the matter. "Miles has been very kind, and I have appreciated that. I feel as though I'm being unfair to him, but I can't . . . I'm not—"

"You don't know how to go about showing that you're grateful for his kindnesses, but you know better than to trust him."

"That's the truth and no denying it."

Mama Jones clearly recognized the saying as one of her own. She smiled and squeezed Elise's fingers. "You've reason to be wary, child. His kindnesses aside, he's not earned the right to your trust."

Elise leaned her head on Mama Jones's shoulder. "What am I to do? I cannot trust him, but I do not want to live every day in fear."

"You do just this: allow yourself to accept his friendly offerings. Allow yourself to be on more friendly terms. But keep a weather eye out."

"Watchful waiting, you mean?"

"Indeed."

There was wisdom in that. She could keep Miles at a safe distance without having to shut him out entirely. She would feel far less ungrateful, and yet she wouldn't be opening herself up to the same pain she'd had before. They could be on friendlier terms without actually being friends.

Mama Jones motioned around the bedchamber. "This'll never do. I'd much prefer a house somewhere in the woods. A grand room like this un makes me feel all closed in on."

Elise knew precisely what Mama Jones meant. That first night at Tafford, she'd felt almost suffocated by the enormity and opulence of her surroundings after the simplicity of their cottage. It was the real reason she'd gone to the library: she'd simply needed to get away from her room for a moment.

"Can you believe I once lived in fanciness like this all the time?" She shook her head at the absurdity of it now. "Perhaps not quite this elegant but every bit as fine. It seems almost ridiculous considering my current circumstances."

"Seems to me the two of us had best make the most out of this ridiculousness." Mama Jones's face wrinkled happily. "Though I do intend to find myself more suitable lodgings, I'll not be turning my nose up at a cup of chocolate while I'm here."

They laughed together at that. Life had been hard the past four years, but they had seen one another through it.

"I am so pleased to have you back, Mama Jones. I don't know what I would do without you."

* * *

"I'm goin' to lose m' mind, Miles Linwood," Mama Jones declared, entering his library with all the assurance of a duchess.

"Is something amiss?" He rose and offered her a brief bow.

"Things like *that*." She motioned to him with her head. "Your staff is bowin' and scrapin' and doin' for me. And you've put me in a fine room."

"You disapprove?"

"I'd much rather be in a cottage with work to do and smaller spaces. I'm like to lose m' mind here with all this openness and bein' treated like I was quality."

Miles felt an ironic smile creep to his face. "Elise said you would not be happy with the arrangements I made for you."

"And you didn't listen to Ella, did you?" She pointed a wrinkled finger in his direction.

"I admit I didn't." Miles was duly chastised. He assisted Mama Jones to a chair near the low-burning fire. "Tell me what I can do to help."

Mama Jones seemed to study him as if uncertain he was truly willing to assist her. "Is it your habit to come to the aid of those who need you?"

"I always have," Miles answered immediately and forcefully.

"Are you sure about that?"

Miles tipped his head and studied her in return. Why would she second-guess his answer? "I have my failings," Miles said, "but I do not turn my back on those in need."

"And you never have?"

"I do not believe so." Wariness entered his tone. Her interrogation was too pointed to be insignificant.

"Think on that, Miles Linwood." She pointed the end of her cane at him, then returned it to the floor with a thump. "And think on a cabin."

"A cabin?"

"Or cottage." Mama Jones shrugged. "You said you wanted to help. I'd be happier in a cottage, like I was before."

She certainly wasn't one to mince words.

"I believe there is an abandoned cottage not far from the house."

"I'll take it." Mama Jones tapped her cane on the floor once more.

"I warn you it has not been used in some time and would need work to make it livable," Miles said. "I believe the roof needs replacing, and it could use an airing out."

"You see to the roof, and I'll see to the rest." Mama Jones nodded her head. "And all m' things that you hauled to that back building when I arrived, you can just cart on over to this cottage of yours."

Miles smiled at the woman's dauntlessness. Very few would have the nerve to order about a peer. Miles liked it. If Elise had had this formidable woman as her ally these years, she had been in good hands.

"This cottage of *yours*," Miles corrected with an appreciative smile.

"I like you, Miles Linwood."

"And I find I very much like you, Mama Jones, even if you don't seem to entirely trust me."

"I have reason to doubt," Mama Jones answered. "But you've shown there's reason to trust you as well. Now you just need to show that poor girl up there." Mama Jones cocked her thumb up at the ceiling.

"Elise?" Miles asked. "You don't think she trusts me?" Miles had suspected as much but felt winded by the confirmation just the same.

"She's afraid to trust you. But I think she does the tiniest bit. And that worries her. Frightens the very daylights out of her, in fact."

"Please." Miles sat on the ottoman near Mama Jones's chair and took possession of her hand. "Tell me what I've done. I have no idea how . . . I don't understand—"

"It isn't m' tale to tell." Mama Jones shook her head but gave him a maternal pat on the cheek.

"But *she* won't tell me either." Miles said. "She barely speaks to me."

"You may be pickin' the wrong topics, Miles Linwood. There's a great many things she *never* speaks of. She told Jim about your fathers' dyin' at the hands of that horrible stranger but never once said anything of it to me. Four years, and she's not spoken of it even once. And she wouldn't often speak of you or her home. She kept that locked away. I'd not be surprised if she won't allow those topics to be discussed between the two of you even now. So you'd do best to avoid those things."

What else was there to talk about? Their entire connection was home and their childhoods, but she didn't talk about them. The few times Miles had attempted to talk to Elise about her life in the years since she'd left Warwickshire, she had not permitted that topic either.

"I took care of her as best I could," Mama Jones said, breaking into his thoughts. "But Ella weren't very happy. She weren't never joyful. Stranger still, she was hardly ever sad or upset. Her feelings stay bottled up. Fights 'em fierce, like she's afraid to feel anything at all. I'd like to see her happy."

"So would I." Miles looked into the woman's pale blue eyes. *She's afraid to feel anything. Fights her feelings.* It fit perfectly what he'd seen. But how could he get past that? "Everything I have tried—"

"Stop trying so hard," Mama Jones said.

Giving up on Elise was not an option, and it never would be. "I want to help her feel more at home here, but I'm not sure what would do the most good. I am hoping you have some suggestions."

"There's nothing in this world so dear to her as Anne," Mama Jones said. "See what you can do for that sweet child, and you'll touch Ella's heart in the doing of it."

"I have been thinking about Anne. Quite a lot, actually. And I do have a few ideas."

"Good." She nodded firmly. "Outside of that, Ella's needs are simple. All she's wanted since leavin' your home was to have her friend back. She mourned losing you more than anything else she left behind. I realized that truth early on, before she was so good at hidin' how she felt."

"Then she did leave." Miles muttered. Mama Jones had just said Elise had left. "She wasn't taken away or forced to go."

"Oh, she was forced," Mama Jones contradicted. "But not in the way you think."

"I don't imagine you are going to explain that remark to me."

Mama Jones smiled back at him. "I do beat all when it comes to sayin' things mysterious-like, don't I?"

"That you do." Miles had to chuckle, though his mood had not lightened much. "Could you possibly tell me a little less mysteriously how I might go about reaching Elise—besides through Anne? I wish to cheer her and lift her spirits."

"She's already mentioned her morning chocolate," Mama Jones said with a mischievous smile.

"Chocolate, then, is the way to soften a lady's heart?" Miles leaned casually against the arm of Mama Jones's chair, feeling very much as though he were a child again, speaking to his old nurse or Elise's.

Elise's old nurse. An idea sprang on the instant, though unformed and very vague.

"Go on and bring Ella some chocolate and flowers."

"I have plenty of flowers." Miles warmed to Mama Jones more with each passing moment.

"That's a start for you." Mama Jones nodded. "An' when that doesn't work, you can always come visit at my cottage and ask for more advice."

Mama Jones rose to her feet and Miles assisted her.

"*When* it doesn't work?" he asked.

She laughed warmly. "It's a start, but Ella'll need more than them tokens."

She would need more, but *what?* Miles would give her the world if she'd let him.

Chapter Twelve

"Miles!"

He spun toward the door of his bedchamber at the sound of Elise's voice. For once, her words weren't reluctant or uncertain. She sounded almost excited. Her face, to a lesser degree, showed that same emotion.

"What is it?"

"Mrs. Ash is here." Thank the heavens she spoke with excitement and not offense. Miles knew he had taken quite a risk sending for Elise's old nursemaid without asking her thoughts first. He'd wanted to do something for Anne, something that would also help Elise.

"She says she's here to be nursemaid to Anne," Elise said. "Was that your idea, Miles?"

"I will admit to my role in this only if you are pleased with the outcome," Miles said. "If you are entirely put out by it, I deny any knowledge of this debacle."

She smiled. Elise actually smiled. "I nearly squealed like a little girl again when I first saw Mrs. Ash. I love her so dearly."

Relief surged through him. Though Mrs. Ash was one of the sweetest and kindest women Miles had ever known, and he well remembered how much Elise had adored her, he'd not been entirely certain of this course of action.

"She has already won Anne over, and that is nearly impossible." Elise crossed the room to where he stood. He'd been about to don his jacket when she'd arrived.

"Mrs. Ash could win over Napoleon if she put her mind to it," Miles said.

"Anne is teaching her to gesture, and Mrs. Ash is already speaking slower and being so very patient with Anne's lack of understanding. And when Anne does speak, Mrs. Ash truly listens as though she means to work at accustoming herself to Anne's odd pronunciation and single-word sentences." Her rush of words reminded Miles forcibly of Elise as she'd been when they were younger: so eager and excited. "They will get on perfectly."

"I thought they might." Miles's smile grew.

"This is the kindest thing I think anyone has ever done for me, Miles." She clasped her hands over her heart. "I don't know how to even begin thanking you for this."

Thanking *him*? Miles was the grateful one. Seeing Elise smile was reason to give heartfelt thanks.

"And Mama Jones finally allowed a few of the maids to help her with the cottage," Elise said, switching topics. "I was worried. She doesn't get about as well as she used to, but she's such a stubborn woman. How in heaven's name did you convince her to accept their assistance?"

"I can be persuasive when the situation warrants it." Miles felt a growing urge to laugh out loud in sheer triumph. Elise was speaking to him. She was even smiling!

"You make me very ashamed of putting a fish in your bed when I was eight." Elise grinned.

"That *was* you. I had always suspected but could not, for the life of me, figure how you got inside Epsworth with a putrid trout."

"It wasn't putrid when I put it in your bed."

The remembered odor scrunched his nose. "How long was it in there?"

"Longer than you were." Elise laughed.

Miles did as well, more from the sound of that cherished laugh than from his own amusement. He hoped, desperately hoped, this meant Elise was coming around, that he had, at least in a small way, regained some of her confidence.

"I told Mrs. Ash we would take our tea in the nursery with Anne," Miles said to Elise, reaching to pull his jacket from the chair back, where he'd draped it upon entering his rooms some thirty minutes earlier.

"Yes, she said as much. She sent me to fetch you, in fact."

"Is this a formal tea, or should I, perhaps, arrive in my shirtsleeves?"

Elise smiled as Miles intended her to. Shirtsleeves were not acceptable at even the most informal affairs. "Mrs. Ash will ring such a peal over your head if you arrive looking half put together." Elise shook her head scoldingly. How often she'd assumed just that demeanor with him.

"Yes, Mama," he said in the mock tone of annoyance he'd always used when she'd begun mothering him.

She rolled her eyes.

Here was a glimpse of his old friend. If only he could find a way to hold on to this moment. He knew she would slip away again. Their interactions had followed that cycle ever since he'd found her in Stanton.

He pulled his jacket on, turned to face his reflection in the mirror, and straightened his lapels.

"You look properly dashing, Miles."

"Don't sound so surprised. I haven't been horribly ugly in years."

Another of her twinkling laughs filled the room. How he'd missed that sound!

"Mrs. Ash will be quite pleased to learn she didn't raise a complete scamp," Elise said.

"I did spend a lot of time in your nursery." He and Elise had been rather inseparable before he'd left for school. "Mrs. Ash had the raising of me every bit as much as my own nurse and tutors."

"And now Anne will have Mrs. Ash in her life." Elise sighed. "I would have loved for Anne to have had that these past years."

What else have you longed for? She still looked a bit underfed, but time would resolve that. She wore clothes made of rough homespun fabric. He would see to it that she had new clothes. She had always loved wearing his mother's ball gowns when she was small, smoothing the silks and satins with her tiny fingers. As a school girl, she'd run across the meadow to Epsworth every time she had a new dress, intent on showing him her finery.

Elise would love a new gown. Several, in fact. At least one needed to be blue, as that had always been her favorite color.

"Miles?" Elise asked uncertainly.

He realized then that he'd been staring at her. "My thoughts were wandering, I'm afraid. I do believe we have a tea appointment. I would rather not keep Mrs. Ash waiting. She'll take a switch to me."

Elise shook her head at him. "She would never, and you know it."

"I was not nearly as well behaved as you were, Elise."

She laughed silently. "Now that *is* true."

He walked by her side all the way to the nursery, glancing over at her repeatedly, attempting to convince himself that he wasn't imagining the lightening he saw in her expression. She seemed less burdened, though heaven only knew how long the change would last. Miles simply had to think of what to do next to keep this change in her from evaporating.

* * *

"For me?" Elise eyed the letter on Humphrey's silver tray.

The butler nodded and, after she took the letter, bowed and left the drawing room, no doubt to see to the many after-dinner duties he had.

She'd had time that evening to reflect back on the day. The arrival of Mrs. Ash had proven almost too much for her. The joy of being reunited with that cherished woman had quickly led to sadness for the loss of her other beloved associates from Furlong House, only to be replaced by relief at Mrs. Ash's ready acceptance of Anne. Then followed gratitude at the realization that Miles had done this for Anne, mingled with elation at the success of Anne's first meeting with her new nurse. Elise wasn't entirely sure she'd prevented herself from spinning in celebratory circles.

She had spent the rest of the afternoon getting herself under control again. Emotional eddies could quickly turn to tidal waves. She was taking Mama Jones's advice to heart. She allowed herself to acknowledge the kindnesses Miles offered her but did so cautiously. Letting her emotions run away with her was hardly the way to keep her head above water and her heart and her daughter safe.

Elise looked back at the letter in her hand, studying it. It was addressed to Elise Furlong, which was odd and yet not odd. No one who had known her as Ella Jones would be writing to her. But she had not been addressed by her maiden name in so many years that seeing it written out felt strange.

She stood alone in the room. Beth had taken herself to the necessary. Miles and Mr. Langley had not yet joined the ladies after their port. Elise crossed to where the candlelight glowed brighter. She slowly opened the missive.

There was no date, no greeting, only a single scrawled sentence.

Should your memory improve, so shall my aim.

The message was cryptic to say the least. She read it once more, and the mysterious nature of the eight words gave way to an ominous and threatening tone.

Elise shivered as she clutched the note. In a flash of remembered pain in her left shoulder, she knew exactly what the note referred to. She'd survived the murders all those years ago only because the shooter's aim had been ever so slightly off, the bullet missing her heart by a mere two inches.

"So shall my aim," Elise reread in a whisper. A threat, blatant and cold.

"Has Beth abandoned you?" Mr. Langley's voice asked from the doorway.

Elise quickly refolded the letter and slipped it inside a pocket in her gown before turning to face the arriving gentlemen. "She will return shortly." She hoped neither Mr. Langley nor Miles heard the slight break in her voice.

Mr. Langley nodded and made his way toward the fireplace. Miles crossed directly to her. Did her distress show on her face?

"I have had another brilliant idea," he said.

"What is this brilliant idea?"

Years of careful study served her well. She'd managed to regain complete neutrality in her tone and return her face to the blankness that had saved her many times from painful questions.

Miles's eyes narrowed, as if sensing she hid something. She didn't allow anything but calm serenity to touch her expression. He continued without pressing for more information.

"I have missed four of your birthdays," he said. "I have settled upon the gifts I mean to give you."

Should your memory improve, so shall my aim. She couldn't dismiss the words enough to respond to Miles beyond giving a nod of her head.

"I would like very much to give you a dress, one for each birthday I've missed."

Should your memory improve.

"Of course, we will put it about that the dresses are from Beth so no one will question the propriety," Miles continued. "Once Mr. Cane has contacted us regarding your account, you can see about anything else you need."

So shall my aim.

"So, was that not rather brilliant?"

"Uh . . . yes . . . brilliant." *Memory. Aim.*

"I will have your measurements sent tomorrow, then," Miles said.

Elise nodded, allowing her eyes to lock with his for the first time since he'd come into the room. Something about those familiar brown eyes made her want to lean against him and tell him everything. But she knew better than that. Without caution, she would never truly be safe. She would address the problem as she'd learned to do.

"I should go check on Anne."

"Anne will be sleeping by now." Miles obviously sensed there was more to her departure than maternal concern.

"But it is her first night having Mrs. Ash with her in the nursery," Elise extemporized. "She will be uneasy."

"Not if she is asleep." His gaze narrowed a bit. "What is it, Elise, truly?"

"Nothing."

His disbelief showed. "Elise."

"Please . . . don't. I—" She stepped back from him and took a calming breath. "It is nothing."

"It obviously isn't 'nothing' if you are worried." Miles closed the distance between them again. "I would like to know, no matter how trivial you may think the matter is."

"You needn't concern yourself, Miles." Elise was on firmer footing here. She'd long since grown capable of seeing to her own worries without his help or anyone else's.

"Allow me to help—"

"I do not need your help."

"But if I can—"

"I solve my own problems, Miles," Elise snapped. Then, appalled at the fierceness of her declaration, Elise bit her lips closed. For four years, she'd managed to subdue all outbursts. What was happening to her?

Miles watched her with a look of hurt mingled with frustration. The rest of the room had gone silent. Mr. Langley stood watching her, brows knit. Beth, who appeared to have only just rejoined the group, stood near the doorway, her mouth open in shock.

Why did everything fall to pieces lately? She wasn't treating them all with forced indifference as she had been, but neither was she pouring out her problems to them all. Perhaps this new approach wasn't working as well as she'd thought. Or maybe she was simply doing it wrong. The arrival of the threatening missive had dealt a blow to her composure.

"Forgive me," she said. "I spoke more sharply than I'd intended. I think I must be overly tired, or . . ." She let the sentence hang incomplete. How could she possibly explain what was happening to her when she didn't really understand it herself? "Forgive me. I believe I will turn in for the night."

No one argued. She didn't slow until she'd reached her bedchamber. She slipped the letter from her pocket and simply looked at it a moment.

She would have to decide what to do about it. A voice in her head insisted she tell Miles, ask him for his impressions. But she'd laid her troubles and most vulnerable worries out to him before, and . . .

No. I will have to do this alone. There was simply nothing else to be done.

Chapter Thirteen

"You missed breakfast." Miles quickly realized it was not the most eloquent of good mornings.

"I am afraid I did not sleep well last night." Elise was back to hiding behind her walls. Gone were the eager smiles of their discussion of Mrs. Ash. "I suppose that is to blame for my late morning."

She pressed her fingertips to her temples, closing her eyes for a drawn-out moment.

"Are you unwell?"

"No."

Would she not even tell him something so commonplace as the state of her health or well-being?

"You are in time for lunch, however." Miles kept to a safe topic, though he could feel the tension in the air between them. "And we are having a picnic."

"A picnic?" She looked up at him. Beneath her solemn demeanor, Miles thought he detected some degree of interest.

Miles silently thanked Mama Jones for the suggestion. "Under the tree, in the meadow."

A hint of a smile crept onto Elise's face. "We picnicked under our tree quite often."

"Do you remember the picnic when you refused to eat anything that wasn't red?" The Epsworth cook had actually enjoyed trying to put together an entirely red picnic. Everyone had adored Elise.

"I don't believe I've ever eaten so many strawberries in a single meal." The memory lightened her expression, though she still looked burdened.

He silently listed those things he'd done for Elise the past few days that had been successful in the hope of hitting upon something that might help now. *Looking after Anne. Pleasant memories. Not pushing her to confide in me.* She seemed to be happy about the picnic. "Mrs. Ash, Anne, Beth, and Langley will be making up the picnic party," he said. "The weather is quite fine."

"And I am quite famished," Elise said with a hint of forced humor.

Miles tried to laugh in response but found himself far too concerned for laughter. Elise did not look well. She was paler and more withdrawn. When she'd been small and her worry lines had appeared, he had kissed her forehead. The gesture had seemed to help then. It would be entirely unwelcome now.

"Anne is still a bit shy with Mrs. Ash," Elise said. "I hope that will improve with time, but she has always been very wary of strangers. Except for you, oddly enough."

"What is so odd about that?" Miles shrugged with as much feigned arrogance as he could muster. "I'm a very likeable fellow. Hardly anyone has disliked me enough to shun me or push me out of a tree or put dead fish in my bed. Hardly anyone at all."

"If I promise not to inflict on you any further bodily harm, may I attend your picnic?" Elise asked.

She *did* want to attend. He hadn't missed the mark so entirely.

"I really ought to extract a promise from you not to teach Anne to push me out of trees," Miles said. "I'm not certain I'm equal to the task of keeping both of you at bay."

"We would be a very formidable combination."

"I believe it." Miles chuckled.

"When is this picnic?"

"Right this very moment, actually." He found her surprised expression immensely enjoyable. It was unguarded and completely honest.

Beth's abigail had taken Elise's measurements after she'd awoken, Miles had been informed, and would be sending them on to the seamstress in Sheffield, who would begin several dresses for Elise and bring a couple at the end of the week for a fitting. The rest of the day, therefore, was open.

When they reached the back doors, Humphrey handed Miles Elise's cloak. He draped it over her shoulders.

"Are the others already gathered, then?" Elise asked as he led her around the house and toward the back meadow.

"I was sent to see if you were up and about and desirous to join us," Miles explained.

No sooner had they reached the picnic blanket than Anne began gesturing frantically. Elise responded in kind. He needed to learn their shared language so he could be part of those conversations. He hated feeling left out of Elise's life. He'd missed far too much as it was.

"The staff will bring out the meal in a few minutes' time," Miles said. "What shall we do while we wait?"

Anne watched him very closely as he spoke. *She has always been very wary of strangers. Except for you, oddly enough.* Though Anne wasn't entirely comfortable with him, she seemed to like him, at least a little. He would work at building on that promising beginning.

"What would you like to do?" Miles asked her, looking at Anne directly as Elise always did when speaking to her. "We can do anything you'd like."

She seemed a bit confused.

"A little slower and with fewer words," Elise suggested. "Your accent is unfamiliar to her. And speak a touch louder, so she can hear more of what you say."

Miles posed the question once more but more simply. "What should we do?"

He asked twice more before understanding lit her eyes.

"Run," she said.

Miles smiled at the hopeful enthusiasm in her face. He nodded encouragingly. Quick as that, Anne hopped to her feet and ran into the open field.

Elise watched her, a look of love on her face that Miles remembered well on his own mother's face. A moment later, Elise was on her feet, chasing her daughter through the grass. Her laugh echoed and jumped. Miles held his breath at the welcome sound of it.

I have been unhappy for a long time. Elise's words reverberated in his mind.

"You seem happy now," he whispered to himself, watching her.

It was suddenly not enough to only watch. Miles slipped his jacket off, tossing it onto the picnic blanket, and ran after them. Anne glanced back at him again and again as if making certain he was still playing her game. Elise smiled broadly, and not even a hint of the weight he'd seen remained in her eyes. He had needed that moment, had needed to see, even for a fleeting instant, a carefree and happy Elise.

He found wildflowers and gave them, with an exaggerated bow, to Anne, who blushed quite endearingly. So Miles suggested they find a flower for the girl's mother. Anne nodded her agreement and selected a daisy from her own bouquet and gave it quite solemnly to Elise. She accepted it and hugged Anne tightly before letting her run free once more.

Though Miles was far from perfect in his attempts to communicate with Anne, he was doing better. An impulse struck him, and remembering a similar experience with his father, he lifted Anne into the air and spun her around in a circle over his head. She squealed the oddest, most wonderful-sounding laugh he'd ever heard, which instantly had him laughing. Again and again he spun her until his own dizziness threatened to bring their game to an abrupt halt.

He set Anne on her feet. She swayed a little. When they were both finally steady, Anne gave him a brilliant smile—and had full claim to her very own bit of his heart. She ran in the direction of the blanket, no doubt to share their game with Mrs. Ash. Miles watched her as she ran, already formulating plans to improve his ability to speak to the sweet child.

He looked at Elise, intending to ask for suggestions on mastering Anne's language, when he noticed a single tear slipping down her cheek. "Oh dear. What have I done now?"

Elise shook her head even as she swiped at her eyes. Miles's handkerchiefs were in his jacket, else he would have offered her one.

"Are you upset?" he asked, unsure why she would be.

"No." She even smiled a little. "Anne doesn't laugh often. Hardly ever, in fact."

Miles sighed in relief—these were tears of joy.

"And she smiled at you. She so seldom smiles. You must come try again." Elise eagerly motioned him toward the picnic blanket.

Miles opened his mouth to answer but was cut off.

"Lord Grenton," a woman called out from somewhere behind him.

He turned around and recognized her and the young lady at her side on the instant. "Mrs. Haddington. Miss Haddington. What a pleasure to see you again."

The Haddingtons were his nearest neighbors, their estate sitting not a half mile up the road. They had been among the first to welcome him when he'd first arrived from the West Indies.

"We were passing by on our way back from Norwood and thought to ourselves, 'We haven't visited with Lord Grenton since his return to Tafford.'" Mrs. Haddington smiled at her daughter. "Didn't we, dear? Didn't we say that?" Her gaze returned to Miles. "We said just that."

Miss Haddington met Miles's gaze, an amused twinkle in her eyes. "Mother has missed you terribly, Lord Grenton."

"I *am* rather missable."

Miss Haddington laughed lightly. "I don't believe that sounded quite the way you intended it to."

"Mr. Haddington has been quite remiss in calling on you, but I am certain he will soon." Mrs. Haddington jumped back into the conversation. "Is that Mr. and Mrs. Langley? I had hoped they would visit again."

"Indeed, my sister and her husband mean to stay for a few more weeks, at least, before returning to their own home."

"We must go bid them a good afternoon." Mrs. Haddington made straight for the picnic blanket, motioning for her daughter to follow. "Offer her your arm, Lord Grenton," she said in a scolding tone. "You are a gentleman, after all, and she is a lady. A gentleman always offers his arm. To a lady, that is. A gentleman wouldn't offer his arm to a gentleman."

"I can't say that is something I've seen often." Miles managed to keep his expression serious.

"Unless, of course, one of the gentlemen had sustained a wound of some kind and was weak from blood loss," Mrs. Haddington continued. "Then it would be the gentlemanly thing to do, offering one's arm."

"Perhaps you should feign a desperate injury," Miles said to Miss Haddington under his breath. "Otherwise, I can make no guarantees."

"A lady need not be grievously wounded." Mrs. Haddington hardly stopped for breath. "She simply needs to be a lady. And my daughter *is* a lady."

"I am aware of that, ma'am," Miles said.

Mrs. Haddington's brows pulled in with confusion. "Then why haven't you offered her your arm?"

"You'd best make the offer, Lord Grenton," Miss Haddington warned him. "Otherwise, this conversation will never end."

He held his arm out for her, and she accepted it with a smile. Mrs. Haddington looked the two of them over, then nodded her approval. She moved swiftly toward the picnic blanket, leaving Miles and Miss Haddington to follow in her wake.

"Forgive Mother," Miss Haddington said. "She can be very single-minded, especially on such crucial matters as to whom a gentleman offers his arm."

"And so she should. If we let matters of such importance slip, what would happen to this country?"

"We'd be France." Miss Haddington managed the comment with perfect seriousness, but her smile won out in the next moment.

They reached the picnic blanket. Mrs. Haddington had already claimed all of Beth's attention, and Langley was doing an admirable job of appearing pleased to be forced into listening to their conversation.

"Who is this?" Miss Haddington asked.

Miles followed her gaze all the way to Elise. *Elise.* When had she left his side? They'd been walking back to the picnic together when the Haddingtons had arrived. She must have walked away then.

"This is Mrs. Jones," Miles said, bringing Miss Haddington to where Elise sat with Anne leaning against her. "And this lovely young lady is her daughter, Miss Jones."

Anne looked excessively uncomfortable, pulling in closer to her mother. Elise didn't quite manage a smile, neither did she look Miss Haddington in the eye.

"Mrs. Jones"—Heavens, it felt strange calling Elise that, but he did know how to make a proper introduction—"this is Miss Haddington of Ravensworth."

Miss Haddington offered a very elegant curtsy. "I am so pleased to meet you, Mrs. Jones. Do you live nearby?"

Elise didn't answer. Her mouth moved about silently. She clutched her hands tightly in front of her.

"Mrs. Jones is a dear family friend," Miles explained. "My sister and I are enjoying some time together with her again."

"Oh." Mrs. Haddington looked more curious than Miles would have expected. "And *Mr.* Jones is . . . ?"

Elise's chin rose, and a palpable surge of pride filled her posture and expression. "My husband was a soldier. He was lost in battle."

Beneath her calm declaration lingered a hint of sadness. Until that moment, Miles hadn't truly contemplated the grief she must have felt at losing her husband.

Her husband. In his mind, she was still the fifteen-year-old girl she'd been before. He couldn't entirely wrap his mind around Elise as a wife and mother.

"I am so sorry for your loss," Miss Haddington said. "This war has brought heartache to so many people."

"It has," Elise said, her voice becoming quiet and withdrawn once more.

The food arrived in the next moment, and the Haddingtons joined the picnic. Conversation became general. Almost. Elise didn't speak a word. Indeed, she sat with Mrs. Ash and Anne, a bit removed from the rest of the party. Anne's unease was expected, but Elise's surprised Miles.

Though she'd not had her come-out before her disappearance, she'd been quite the social butterfly amongst the neighboring families. She had easily interacted with young and old. She had lit up every room she entered. Why, then, did she seem so intent on suddenly disappearing into the scenery?

Perhaps she meant only to shield Anne from the discomfort of interacting with strangers. It was a reasonable explanation, and yet he sensed there was more to it. That part of her personality had changed. Here was yet another mystery surrounding the one person he'd always thought he knew best.

Chapter Fourteen

IF ELISE NEVER AGAIN WENT on another picnic, it would be too soon. It had begun well. Anne had laughed so joyously. She'd run and spun about and giggled like the happy little girl Elise had always wanted her to be. Life had been too hard, too full of worry and need. But for that one moment, that lovely, lovely moment, Anne had been carefree. Elise's heart had nearly burst.

Then the Haddingtons had arrived, elegant and perfectly at ease in the company of wealthy, elegant people. Elise's longstanding friendship with Miles and Beth had momentarily blinded her to how very different their new places in Society truly were. Her old friends had land and money and positions of influence and importance. Elise was nobody, honestly and truly nobody, with nothing she could claim as her own beyond difficult memories and forgotten dreams.

Miles had explained to his visitors that Elise was a family friend who was visiting Tafford. The Haddingtons had accepted the explanation, though Elise had felt the dismissal inherent in their postures and expressions. She still remembered the nuances of interactions in Society. Four years hadn't erased that bit of her education. Miles and Beth didn't make a point of how far beneath them she now was—they might not have truly given it much thought yet—but the truth was there. Nothing would change that. In her mind, she understood it, but her heart still hurt.

* * *

Mr. Cane came to Tafford two days after the picnic. Elise offered an appropriate curtsy after Miles introduced him. Mr. Cane had been her father's and Mr. Linwood's solicitor. She remembered him vaguely from his visits to Furlong House. His hair had been thicker then, his waist a little less thick.

"Mr. Cane, I am certain you recall Mrs. Jones," Miles completed the introduction.

"I do, indeed," Mr. Cane answered with a bow. "Though she was much younger when I last saw her." He addressed Miles, though he spoke about Elise. She'd grown quickly accustomed to just that sort of dismissal over the past four years. She was no longer a lady of station or wealth. "I suggest we begin directly, as I have no wish to monopolize your entire afternoon."

Miles nodded to Mr. Cane and indicated that he should take the chair behind the library desk. Elise sat in a chair facing the solicitor. Miles sat beside her but didn't speak.

They hadn't said much to each other since the picnic. For her part, she didn't know what she might possibly say. It was hardly Miles's fault they were no longer equals. And Miss Haddington had, in all actuality, been perfectly cordial, considering their very disparate situations were so very obvious. Elise had no real reason for complaint. She simply felt so utterly out of her element.

"Forgive the interruption." Humphrey stood in the doorway with something in his hand. "I did not realize your meeting had begun. A letter has arrived for Mrs. Jones."

A letter. Another threatening one? She'd received the first only two days earlier, then another yesterday. Both were unposted, brief, and undeniably threatening. She knew with perfect certainty the messages were from the unidentified murderer who'd brought such devastation to her life. The man who'd taken so much and then laughed about it.

She took this newest letter from Humphrey, offered him a quick thank you, then studied the missive in her hand. It was addressed to her and postmarked from Leicester. She didn't know a soul in Leicester. It was too far from Stanton for her to have made any acquaintance there during her four years away and too far from Epsworth for her to have known anyone there during her first fifteen years.

The other two letters hadn't been posted, which worried her. The letter writer had to have been near enough to Tafford to arrange for a hand delivery. Perhaps this one was not another threat but something less alarming. Elise looked up at Miles.

"Please, take a moment to read your letter," he said. "We'll wait."

Mr. Cane was bent over his papers and didn't seem to mind the delay.

Elise turned the letter over and broke the seal. She unfolded the parchment. All hope of this being a benign, friendly note evaporated in an instant. On the paper was written but one sentence.

Good day, Elise.

Good day? What did that mean? She didn't believe for a moment the greeting was friendly or genuine. *Good day.* It was so commonplace she had likely heard those words from hundreds of people.

Hundreds of people. Had she been greeted that way by the murderer himself? Was he telling her of a conversation he'd already had with her? Such an insignificant thing might have been said by anyone.

Elise tried to calm her mind. She would give it some thought when she was alone again. But now was not the time to sort all of it out. She quickly folded the letter once more and looked up at the two men.

"My apologies for the delay. Please, continue."

Miles leaned a little closer. "What was in that letter?"

"Nothing of importance."

His gaze narrowed.

Elise turned quickly to Mr. Cane. "Let us begin, please."

Mr. Cane looked to Miles. "My lord?"

Miles watched Elise a moment longer before silently indicating Mr. Cane should proceed.

"Many years have passed since this account was created, but I believe you will be pleased with the changes you will see in it," Mr. Cane began.

His voice continued on in the background of Elise's wandering thoughts. *Good day, Elise.* She would likely never hear those three words again without worrying that the remark was pointed. How would she know if the greeting was offhand or in reference to this letter? She wouldn't.

"Elise?" Miles's voice broke into her distraction.

She opened her eyes to find both men watching her closely. "Forgive me," she said quietly. "I was wool-gathering, it seems."

Mr. Cane watched her with palpable patience. "Would you rather we postpone this?"

"I am fine," Elise insisted.

Miles had taken to very pointed studies of her the past few days. He did so again in that moment. It was enough to make Elise squirm, though she managed to subdue the impulse.

"I will be brief," Mr. Cane reassured them. "You may remember I served as solicitor for your late father. After his affairs were settled, a small amount of money remained, which, wisely, Lord Grenton"—Mr. Cane looked in Miles's direction—"as your guardian, set aside in an account in your name."

"You did?" She'd heard nothing of this before.

"I thought, at the time, it could become something of a dowry," Miles said. "You were only fifteen years old, and after a few years had passed and you were of an age to marry, the investments made on your behalf would, I hoped, have increased the amount to a respectable total."

Elise smiled sadly. "And I told Jim I brought nothing to our marriage. He could have been wealthy." She laughed lightly. Thoughts of Jim brought the usual sadness, so she pushed them firmly from her mind.

"The man of business you appointed to oversee the investments has given me a full accounting," Mr. Cane told Miles. "I believe you will be pleased with the results. The original amount was only a little over two thousand pounds."

Elise barely managed to hold back a gasp. *Two thousand pounds.* That would have been a vast fortune the past four years.

"Mrs. Jones is now in possession of nearly twenty-five hundred," Mr. Cane continued. "As requested, your man of business has looked over the investments as well. He has declared them to be wise and likely profitable in the long term."

"I could have an income off these investments?" Elise asked, hardly believing it.

Mr. Cane nodded. "Though it would not be a large amount, it would certainly be enough to support yourself."

"And my daughter?"

He nodded again. "You would not be in a position to live in style, but you would be comfortable." Mr. Cane held a paper out to her. "The details are all here. I would be happy to answer any questions you might have."

She took the paper and looked over it quickly. The upper classes would have scoffed at the amount, but it was more than ten times what she'd been living on. "Thank you for this, Miles."

He smiled a bit. "I only wish it were more. There was so little left after settling your father's estate."

"This is more than I could have hoped for," Elise said. "And far more than I've had the past years."

"You aren't disappointed?" He seemed to have genuinely expected her to be.

"Not at all. Not at all."

Though she didn't yet know what path her future would take, she had money enough to support Anne and herself. That lifted an enormous weight from her shoulders.

But what was she to do about the letters?

* * *

"She's keeping something from me. I can sense it." Miles turned to make a fourth circuit of Mama Jones's small parlor.

"An' how long did it take you to decide that, Miles Linwood?" Mama Jones asked, rocking rhythmically, as always. And as always, she seemed a moment away from laughing at him. "Somewhere between disappearin' without a word all them years ago an' hardly speakin' to you now she's been found? Somewhere in there, was it?"

Miles couldn't help a begrudging smile. "I meant something *new*, something recent." He would wager the letter she'd received during Mr. Cane's visit was connected to the increased tension he saw in her.

Mama Jones narrowed her eyes. "I've seen it too. Something's weighin' heavy on her mind."

"Precisely." Miles began a fifth turn around the room. "She hasn't confided in you either?"

"Ella's always kept her own counsel. She keeps everything to herself, her worries and joys, her struggles and triumphs. She keeps it hidden."

"She didn't used to do that," Miles said.

"Ah," Mama Jones said, the sound one of feigned discovery. "Perhaps, then, that's your next clue."

"Clue?"

"She keeps her feelin's bottled up," Mama Jones explained in that mysterious-like way she seemed so proud of. "But she didn't used to. Seems there must be a reason for the change."

Miles stopped his pacing to study the woman watching him from her rocking chair. Again she wore a look of ill-concealed amusement. And yet Miles didn't truly think she found the situation funny.

"Was she always so closed up in the years you have known her?" He didn't know if she would answer his question. Mama Jones could be very close-lipped herself.

"Aye, that she were." Mama Jones nodded in time to her rocking. "Ever since Jim brought her home to me. 'Mama,' he says, 'here's m' wife, Ella.' 'Twere a surprise to me. Jim roared out laughin' when he saw my face so bewildered. He finally told me all 'bout how they came to be man an' wife. But through the whole story, Ella just stood silent and still, holding to his arm as if she was terrified of him leaving her. She didn't smile, didn't laugh when Jim got to tellin' things in his funny way. She just stood there with sad eyes an' listened."

"She and your son were married already when you met her?" For some reason, that surprised him.

"Aye." Mama Jones nodded once more. "He were away from home, soon to be joinin' up with the army, he was. I expected him home sooner, but Jim was wont to wander at times. Came home a few weeks late and with a bride."

"How long was he gone?" He hoped Mama Jones would continue her revealing story. It was more information than he'd had from her yet and far more than Elise was likely to provide.

"Near about a month." A certain twinkle in Mama Jones's eye told Miles that bit of information was significant.

"And you didn't know Elise before that?" It did indeed seem strange.

Mama Jones shook her head. "Jim didn't know her neither." Her look became pointed.

"They met and married within a month?" Miles blurted the question as he began pacing again.

"An' posted the banns," Mama Jones added.

Having the banns read required three weeks. Which meant Elise and Jim Jones had become betrothed within a week of meeting each other, less if any amount of traveling had been completed in that time frame.

"Were they so much in love, then?" He wondered at the odd growl in his voice as he spoke.

Mama Jones laughed out loud, thoroughly annoying Miles. "I'd wager a yellow boy you're jealous, Miles Linwood." She chuckled. "You, who had her love, jealous of m' boy, who only had her gratitude."

Mama Jones continued to chuckle, but Miles's mind was spinning. *Her love.* Had Elise loved him all those years ago? She'd been so young when she'd left home. He couldn't imagine fifteen-year-old Elise nursing an unspoken passion for him. Lands, he'd only been nineteen himself. They'd been more like siblings than sweethearts.

"Now don't go frettin' your breeches into a bundle." Mama Jones chortled when Miles stared wide-eyed at the rather descriptive admonishment. "Ella left her heart behind her when she came to us, but she weren't pining away over some flimmy-flammy romantical notion. She *did* love you in her sweet little way. I knew it. And Jim knew it."

"Jim knew it?"

Mama Jones's amused smile slipped to one of almost reverence. "I wish you could have known Jim. You'd've liked him. Good to the soles of his feet, he were."

"Sounds like a paragon," Miles muttered.

Mama Jones ignored him or didn't hear. "I think you're like that too."

"Perfect?" Miles half laughed, half snorted.

"*Good.* An' you care about people, almost so much it hurts." She tapped at her heart. "I do suspect you're quite a bit like him, excepting, of course, that Jim did for Ella what you wouldn't."

Something in the sudden sharpness of her voice made Miles's stomach twist with immediate guilt. "And what was that?" he asked, though unsure he wanted to hear.

"He listened."

Miles leaned against the wall very near a narrow window and watched as the rain came down outside. *He listened.* Miles had listened to her all his life. He had been the person she had always come to in times of crisis, sometimes even before turning to her own father.

"There be a box on that mantelpiece, Miles Linwood. Bring it to me."

Miles obeyed, intrigued by the rough, hand-hewn box Mama Jones was so intent on having. She lifted the ill-fitting lid. "Ella made me this box." She paused in opening it. "It ain't the most beautiful of things, but she tried so hard at it, bless her."

Mama Jones lifted from inside the box a single sheet of paper, not of the highest quality but very well cared for. There did not appear to be a single crease or wrinkle on it.

"This here's m' Jim." Mama Jones turned the paper around.

It was a very well-executed pencil sketch. The details were precise. Miles likely would have recognized the young man based only on this sketch had he run into him on the street. He could even tell Jim's hair had been dark while his eyes were of a lighter hue. And Jim's mischievous smile had precisely matched his mother's. But it was his youth that proved most surprising.

"He's just a boy."

"Aye. He was but eighteen when Ella sketched this here likeness before he left with his reg'ment." Mama Jones returned the picture to the box. "Ella was, of course, younger than that."

"And they were married?" Miles couldn't help the disbelief in his voice. "They were only children."

"Part of the reason Stanton folk didn't take to Ella. Raised their eyebrows at her." Mama Jones closed the lid of her treasure box and began rocking once more. "Said she tricked him into marryin' her somehow. Said she weren't no better than she should be."

"The innkeeper in Stanton gave her a look that communicated a very similar sentiment." He returned his gaze to the rain outside. How awful to be so regarded when Elise was, he knew, nothing like the citizens of Stanton had labeled her.

"She's had a very difficult four years," Mama Jones said as if in agreement. "I know the things that were said hurt her fiercely, but she never let it show."

Was that part of the reason she held back her emotions? So those who'd hurt her couldn't guess that they had? Was that why she hid her feelings from him, because he had hurt her?

"When did she first come to live with you?" He felt as though he were only a few pieces away from finishing the puzzle of Elise's life away from him.

"Wondered when you'd get around to askin' me that."

Miles looked over his shoulder to where Mama Jones sat rocking back and forth. "Jim brought her home late in January. Four years ago."

Miles thought on that as he rode back to Tafford. Elise had disappeared from Epsworth on December 14, 1810. Four years ago late January was only six weeks after that. Where had she been during that time? he wondered. At least three weeks of that was spent posting banns wherever it was that she and Jim had married.

She couldn't have been with any family friends—Miles had inquired and come up empty-handed. According to Mama Jones, Jim had been away from Stanton for only a month. Even if he had looked after Elise during the entirety of those four weeks, there still remained a fortnight unaccounted for. Considering she had been very young, unaccompanied, unprotected, and likely very low on funds, the possibilities were not comforting.

Elise had married within six weeks of disappearing from Epsworth. But she hadn't loved her husband, according to Mama Jones. Jim was, it seemed, quite without fault, so Miles doubted Elise had been cajoled or tricked into the union.

Mama Jones had said when she'd first arrived at Tafford that Elise had told Jim about the murders but had not told her. To Jim, she'd confided her difficulties and worries. How had he gained her confidence on such short acquaintance when Miles, who had known her all her life, did not warrant the same trust now?

He listened, Mama Jones's voice echoed in his thoughts.

But, Miles countered, so had he. And she hadn't said a single thing to warn him of her departure. Miles reached the stables and left his horse in the care of his groom. With his mind heavily preoccupied, he made his way to the house and up the stairs to his library. He let out a deep breath and dropped into an armchair, feeling suddenly exhausted. No matter how often he reviewed what he knew, nothing made sense.

Chapter Fifteen

ANOTHER LETTER. ELISE TREMBLED AS she looked at it. Miles, Beth, and Langley were all present.

She wouldn't allow her distress to show. She hadn't found an answer to this particular difficulty that felt right. She had considered fleeing, though she didn't at all like the idea. However, she had the means of supporting herself should that prove necessary. There was no guarantee the writer of the letters wouldn't follow her wherever she chose to relocate.

Elise felt the others' eyes firmly fixed on her. She nervously let her gaze flicker to the envelope and very nearly breathed an audible sigh of relief. This letter had been posted and bore a return address: Mrs. Gibson in Warwickshire.

"It is from Mrs. Gibson," Elise told the others, proud that she'd kept both the earlier panic and the relief that had followed out of her voice.

"Word of your return must have reached the neighborhood," Beth said, returning to her finger sandwiches.

"I wrote to the Hudsons the day after we returned to Tafford," Miles said.

Word had reached their former neighbors in Warwickshire before the arrival of Elise's unwelcome letters. Could there be a connection? She'd often wondered over the past four years if the murderer was someone known to her. She had found it increasingly hard to trust anyone she came in contact with. That feeling of imminent danger had subsided during her time in Cheshire, but Elise felt it creeping up on her once more.

Who else knew she had returned? Anyone near Tafford. Everyone in the neighborhood where she'd grown up. Mr. Cane. Miles, Beth, and Mr. Langley, though thinking of any of those three as murderers was ridiculous in the extreme. Miles had, she understood, received at least one letter from his cousin, Lady Marion Jonquil, and had written a reply. So anyone Lady Marion might have told would now know.

There were too many possibilities. She couldn't hide from the entire world. Again, that feeling of lurking danger swept over her. She bit down once more, tensing every muscle to keep herself calm.

"What does Mrs. Gibson have to say?" Beth asked after another bite of her sandwich.

Elise opened the letter and began swiftly scanning the words written there, her heart pounding in her head. "A few pointed statements about my being gone for four years." Elise kept her eyes on the letter. Miles and Beth no doubt were wishing for the same answers for which Mrs. Gibson was fishing. "Gilbert Gibson is married," Elise added. They probably already knew that. "Miss Harriet is not." Then, under her breath, Elise added, "That is not surprising."

Elise thought she heard Miles laugh. She looked up. He smiled broadly, though his eyes were on his plate. His smile eased her discomfort in an instant, like it had so many times before.

"This means she now knows where you live, Miles." She could not resist revisiting one of her favorite topics on which to tease him from years earlier. "Perhaps she will discover a relation nearby, and you can finally have the perfect opportunity to make her that long-awaited offer of marriage."

Miles looked up then and raised an eyebrow, frowning far too severely for sincerity.

"She is such an accomplished young lady," Elise added, feeling an uncharacteristic urge to laugh.

Miles's face split into a grin. For no reason whatsoever, Elise's heart lurched. Color flooded her cheeks without warning, and she couldn't do a thing to stop it.

"I do not believe I have ever heard a young lady play the pianoforte with as much *enthusiasm* as Miss Gibson was wont to display," Miles said dryly.

He'd told Elise repeatedly of Miss Harriet Gibson's almost overwhelm-ingly loud performances. They'd often sat under their tree in the meadow the day after a neighborhood musicale or dinner, laughing over Miles's retellings.

"I never could command the undivided attention she did." Elise felt a laugh bubbling inside. She allowed a smile but nothing beyond.

"You were always too talented for the kind of theatrics she employed," Miles said.

"I haven't played the pianoforte in four years," Elise whispered, unable to meet his eyes any longer.

Her face felt too warm for her blush to be unnoticed. If asked, she couldn't have accounted for her reaction to what ought to have been a simple conversation. He had offered a compliment, yes, but nothing to make her flush the way she was.

Elise heard chair legs scrape the ground, and in the next moment, Miles stood beside her. He leaned down, whispering in her ear. "Four years is far too long."

Her heart had stopped before. Now her pulse was pounding in her neck.

Miles picked up her plate and held his free hand out to her. How she wanted to accept it. She'd held his hand so often as a child and as a young lady. A person would have been hard-pressed to find them together without their hands entwined, so common had the gesture once been between them. She'd missed that so deeply. But returning to that symbol of their once-close relationship felt too risky, too vulnerable. If she let him take her hand, how would she ever keep him from breaking her heart again?

She rose from her chair but kept her letter in her hands as an excuse. His disappointment was obvious but fleeting.

"You must come thumb through the pieces of music in the music room," he said.

"You have a music room?" she asked as Miles led the way down the corridor.

"Have you not been given the grand tour, then?"

"No." She'd felt enough like an interloper without pulling Mrs. Humphrey from her duties.

"We do, indeed, have a music room, complete with a harp, a pianoforte, and seating for as many delighted listeners—or horrified, depending on the performer—as one could hope for."

"You, Papa, and Mr. Linwood were the only listeners I ever forced my efforts upon," Elise said as they stepped inside a room she hadn't yet visited.

"Forced?" Miles laughed. "You were always a fine musician, Elise."

The music room was everything she could have hoped for, with exquisite furnishings and silk-hung walls. Decorated in shades of blue and gold, it was both tasteful and elegant. The air was not stale or damp, testament to a staff who kept the house in good working order and a household income sufficient for low-burning fires. No matter the effort they'd employed, she and Mama Jones never had been able to quite rid their small home of the dampness in the air.

Miles set Elise's plate on a small end table not far from a highly polished Broadwood grand. Elise had never in all her life played such an elegant instrument.

"This is your seat, Elise." Miles pulled her to the instrument stool. "The music is housed in this cabinet here." He indicated a deep-cherry armoire. "And you are to play whenever you please, for as long as you please."

"Thank you, Miles." She turned to face him at the exact moment he turned to face her.

They stood mere inches apart, looking into each other's eyes. Something in the atmosphere around them turned thick. Elise couldn't have looked away from those beloved brown eyes if she'd tried.

Too much lay between them for anything to be as it had been, but for all of that, he was her Miles—her dear, sweet Miles—and she had missed him acutely.

"Four years is too long," Miles repeated his earlier declaration in an almost breathless whisper.

She had the very distinct impression they were no longer speaking of the pianoforte. He didn't step back away from her.

"I was across an ocean, Elise, but still, I thought of you. Every single day, I thought of you and worried about you."

Elise felt a sting at the back of her throat and a prickling behind her eyes. "I have had people looking out for me," she replied in a whisper, feeling compelled to reassure him. Miles looked as if he blamed himself for her suffering in the years of their separation. She, somehow, couldn't bear to have him take the entirety of that weight on his shoulders, no matter the role he'd played in her desperate flight.

He set his hand lightly on her arm. "Was Jim good to you?"

"He was very kind to me." Her heart grew heavy as it always did when she thought of poor Jim Jones. "He stood my friend when I was entirely alone."

"Was I not your friend?" Miles pressed, his brows knit together.

She knew an honest answer would break his heart, so she didn't reply. Her silence, however, seemed enough.

"I'm sorry, Elise," Miles whispered, dropping his hand and stepping back. "I am not even sure what I did to lose your faith so entirely, but I am sorry for it—more sorry than I can even say."

Elise had to look away from his pained expression. His suffering pierced her usually impenetrable armor. It had always been that way. They'd shared everything and had understood each other better than any other person on earth. To see him hurting, knowing she had caused it, pricked at her.

"What can I do to regain your trust?" Miles asked.

Her trust? Her trust had died long ago.

"I don't know." Elise shrugged, fighting the loneliness that suddenly engulfed her.

A heavy silence hung between them. Elise could hear Miles's long, tense breaths. She forced back the tears that threatened to fall.

"I wish you would give me a chance," Miles muttered before turning on his heels and leaving her alone with her unsettling thoughts.

* * *

"In all honesty, Langley, I'm beginning to lose patience with her." Miles felt like a traitor saying such a thing about Elise, but he had to release some of the pressure building inside.

"'Beginning to lose patience with her?' Is that your gentle way of saying 'tempted to throttle her?'" Langley grinned at him as they made their way down the corridor. "I'd say you have reason to, though I suggest you not actually follow through."

Miles was grateful for a reason to smile amidst his frustration. "Good of you to look out for her."

"Nothing of the sort," Langley said. "I am looking out for *myself*. If you throttle poor Elise, it will put a damper on Beth's current pet project and that would prove disastrous for me."

"Will it?"

"If this ball falls to pieces, she will insist on throwing a ball every week for the rest of our lives to make up for her current disappointment." Langley pretended to grow worried. "No gentleman should be expected to endure that."

"Beth is planning a ball?" Miles hadn't heard as much. "While she's here, I would imagine, which means I am hosting it."

Langley grinned at him. "Congratulations."

Miles sighed. "Do you happen to know when this ball is meant to take place?"

"On Friday." Langley stopped in front of the sitting room and pointed toward the closed door. "Beth is in there even as we speak, making unnecessarily extravagant plans with Mrs. Haddington."

"Mrs. Haddington? In other words, there should be a great deal of talking at this ball."

"Talking. Eyelash batting. Coy fan waving."

"Run while you can, Langley." Miles tugged at Langley's jacket sleeve. "Save yourself."

"Laugh all you want, Miles. I *can* run. You, however, cannot escape this." They continued down the corridor. "You are a peer with an old and respectable title, estates, and an income few can even fathom. All of that would likely be enough to garner you invitations to every social event ever planned. But, Miles, you are all of those things *and* unmarried. That is a combination no mother with an unwed daughter and any degree of social ambition could possibly be expected to resist. You, my poor brother, are fresh meat."

They stepped out the back doors and onto the terrace. "You are certainly building my enthusiasm for this ball," Miles said dryly.

Langley laughed and slapped Miles on the shoulder. "Only offering a friendly warning. You have escaped the marriage mart longer than anyone could have predicted, but they have your scent now. The ladies of Society will not leave you be until you are either married or dead."

"I expect you to extricate me if the ball grows dangerous." Miles chuckled. "We can plan an escape route ahead of time, just to be safe."

"An excellent idea, beginning now. I propose we spend the rest of the afternoon going for a bruising ride; that way the ladies cannot talk us into helping plan anything."

"Genius." Miles gladly made his way to the stables. He hadn't anticipated a ball, but there seemed no way of avoiding it.

He'd last been in London for the social whirl when he was only nineteen, too young to be anything but annoyed by it all. He likely wouldn't mind it now, but the timing and location were far from ideal. The house and title didn't yet feel like his. He was still finding his way in this strange new existence he had inherited.

Perhaps a ball was exactly what he needed. A lighthearted distraction. And Elise might enjoy it. She'd often talked about making her debut. She had shared in great detail what she'd imagined her come-out ball would be like, the soirees and musicales she meant to attend. She'd dreamed about it but had never had her Season, never attended a single ball.

Here was a start. He could give her back bits and pieces of all she'd lost, and maybe in time, things would go back to the way they'd been.

Perhaps a ball wasn't such a bad idea after all.

Chapter Sixteen

Six lovely morning gowns on Wednesday. *Six.* She'd not been expecting so many, nor anything quite so fine.

"I cannot accept these," she said.

Beth looked down her nose at Elise, her posture suddenly quite haughty. "Are they not fine enough for you?"

Elise's heart sank. She hadn't meant her comment as a complaint. Not at all. Her plain dresses of humble fabric quite obviously told everyone who saw her that she, of all people, was in no position to judge any gown, especially a fashionable one, to not be fine enough for her taste. For all intents and purposes, she was a beggar, one who had inadvertently offended her benefactress. "They are all beautiful, certainly far nicer than anything I have worn these past years," Elise said, feeling wave after wave of humiliation. "I hadn't meant to—"

But Beth smiled and took Elise's hands, squeezing them. "Miles says I have become terrifying when I put on my 'lady of the manor' facade." Her expression quickly turned apologetic. "I had only meant to tease you, but clearly I did it ill."

Though Elise had accepted her lowered status four years earlier, she hadn't felt the change so acutely as she did now. Seeing firsthand the life she'd lost, seeing it day after day, was chipping away at her fragile confidence. "I suppose I am a touch too sensitive about some topics."

Beth put an arm around her shoulder and guided her over to the chairs set beside the fireplace in her bedchamber. "There are more yet to arrive. You'd best tell me what it is about the dresses you don't care for."

"It isn't that. I assure you." How did she explain it without sounding terribly ungrateful? "I simply feel like such a burden. Miles said he was giving me four belated birthday presents. Six gowns with more on the way is—"

Beth cut off her protest with a raised hand. "We have missed your last four Christmases *and* birthdays. And as your guardian, Miles would have seen to it you had the proper wardrobe for your come-out."

Her come-out. Elise hadn't allowed herself to think of that since leaving Epsworth. She'd looked forward to making her London debut all her life, but fate had ripped that from her.

"Consider these additions to your wardrobe payment on a debt, Elise. And please allow us to do this."

Elise was too aware of just how much Miles and Beth were doing for her to not feel some degree of weariness at yet another offering. And yet, to refuse would be an unnecessarily stubborn stance. "I *do* need new dresses."

Beth looked immediately relieved. She motioned Elise back over to the gowns. "I think you will like these. They are quite in line with current fashions but are wonderfully simple."

Simple? Elise eyed the ivory lace edging the neckline and cuffs of the dresses, the colorful fabrics. One gown even had a sheer overlay. There was nothing at all simple about the gowns Beth had ordered when compared to the utterly unadorned dress Elise wore day after day.

"Thank you for these," she said. She was grateful, but she was also terribly uncertain. Wearing the dresses would feel almost like a lie. Fine gowns and fancy fabrics were no longer who she was. She hadn't rejected those comforts; she had actually missed them terribly. But a person didn't simply return to the *ton*. That was a door that once shut was never reopened.

She would always be poor, insignificant Ella Jones. Nothing could really change that. Being a guest in the home of a peer didn't make her his equal. Wearing a fine gown didn't make her a fine lady. Still, she could pretend for a time, if only to make Miles and Beth happy.

She ran her fingers down the skirt of one of the dresses. "I'd forgotten how soft muslin is. I never did grow accustomed to the itchiness of homespun. Though, in its defense, it is very warm in the winter."

Beth took up one of the dresses laid out on the bed and held it up for closer examination. "Miles said your favorite color was blue. I hope that is still true. I did favor blue in the order I placed."

"I love blue." Elise was impressed and touched that Miles would recall that. But, then again, she still remembered that he was quite fond of green. That came of growing up with a tighter bond than many siblings had. They had always been so much a part of one another's lives that their knowledge of even the most trivial things about each other had come about without effort.

The color blue, in that moment, joined all the other bits and pieces of her past life, tiny reminders of what once was and might have been. She had an entire collection of such things—memories she pulled out when her heart was heavy and her mind reflected on years gone by.

"There is a particularly lovely ball gown set to arrive on Friday," Beth said.

"A ball gown?" What need had she of a ball gown?

But Beth's nod was quite matter-of-fact. "There's to be a ball, you realize."

She'd heard no such thing. "A ball *here?*"

"Indeed. All the local families are coming, as well as several neighboring ones." Beth carefully laid the dress back down. "This is the Season in London, so our gathering will be small compared to what we might have planned were more people in the country just now. Still, I think it will be a wonderful evening."

"You are expecting me to attend?" Elise felt certain Beth was, though the very idea terrified her. She didn't belong in a ballroom. The past four years she'd been beneath the notice of even the staff in a fine home such as this.

"Of course." Beth smiled as though she truly thought Elise's question had been nothing but a bit of humor. "And you'll love the ball gown." She rubbed her hands together. "It is positively delicious."

"Am I supposed to wear it or eat it?"

Beth laughed, her hands pressed to her heart. "Oh, my dear friend. How I have missed your humor these past years. You forever had us laughing so hard we could hardly breathe."

Those had been lovely times. "Do you ever miss the carefree days of childhood?"

"I think every adult does, but I believe our joy grows as we do because our challenges are greater. The contrast magnifies our triumphs."

Triumphs. Elise could do with a triumph; she'd known too many defeats.

* * *

Friday afternoon found Elise hiding away at Mama Jones's cottage. The world of glittering fanciness had begun to wear on her. She'd missed it the past years yet didn't at all feel ready to jump back in feet first. She needed a momentary respite. And she needed time and space to think.

She'd received another letter, unposted, unsigned.

Be wisely tight-lipped, or you'll be silent as the grave.

A reminder that the murderer didn't want her revealing anything she remembered about the murders. But she had no memories beyond the ones she'd told the Bow Street Runner who'd handled the investigation. There was nothing more to tell. And she had no intention of speaking of that awful, harrowing night ever again.

So long as her silence was in question, her life was in danger. She knew that. But what could she possibly do? A cottage tucked away somewhere could either be safe or dangerously isolated. Anything might happen, and no one would ever be the wiser.

Anne danced about the parlor. Mrs. Ash had recently introduced her to the same childish songs she'd taught Elise as a little girl, and Anne clearly didn't hear the tunes in their entirety but made out enough to have fallen in love with the music. How often Elise wondered just how much her daughter could hear and if anything could be done about it. As soon as she knew precisely her income, she meant to take Anne to a man of medicine.

Elise sang the songs and clapped in rhythm, her heart swelling as she watched her once-solemn little girl blossoming before her very eyes. Anne would likely never be praised for her grace as a dancer, but no one could fault her enthusiasm. Would all of that crash down around them if Elise had to pull her away from this new life they were building? Was not that, perhaps, a direction more fraught with risk than remaining near Miles?

"My turn," Mama Jones jumped in. "I remember so well Jim's favorite song when he was a tiny thing."

She began a boisterous rendition of "Oh, Dear, What Can the Matter Be?" Anne swayed back and forth, the movement more than a touch awkward. She sang along, the same tuneless singing of nonsense sounds she'd engaged in the entire afternoon. Elise couldn't imagine anything more beautiful. Anne had never sung before, not even once. Tafford had been very good for her.

A mere few weeks with Mrs. Ash in the fairy-tale nursery and free of the worry of poverty and Anne had become a new child. While Elise wanted to believe the difference was money and opportunity, seeing the light in Anne's eyes as she danced in Mama Jones's parlor, Elise couldn't deny the source of Anne's transformation had far more to do with simply being allowed to be a child.

A weight settled on Elise's heart. She had given Anne so little to be happy about and now stood poised to rip it away again. *I am a terrible mother. Terrible.*

Jim had deserved a better wife than she had been. He ought to have been loved deeply by someone capable of it. She had been in too dark a place to have cherished him the way he'd deserved. Mama Jones had cared for her the past four years, and what had Elise given her in return? Two extra mouths to feed and not nearly as much happiness as she deserved.

How could Elise protect herself and Anne while still making certain her darling little girl could grow up happy and whole?

She had no answers, only the firm realization that she had to do something. She couldn't allow herself to snuff out the flickering flame of joy she saw in Anne. But neither could she permit her sweet girl to be in danger.

Chapter Seventeen

"You are no longer my favorite sister," Miles muttered under his breath to Beth as they greeted the last of an unexpectedly long line of guests at the start of the ball.

"Well worth it, I assure you." Beth was firmly in her element. Social gatherings and miserable crushes of people were to her what dolls and toys were to small children. She couldn't possibly have looked more pleased. "My next goal will be to plan a house party—held here, of course—of such grand proportions that you will disown me in the most public and vitriolic way imaginable, and we shall make the social column of any and every newspaper within a four- or five-county radius. And I will love every moment of it."

Miles couldn't be at all certain she was exaggerating. Indeed, he was leaning toward believing every word.

He offered Beth his arm. Balls required siblings to set aside their propensity for pricking at one another and act civilized for an evening. Fortunately, he *did* like his sister despite his insistence otherwise. "You must be pleased with the number of guests," Miles said. Beth had worried a little that they'd have a disappointingly small response.

"I am," she said. "Though I've been so busy I've not had a chance to see Elise in her ball gown."

Miles hadn't either, though he knew the gown had arrived. He'd feared it wouldn't. Elise had never attended any of the balls she would have had their lives played out differently. He didn't want this first one to be a disappointment to her.

"I admit I'm a little jealous," Beth said. "The fabric I selected is simply divine."

"You need only tell your husband how heartbroken and disappointed you are," Miles said. "I've noticed how firmly wrapped around your finger he is. He'll buy you every ball gown you want if you only pout a little."

She shook her head at his teasing but smiled knowingly. Langley really was a rather happily browbeaten husband. They walked into the ballroom, offering nods of acknowledgment and greeting as they passed their guests but continuing their conversation in muted tones.

"I do hope Elise is happy with her gown," Beth said.

"I am certain she is. She always adored finery." Miles couldn't count the number of times she'd begged his mother to allow her to dress up in her gowns and fine things, her own mother having died when Elise was only four years old. After Miles's mother died, Elise had taken to borrowing Beth's fanciest gowns for her imaginary balls and outings.

"I am not as confident as you are in that," Beth admitted. "Elise's childhood was filled with such things. But as an adult, she has built her identity in a world devoid of them."

"She seemed comfortable enough in the morning gowns that arrived earlier this week."

"A ball gown is something quite different," Beth said. "It is meant for an evening such as this. If she is not ready to make that step back into her former life, the gown itself might not be welcome."

Langley approached in the next moment. Beth happily abandoned Miles for the greater pleasure of her husband's company. For his part, Miles began searching about for Elise. She was never far from his thoughts, but Beth's uncertainty had him particularly anxious.

"Lord Grenton." Mrs. Haddington hurriedly reached his side. "What a lovely night this is proving to be. Such an impressive assemblage. The staff carried out instructions perfectly. Everything is just as it should be. Such a triumph for the neighborhood."

Triumph? Miles had managed to avoid evicting his father's tenants in the aftermath of his unpayable debts. He'd survived being left without a home or a guinea to his name. He'd found his long-lost dearest friend. Those were triumphs. This was simply a ball.

"I am pleased you are enjoying the evening," he said. Though he didn't place upon it the same importance she did, he was happy she was satisfied with the fruits of her efforts. "And I know Beth is quite grateful to you for the assistance you offered."

Mrs. Haddington waved off the gratitude. "Someday we will have a Marchioness of Grenton to take on such things. Until then, I am more than happy to help where I can." She waved her daughter over. "I am simply happy that the neighborhood has one of its principal families again. That lack has been acutely felt since the late marquess's passing."

"Who would throw a lavish party such as this, after all, if there were no marquess?" Miles allowed a bit of his underlying dryness to touch the words.

Mrs. Haddington playfully swatted at him with her fan.

Miss Haddington's response was a touch more serious. "Surely you realize a marquess is more than that. Whilst this estate and title were in limbo, so was the area. The tenants were at risk of losing their homes and livelihoods. Most of the staff was let go. The shop owners suffered as a result. And the Marquess of Grenton holds a position of influence in Lords, which is important for those whose lives his decisions there will impact."

She held a very high view of one man's importance. "You left off a marquess's duty to control the weather and dictate the movement of stars."

Miss Haddington smiled. "I believe only dukes can do that."

"Well, that is a relief. I do have rather a lot to see to without adding the functioning of the heavens to my responsibilities."

"Then it is with deepest regret that I find myself obligated to point out that you are, at this very moment, neglecting one of your more pressing responsibilities."

He understood in an instant. "I am meant to be dancing, aren't I?"

"At the very least, you are expected to mingle with your guests."

Miles hung his head dramatically. "Shabby through and through."

He'd nearly forgotten Mrs. Haddington stood nearby until she jumped unexpectedly to defend him . . . against himself. "You are simply out of practice with such things, living away from England as you have. You only need someone versed in such things to offer you a bit of guidance."

He bowed quite properly. "Again, I thank you for your offers of help."

"Nonsense. Camille will walk you through this evening. She has attended many balls and is quite in demand at any social event, no doubt because her grace and manners are second to none. You could not hope for a more helpful young lady to have at your side."

Miss Haddington looked utterly amused at her mother's ham-fisted attempts at playing matchmaker, though she managed to keep most of the laughter out of her expression. "I *am* quite indispensable. However, an unmarried young lady cannot act in the capacity of hostess for an unmarried gentleman, even informally, without implying some degree of understanding between them."

Miles hadn't immediately thought of that, though he knew in an instant she was absolutely correct. By the quick flash of disappointment in Mrs. Haddington's face, that lady *had* realized the implications.

"Rely upon your sister's guidance. Mrs. Langley knows what she is about," Miss Haddington said.

"She was not, despite her reliability, able to point me in the direction of our friend, Mrs. Jones," Miles said. "I want to make certain she is at ease. She has no friends or acquaintances in this neighborhood beyond our small family circle."

Mrs. Haddington seemed surprised. Miss Haddington, however, did not. "She is sitting along the far wall, a bit removed from the French windows. And, I am sorry to say, seems excessively uncomfortable."

Miles's heart dropped. He had feared exactly this. Perhaps he ought to have discussed these plans with her as soon as he'd heard of them. He ought to have found out for himself what her feelings were and what she needed in order to enjoy her first Society event.

"Thank you, Miss Haddington." He bowed over her hand, offered her mother an acknowledging dip of his head, and made to follow Miss Haddington's direction.

He was waylaid, however, by Mr. Haddington before he'd gone more than a dozen steps. "My apologies, Lord Grenton, for not having come for a visit these past few weeks. I've been neck deep in a great deal of business."

Miles waved off the apology. He'd not been the least offended. He'd been rather too occupied with his own concerns to have even noticed. "I am pleased you could come this evening, you and your family."

Mr. Haddington nodded, his brow and mouth both turned down in deep thought. "I understand you've had some house guests."

"Yes, my sister and her husband, as well as a dear family friend."

"Yes, the soldier's widow." He nodded. "My wife and daughter told me about her. Quiet thing, they said. Has a little girl."

Miles's limited interactions with Mr. Haddington had proven him a blunt and somewhat nosy man, inclined to jump directly into another's affairs without bothering to think whether the intrusion was appreciated or appropriate.

"Mrs. Jones and her daughter are both very dear friends." Miles hoped he had conveyed the necessary warning. He would not permit Elise or Anne to be spoken of unkindly.

Mr. Haddington barreled on. "I think I may have known Mrs. Jones's father. Furlong was the name, I believe."

"It was, indeed." Miles hadn't been expecting that. He knew Mr. Haddington had known his father but didn't realize the acquaintance had extended to Mr. Furlong.

"We belonged to the same club, attended some of the same races, and, in our more intellectual moments, attended the same lectures and demonstrations. We weren't the closest of friends, but we were more than passing acquaintances."

"I didn't realize your connection to my father and hers was as extensive as this." Miles didn't think he remembered his father ever mentioning a Mr. Haddington. But, then again, Father had never mentioned his mountain of crushing debts either.

Mr. Haddington shook his head. "As I said, we weren't the closest of friends. But I knew him. Good men, both of them. I was sorry to hear of their passing."

"It was a grievous loss, certainly." Miles never knew whether to thank people for expressing sorrow at Father's death or to simply agree with them. Agreeing seemed the best response in that moment.

"Well, I'll leave you to your guests," Mr. Haddington said. "I only wanted to know if Mrs. Jones was Mr. Furlong's daughter. The world seems smaller the older I get. More connections between us all."

Miles could only imagine how ceaseless the chatter was at the Haddington house. Neither the master nor mistress were prone to bouts of silence. He left Mr. Haddington behind and continued his search for Elise.

Miss Haddington's directions proved entirely correct. Elise occupied a chair a bit apart from any of the others. She sat ramrod straight, her bare hands clutched tightly in her lap. She watched the dancers and other guests with a look of pending doom, as though she expected someone to attack her or toss her out on her ear.

So distracted was she that Miles managed to take the seat next to hers without being noticed. "Do you not wish to join them?" he asked, fully expecting to startle her.

She didn't bat an eyelash. "I am quite content exactly where I am."

"You *did* see me approach."

"Of course I did." She looked at him at last. "You are quite dashing this evening. I don't imagine anyone hasn't taken note of you."

Miles made a show of tugging at his cuffs, then pretended to smooth back his hair.

A whisper of a smile touched Elise's face. "You used to do exactly that whenever I forced you to come have tea with me in my nursery," Elise said. "For years, I thought that was an integral part of any social call."

He could easily imagine that. "I was a bad influence on you."

She shook her head. "You were the best part of my childhood."

And she had been the best part of his.

"You look lovely this evening," he said. "That gown is new."

She nervously smoothed her skirt. "Beth ordered it for me. It is the finest gown I've ever owned."

"I know very little of fashion, but I think it's perfect."

"How comforting that someone who knows little of fashion has given his approval of my fashion choices." The tiniest glimmer of mischief twinkled in her eyes.

"I clearly remember how often you gave me advice on fisticuffs and how to strut about in the manliest way a schoolboy could possibly manage, though you had no experience with either one."

"That is different." If not for the smile tugging at her lips, Elise would have looked entirely in earnest. "*I* was always so clever that experience was not at all necessary."

Miles chuckled lightly. He looked out over the dancers and other guests. "What does your cleverness say about my very first ball as a marquess? Is it a success?"

"Inarguably," she said. "If nothing else, you have quite a collection of matchmaking mamas rubbing their hands together schemingly whilst their daughters adopt a very proprietary air when looking your way."

"And more than one of the fathers has been a bit too pointed in his sudden interest in being my newest associate," Miles said. "Makes a man feel like a horse at market."

Elise smiled at him. He had the oddest urge to simply hug her.

"A marquess is rather a catch," she said. "Even if he has spent the past four years working in the sugar fields."

"Perhaps I should pull out some of my old, mud-stained work clothes and see how interested the young ladies still are."

"A single gentleman with both a title and a vast deal of wealth could arrive at a ball in only his dressing gown and would still be in high demand." Her smile faded a bit. "A woman of no fortune, however, could arrive spectacularly gowned and perfectly coiffed and still be rejected out of hand."

"Is that what is worrying you, Elise? You fear their rejection?"

"I am too far beneath their notice to even warrant the effort of a rejection," she said quite matter-of-factly.

He set his hand on top of her hands, still clutched tightly together in her lap. "You underestimate yourself, my friend."

She didn't pull away. She didn't pull away!

"You think no one has even noticed you," he said, "but Miss Haddington knew precisely where you were when I asked. She had noticed you."

"From what I have seen of her, Miss Haddington is a very kindhearted person," Elise said. "I will say this though: she may have noticed where I was sitting, but she hasn't yet lost track of *you*. Very few people have, in fact."

Miles returned his gaze to the other guests and realized Elise was absolutely correct. Several people were approaching them at that very moment.

He rose as his guests arrived at the small grouping of chairs where only he and Elise sat. Doing so necessitated that he release her hand, and he regretted it on the instant. But, he told himself, that she had allowed the once-familiar connection was progress.

She stood, apparently remembering that doing so was expected. Miles bowed. Elise curtsied. The new arrivals curtsied as well.

"We had wondered where you disappeared to," one of the matrons said, a hint of real reprimand beneath her teasing tone.

"I was speaking with Mrs. Jones. She is a very close friend of the Linwood family."

"Yes, so we have heard."

Another of the local ladies took up the discussion. "That is a lovely color, Mrs. Jones, and a very fashionable style. Who is your modiste?"

"I am not certain," Elise said, her voice low and quiet. "Mrs. Langley placed the order on my behalf."

"On your behalf?" Such doubt filled the lady's question. "I was under the impression she undertook the task entirely."

Elise's coloring dropped off noticeably. Her gaze dropped to the floor. "Mrs. Langley is very kind to me."

"Indeed," was the noticeably haughty response.

One of the younger ladies spoke to Elise next from behind her hand, as though wishing to keep her remark between the two of them, though she didn't lower her voice enough to keep the conversation private. "You have neglected to wear your gloves, Mrs. Jones. You did realize you were supposed to, did you not?"

"An unfortunate oversight, I'm afraid." Elise spoke as though she were a chambermaid being reprimanded by her mistress rather than a lady of the gentry in conversation with other ladies belonging to that same class.

Elise slowly disappeared into herself. The gathered guests took their cues from her and seemed to forget she stood among them. *I am too far beneath their notice to even warrant the effort of a rejection.* Miles wished in that moment the ladies had, in fact, not noticed her enough to be unkind. Listening to their haughty words of dismissal was far worse.

"The next set is about to begin." Miles addressed Elise. If he asked her to dance, his other guests would have to acknowledge she was their equal. Perhaps Elise herself would begin to believe it.

She didn't allow him to even begin his invitation. "Then this is the perfect moment for me to slip away. I wish to offer Anne a good night before she falls asleep."

"You—"

She made a quick, awkward curtsy to all of them at once and hurried from the ballroom before anyone could offer an objection.

For a solid hour, Miles attempted to slip out of the ballroom and follow her, wanting to make certain she had left for the reason she'd claimed. Though the ladies hadn't said anything to her that on the surface was clearly insulting, their tones and postures could not have been misunderstood. Elise had been so fragile since they'd been reunited, no longer the quietly confident, seldom ruffled young lady he'd once known. He couldn't bear the thought of her being hurt in his home.

Finally, he was able to step out and hurry up the back stairwell to the second floor, where the nursery was. Elise said she meant to tuck Anne in. The nursery would be the best place to look first.

A low light burned in the pink bedchamber Anne had claimed as her own. Miles peeked inside. Anne slept soundly on her bed. Heavens, but she looked exactly like her mother at that age. It was like a glimpse directly into the past. He stepped quietly over to Anne's bed and pulled her blanket up over her shoulders.

She had warmed to him a bit over the weeks, but it was a slow process. He'd grown very fond of her and wanted to see her smile, to see her as happy as Elise had been as a child.

He pressed a kiss to Anne's forehead. "Good night, sweet girl," he whispered. "Sleep well."

"Miles?" Elise's confused, quiet voice broke into the silence of the room.

He glanced back and saw her sitting in a chair not far from the bed. She still wore her ball gown, but there was no mistaking the fact that she'd been sleeping in the hard, spindle-backed chair.

She blinked a few times. "I think I fell asleep."

"I believe you did," Miles said. "And not in the most comfortable place."

She smiled a bit. "My neck most certainly agrees with you." Elise turned her head from side to side, her expression twisting with obvious discomfort. "If only Wellington had been aware of this acute form of torture. Napoleon would have surrendered after one night of this."

Did she have any idea how much she tortured *him* with these fleeting glimpses of the girl he'd once known and cared about so deeply? She remained just out of reach.

Elise's gaze settled on Anne. "She wanted to sing a song for me. That one song turned into at least a dozen." She smiled fondly at her daughter. "She fell asleep only after she was entirely exhausted."

Miles sat gingerly on the edge of the bed, careful not to wake the sleeping girl. "I didn't realize she sang."

"A recently acquired talent," Elise said with a quiet laugh. "She will never be invited to perform for anyone, but she enjoys it so very much one can't help enjoying it with her."

Elise yawned. She did indeed look tired.

Miles picked up the lantern from the bedside table. "There's no point being uncomfortable the rest of the night." He held his hand out to her, praying she would take it. "I'll walk you up to your bedchamber. I know a back way so you'll not have to stop and talk with any of the guests if you'd rather not."

"You know me well." She took his hand.

A mixture of triumph and utter relief settled over him. No matter that she remained aloof most of the time; she had allowed him to hold her hand twice that night. He was, somehow or another, getting through to her.

"I did know you very well once," he said gently. "Lately, however, I feel . . . a little lost."

Sadness touched her eyes. "I feel more than a bit lost myself."

"Life has not played out the way either of us expected, has it?"

She shook her head. "Not in the least."

Miles lifted her hand to his mouth and pressed a kiss to her fingers. "We'll sort this all out. We simply have to find our way."

"Then it is a very good thing you have the lantern."

Miles squeezed her fingers as they walked from the room, the lantern held in his free hand. They pretended to be very sneaky as they made their way around the back corridors and down the stairs to her bedroom. It was a game they'd often played as children. She smiled and looked like she was biting back more than one laugh. Miles's heart lightened during that quick journey about the house. The longer Elise was there, the more hopeful he grew.

Chapter Eighteen

MILES, BETH, AND MR. LANGLEY slept straight through breakfast the next morning. Only Elise awoke at the usual time. The others had been up late, enjoying the ball.

Elise sat at the windows of the morning room, looking out over the back meadow of Tafford. She'd worked quite hard the evening before to appear as though she was happy to leave the ball. But that had been far from true. She had been nervous and a little unsure of herself, but flutters of excitement had built throughout the day before.

She had dreamed of attending a ball since she was a child. She'd imagined herself in an elegant gown, dancing with a handsome gentleman, being an inarguable part of the gathering. Last night would have been her first taste of that long-awaited dream. And there she'd sat, gloveless, wearing her worn boots beneath a gown she'd received out of charity—well-meaning charity but charity nonetheless—and feeling like a weed among the roses.

She was every bit as lost as she'd told Miles she felt. Sitting by herself at the ball, she'd finally admitted to herself that she had to decide the direction of her future. She needed to find a place for herself and Anne, a place that was permanent and comfortable and fitting. She didn't know how far away she would settle, couldn't say for certain how much danger she might be in from the writer of the letters, but she could no longer sit idly by and wait for fate to deal another telling blow; neither could she continually uproot Anne. They needed to find a place that could permanently be home.

"Mrs. Jones."

She looked back toward the door.

One of the footman stood in the entryway. "Mr. Cane is here to see you, ma'am," he said. "Mr. Humphrey has placed him in the library."

"Thank you."

Elise stood. She smoothed out the front of her morning dress, grateful for the option of dresses that made her appear at least somewhat important. She likely would have been quite intimidated meeting with a solicitor on her own were she still wearing her old dress of homespun. Looking more like a lady of means increased the likelihood of being treated like one.

Mr. Cane was, in fact, in the library. He stood behind the desk as she stepped inside. Elise inclined her head, allowing that to serve as a greeting. She chose a seat slightly to the side of the desk rather than sit across from him like a petitioner. He was in her employ, in a manner of speaking. She would do well to at least pretend that didn't feel odd to her.

He retook his seat but didn't wait for her to indicate he should begin their discussion. "After I last left here, I returned to my offices fully intending to set in motion those arrangements necessary for your first quarterly payment to arrive as expected. Unfortunately, there have been some difficulties. I am sure you will understand when I tell you that you may be required to wait longer than you had anticipated. It could not be helped, after all."

Elise rallied her determination. "If you would, please begin your explanation again but with at least a little detail. What were the difficulties? How did they disrupt the payment? And when can I expect this problem to be resolved?"

Mr. Cane's air was patient but with just enough condescension to set Elise's teeth a bit on edge. She could have predicted what came next. "Financial matters are complicated, Mrs. Jones, especially to one not schooled in the intricacies of money. A woman of your humble financial circumstances would be overwhelmed by the details."

Though the emphasis on *woman* and *humble* was subtle, it was unmistakable.

"Humor me," Elise said, doing her best to mimic the confident tone she'd heard Beth employ again and again. She might not understand everything Mr. Cane told her, but she meant to try.

"When Mr. Linwood—that is, *Lord Grenton*—asked me all those years ago to invest on your behalf the funds left to you after the sale of your late father's estate, I couldn't do so in Lord Grenton's name, else the funds would have been enveloped by his late father's estate, which was at that time in the process of being liquidated. But neither could I place the account exclusively in your name, as you were underage at that time, in addition to being female, either one of which prevented you from legally being permitted to have sole control of the account."

Elise knew perfectly well the dim view both lawmakers and businessmen took of a woman's ability to make decisions of any kind. She simply nodded her understanding of what Mr. Cane was telling her.

He continued. "The account I created was in your name, with young Mr. Linwood named as trustee. But his recently acquired title and transfer of his interest to the keeping of a different solicitor as well as a different man of business than he had been using have prevented me from directing the monthly payments on my own. I will have to collect the proper signatures and make arrangements with the Grenton solicitor, who is in London, a journey I hadn't anticipated making and which will require a bit of planning."

"That satisfies the what and the how," Elise said, "leaving the when to be answered. When will I receive my quarterly payment?"

"I am not entirely certain."

Elise pushed back the worry growing inside. She needed her income in order to begin planning for Anne's and her future. "The next quarter day is the twenty-fourth of June, some three weeks from now. Do you require longer than that to make a journey to Town?"

"I imagine it all seems very simple to you," Mr. Cane said. "But I assure you, there are complications you wouldn't have thought of."

Elise had been talked down to in just that tone again and again the past four years. A few weeks in Miles's house and she found she was no longer accustomed to it, nor did she have as much patience with it. "Then in lieu of recounting these details of which I haven't yet thought, I will simply ask again how late you anticipate the payment being?"

"Likely not more than a week or two, three or four at the most."

Four weeks? That would certainly put a stop to any plans she might make. But there seemed little to be done. "Thank you for the advanced notice," Elise said. "I will give this some thought."

He nodded but almost mechanically, as though he did so simply to be doing something, not because he actually approved. It was an unspoken dismissal, one with which she was painfully familiar. Even in her finer dress and as the guest of a marquess, she was still poor Ella Jones from Stanton. Mr. Cane could see that. The ladies at the ball the night before had sensed it.

Elise rose. "I will leave you to gather your papers and such," she said. "Feel free to pull the bell if you need the staff's assistance."

"Of course, Mrs. Jones." Mr. Cane gave her a very abbreviated bow.

Elise kept her chin up and her shoulders back as she left the room with all the dignity she could manage. She didn't allow her churning emotions to show. She was finding her new place in the world, somewhere between poverty and affluence. Mr. Cane's visit had added a bit more complication to the endeavor, but it had also given her a moment to recall the confident person she'd once been. She'd kept up her end of their conversation and had insisted on details from her solicitor, even when he'd been reluctant to give them. She could certainly be proud of that.

She spent the remainder of the morning with Anne, singing songs and drawing pictures in the nursery. Mrs. Ash looked on from nearby as she worked on a bit of mending. It truly was something of a fairy world. All the worries of life seemed miles away when surrounded by the magical beauty of the nursery. Someday when she had her own house, Elise would find a way to recreate at least a small bit of this wonderful space.

But I cannot do that without money. What was she to do if the quarterly payment was even later than Mr. Cane had predicted? She couldn't continue on as a guest in Miles's house indefinitely. She could move in with Mama Jones, but what would the three of them live on? She couldn't look for employment in the village. No one would hire a woman who had been a guest in one of the finest houses in the neighborhood. A woman with a child in tow wasn't likely to be hired as a governess or lady's companion.

Elise kept a smile on her face as she played with Anne. When she had a quiet moment, she would think things through and find some kind of solution. In the meantime, she would pretend she wasn't worried.

* * *

Miles took his lunch on a tray in his room the day after the ball. He'd slept later than he had in recent memory. Society kept the oddest hours. He dressed and headed out to the back meadow for some much-needed fresh air and exercise to wake him up fully.

After a few circuits of the meadow, he passed the back garden. On a bench under the rose bower sat Elise. Miles didn't have to give it even a moment's thought but turned immediately up the path toward her.

The few moments he'd spent with her the evening before in the quiet sanctuary of Anne's room had been by far the highlight of the night. He'd known very few of the guests and hadn't particularly cared for all the bowing and flattery and empty conversations required at the ball. He hadn't enjoyed the dancing either. Elise had laughed with him and smiled. Those moments had stayed with him all night.

Elise had yet to realize he was there. She sat on a small garden bench, flipping through a stack of opened letters, her eyebrows knit in obvious concern. *Those letters.* She'd received at least two over the past week or more, but every time he asked her about them, she immediately changed the subject.

What was in them? Why didn't she want him to know? He'd been trying to show her he could be trusted. He'd not pressed her but had offered help at every turn, and she'd rebuffed him again and again.

"A penny for your thoughts?"

Elise's head snapped up, surprise written on every inch of her face. She hastily stuffed the letters into her reticule. "I did not realize you were there."

"Obviously, else you would have been certain to keep your letters out of sight."

She dropped her eyes, fussing over the lay of her skirt.

"Why are you so secretive about those letters?" He sat beside her on the bench.

He could see it was not something insignificant. Indeed, the worry in her eyes could not be mistaken.

She turned a bit on the bench and faced him, her sudden smile not the least believable. "How was the rest of the ball? Did no one attempt to wring a proposal from you?"

He would not be so easily turned from the topic. "I know perfectly well the ball is not what you were fretting over just now. Talk to me."

"I *am* talking," she said a bit defensively. "How was the ball?"

"Why are you so unwilling to tell me about these letters? I can see they worry you. You didn't used to be so secretive."

She stood and turned away again, her eyes focusing decidedly in the other direction. Her posture stiffened, and her expression turned determinedly unemotional. She was pulling on her suit of armor.

"Elise." He took hold of her arm, keeping her there as he rose and came to stand behind her. She did not turn back to look at him. "I am not going to insist that you confide in me." It was a difficult promise to make, sorely tempted as he was to press the matter until she spilled her budget. "But I want you to know that you can. More than that, I need you to realize you are not alone any longer."

She didn't respond, didn't turn back to face him.

"You have been my friend all my life." He did not know which words would prove the ones that finally broke through to her. "If you are worried over something, I hope you will come to me."

She shook her head, silent and unrelenting, still turned away from him.

"Truly, Elise. I would do anything in my power to help you if you are in some kind of trouble."

She spun about. He took an involuntary step backward at the flash in her eyes. This was not the look of trusting friendship he had anticipated. Indeed, Elise looked very nearly livid. After weeks of only the slightest hints of emotion, it was a shocking sight.

"Trouble?" she repeated, her jaw noticeably tensed. "I suppose all I would have to say is 'Miles, I am in trouble' and you would rush to my aid?"

"Of course." His words seemed only to increase her apparent anger. If a look could ignite a fire, Miles would have been nothing but a smoking pile of ashes.

"I tried that," Elise snapped. She was physically shaking. "'Please help me,' I said. 'I am in trouble.' My exact words. You were the only person I trusted, the only one who could have helped."

"What—?"

"I begged, Miles. Pleaded." Elise was shaking so hard Miles worried she wouldn't be able to remain on her feet. Her eyes snapped with something very near rage. "'Help me,' I said. And what was I told in return?"

Miles felt his heart thud. He had no memory, no recollection of this conversation she was, apparently, quoting to him.

"'Grow up,' you said. 'Grow up and solve your own problems.'" She all but spat the words. "Do not talk to me about friendship and loyalty, Miles Linwood. And do not lecture me about trusting you and believing you will help me. I grew up, just like you told me to. I grew up and learned that trust is nothing but a lie."

She pulled away from him with a jerk, then ran from the garden without looking back. Miles was too shocked to so much as move. What in the world had just happened? And how was it everything kept going so terribly wrong?

Chapter Nineteen

ANOTHER TEAR FELL UNCHECKED. IN all the years she had lived in Cheshire, Elise had seldom allowed her emotions to get the better of her. And she'd almost never cried. In the few short weeks since Miles had returned to her life, she couldn't seem to retain control of herself. She'd yelled at him in the garden. She'd let every ounce of anger and disappointment and hurt enter her words and voice. Now she was crying. Sobbing.

Grow up, Elise. Grow up and solve your own problems. She could hear Miles's words as clearly as if he'd only just uttered them. He had never, until that moment four years ago, turned his back on her so entirely.

Miles had always been her hero. He'd rescued her from scrapes her whole life. He was her very dearest friend, who had loved her through her darkest moments. But everything had changed after the murders.

Elise had spent more than a month crushed under the weight of her situation and all that had happened, a weight of such enormity she couldn't even begin to fight her way free of it. She hadn't for a moment doubted that he would help her. He always had.

But in that moment, that time, everything fell apart.

"Miles, I am in trouble."

He had looked up at her from his father's desk in the Epsworth library. Dark circles under his eyes spoke of too many sleepless nights. She had faltered for a moment. How could she add to his worries? But there had been no one else she could turn to.

"I need your help. Please, Miles." Tears clogged her throat. "I am in a great deal of trouble."

He didn't answer. Miles simply watched her with a look of pique, as if her words, her very presence irritated him.

Elise took a slow breath, trying to keep her thoughts calm and rational. "I am frightened, Miles. I don't know what to do." Her voice broke on the last words. She'd so desperately kept the fear at bay but knew she couldn't hold up on her own any longer.

"Will you help me? Please?"

Miles's fists clenched, his jaw growing tight. Every inch of him tensed with anger and frustration.

"Please, Miles," she begged, stopping just short of actually dropping to her knees. She came and stood beside the desk, pleading with her eyes and words. "Please help me."

Miles's eyes snapped as he looked at her standing there. Voice tight, he answered her inquiry. "I am sick of saving everyone. Grow up, Elise. Grow up and solve your own problems."

He lowered his eyes back to the account book on the desk in front of him. He didn't so much as glance back up. Elise stood beside the desk, unable to move.

He had spoken. She had asked for his help—begged for it—and he had said no.

"Please, Miles," she whispered in a last attempt.

His pen scratched across the open page of the account book as if she wasn't even in the room.

The walls of the book room began closing in around her. Dizziness and nausea threatened to send her toppling to the ground. Fear like she hadn't felt since the night she'd seen two men shot dead before her very eyes gripped her insides. She was in real and immediate danger and not a soul on earth cared.

Elise walked in an unseeing daze back to her bedchamber at Epsworth and sat on the edge of her bed. Miles had said no. He who had always helped her, who had stood beside her in her most difficult moments, had turned her away.

"Solve your own problems," she had whispered into the silence of her room. "Solve your own problems." What else could she have done but that?

Elise pulled the rag quilt more tightly around her shoulders and leaned her head against the cold glass of the window in Mama Jones's parlor. She forced herself to breathe slowly. A moment more and the memories would be safely tucked away again.

Rain trickled down the window, the trees outside rustling in the low wind. The house was warmer than their tiny house in Stanton had been.

Warmer. Bigger. Nicer. Miles had arranged for Mama Jones to remain in the cottage free of rent and to receive a small annuity, less than he had originally attempted to provide for her, Mama Jones being both stubborn and proud, but more money than she had ever known before. Miles had appeased her sensibilities by explaining that he owed her that and more for caring for Elise, who had been, after all, his ward.

For all of his refusal to help Elise in her hour of need, he'd certainly risen to the occasion with Mama Jones.

"How much did you tell him?" Mama Jones abruptly asked. They hadn't spoken much since Elise and Anne's arrival nearly thirty minutes earlier. Anne lay on the rug before the fireplace, sketching trees and flowers.

"Not very much." Elise's voice quivered. Her emotions sat so near the surface.

"So is Miles Linwood less confused than before or more, I wonder."

"I do not know." She turned enough to watch Anne as she silently worked.

"He is trying hard, Ella," Mama Jones said almost scoldingly. "And though he disappointed you in the past, I think he is a good un.'"

"You believe I should confide in him?"

"Why did you trust my Jim?" Mama Jones asked in turn, rocking slowly.

"He was eminently trustworthy."

"An' who was it, Ella, that raised that trustable young man?"

"You did," Elise acknowledged with a slight smile in Mama Jones's direction.

"I know a good man when I sees him. Miles Linwood's good to the tips of his fingers."

A sting of emotion clasped Elise's throat. Had she not shed enough tears? She turned back to the window. "I do not want to be hurt again."

"Can't be helped. We all are hurt now and again. It is the misery that buys the joy."

Elise wiped at an escaping tear. If she didn't stop soon, the dam would burst.

"You've been long enough without joy, my Ella," Mama Jones said in her authoritative way. "Time to turn over your misery."

"Suppose things only get worse."

"Worse than you cryin' at m' window?" There was some wisdom in that. "You say you're not able to trust Miles Linwood. So trust me instead. Tell him your troubles. Some of them, anyway. See if he doesn't help you like I think he will."

"I am not sure I can," Elise admitted. "There is too much."

"*Give* a little, Ella. Just a little."

* * *

It was no use. Miles had racked his brain all afternoon and evening only to come up blank. Nowhere in the recesses of his memory was there a conversation like the one Elise had referenced earlier in the day. Yet her words had a horribly familiar ring to them.

Grow up and solve your own problems.

Perhaps it was merely Elise's almost constant insistence that she dealt with her own troubles that sparked that feeling of recognition, but he doubted it. Miles was convinced despite himself that he had indeed said such a heartless thing to her, and he would wager he'd done so very near the time she'd disappeared. The memory, it seemed, had become lost in a quagmire of tense and overwhelming recollections.

He sat in the chair behind the desk in the library, flipping absent-mindedly through the Tafford accounts. His foot tapped. The fingers of his free hand drummed the arm of his chair.

How long before Elise's disappearance had they had that painful interaction? What problem had she been attempting to get his help to solve? Had he ever addressed it? Had she tried to ask him again? Miles wished he could remember.

The house was so still he actually heard the quiet footsteps of someone's approach. He looked up from the account book and experienced the strongest rush of déjà vu. Elise stood not far from the desk, watching him, her expression wrought with anxiety. She clasped her hands tightly in front of her.

"Might we talk?" She sounded oddly resigned, as if she were pursuing the conversation under duress.

"Of course." Miles rose from the desk and hurried around to stand directly beside her.

Elise's eyes darted around the room. "Somewhere else?" she whispered, her cheeks pinking slightly. "Please."

Why not the library? "Certainly," he said. Beth and Langley were in the drawing room. "The music room?" he suggested.

The slightest hint of a smile turned her mouth. She nodded mutely.

Knowing the music room would be empty and most likely dark, Miles brought a brace of candles with him as they left the library. He offered his hand, unsure if she would take it.

What precisely did Elise intend to say to him? Was he to be raked over the coals once more?

She slipped her hand inside his as naturally as she had at three years old. A very good sign. Before they'd even reached the library door, Miles realized Elise was shaking. With anger like before?

Miles squeezed her hand inside his and glanced at her face. Her expression was a study of neutrality. She was making a concerted effort to appear unaffected, like always. Her trembling hand told another story.

They spoke no words between them. Elise didn't look up at him. He hoped she wasn't having second thoughts. If her demeanor was any indication, the topic she meant to broach was significant. This was the opportunity he had been hoping for, if only she didn't change her mind.

The music room stood empty when they arrived. Miles lit several of the wall sconces. Elise held herself perfectly still in the middle of the room, noticeably pale and utterly silent. She pushed a loose strand of hair from her face with a trembling hand.

Oh, Elise. You do not need to be so afraid of me.

Miles stood facing her. She studied her clasped fingers. He could hear her take several slow breaths.

"I am in trouble, Miles," she whispered.

Again Miles was struck by a sense that he had lived this moment before.

"And . . . I need your help." She looked up at him. Her eyes were troubled, her expression anxious.

"Tell me what it is," he said. "I'll do anything I can."

Elise reached into a cleverly hidden pocket of her dress and pulled out a short stack of folded parchment—the letters she'd been hiding from him, no doubt.

"You want me to read them?"

Elise nodded.

He accepted the pile, his thoughts swimming. He'd sensed there was something unsettling about her correspondence but had given up hope that she would share it with him.

"Shall we sit, then?" He motioned to a short sofa not far from where they stood.

In a moment, they were seated side by side. He opened the first letter.

"I received that one the day Mrs. Ash arrived," Elise whispered. "It was the first."

The letter bore no return address. He read, *Should your memory improve, so shall my aim.*

Miles breathed out a mild oath. He read it again to confirm he'd not been mistaken at the implied threat.

"The next one arrived the next day," Elise said, her voice no louder than before, still without emotion.

Miles opened it. *You have been warned.*

"The next is the letter that came during our meeting with Mr. Cane."

"*Good day, Elise.*" An odd thing to write.

"I believe that was meant to be taunting," she said.

Every letter was more of the same. Either innocuous greetings that felt somehow sinister or words that were clearly threats, pointed enough to be taken seriously but too vague to identify the issuer.

"Upon my soul, Elise." Miles stared at the papers in shock.

"I know." A detectable quiver of fear shook her words. "Some are posted, some are not. So I have no idea how near or far the writer might be from Tafford."

"And the handwriting changes." Miles flipped back through the letters.

"This one came this afternoon." Elise handed him one more letter. "I was reading it when you came upon me in the garden."

Miles looked at her as she sat. Her eyes were focused on this last letter, her face paler. Miles slowly opened it. *She will not hear me coming.*

"Anne," Miles said in a breath, shocked.

"Yes." Elise abruptly rose. "Whoever is sending me these letters is now threatening Anne or at least mentioning her. That frightens me most of all. This person knows about my daughter. Is willing to threaten her, to use her that way."

"Do you have any idea who might be sending these?" He wondered if his suspicion matched hers.

Elise turned back to look at him. She nodded slowly. "The man who killed our fathers."

Chapter Twenty

THE MURDERER. MILES HAD SUSPECTED that from the very first letter.

"He fears you can identify him," Miles said.

"I couldn't four years ago," Elise said. "I certainly cannot now."

"It seems he doesn't want to take that risk." Miles scanned the single-sentence letters again.

"But why send the letters in the first place?" Elise rose from the couch, pacing away. "If not for these letters, I would have given very little thought, if any, to his identity. Sending these has increased the chance of my thinking on his identity, not *decreased* it."

There was no arguing that. "He must think the chance of your remembering high enough, even without the topic being forced, that forewarning you is necessary."

"I think he must be nearby," Elise said, her voice far less steady. "Some of these were hand delivered. And he knows Anne doesn't hear well." She wrung her hands. "I didn't want to bother you with this, but I don't know what to do. I—"

"Elise." He jumped across her unnecessary justification, rising and standing beside her. "Elise."

She looked up at him, and a tear rolled from her eye. Elise had never been the sort of female who could or would employ emotional trickery for the sake of gaining sympathy. Her emotions, which were as plentiful as they were varied, had always been genuine. He'd been waiting for weeks to see them. That single tear was like a brick knocked out of the wall she'd erected.

Miles tentatively reached out to her. His fingers brushed away her tear, a light and fragile connection.

"I am afraid," she whispered. "I know what this man is capable of, but I have no idea who he is. He could be the gardener. Or one of your tenants. Anyone except for you."

"I was exonerated by the inquiry," Miles acknowledged.

Elise shook her head. "I never suspected you, Miles." Her fingers slipped into his. She had reached for him. "You could never do what that man did."

"No. I couldn't. And I think we can safely remove Langley from your list of possible murderers. Not only is he one of the most even-tempered and upright gentlemen I have ever known, but he too was cleared in the inquiry."

"*Everyone* was cleared in the inquiry, Miles," Elise whispered. "The inquiry didn't answer anything."

Miles rubbed her hand between his, resisting the urge to pull her into his arms. She was opening up, a little bit. Her trust was so fragile; he didn't dare risk breaking it. Yet her anguish cut at him.

"I still have the inquiry papers," Miles said, thinking aloud. "We could look through them again to see if there is anything we missed."

Elise pulled back instantly. "But that is just what he warned me not to do. If we start trying to identify him, he might . . . he would—"

"I would never place you in danger, Elise." When she didn't look back up at him, Miles laid his hands on her shoulders. "*Never.* The papers are here in the Tafford safe. No one would even know we were looking at them. Not even Beth and Langley, if that is what you wish. But I cannot simply stand by and let this man threaten you."

Elise looked at him then. He still saw uncertainty in her eyes. "You would truly help me?"

Miles didn't think he had ever felt such a sinking sense of disappointment. One careless moment he couldn't even remember had undone what had once been complete confidence.

"I would do anything for you." Miles held her gaze, hoping to communicate his sincerity, his determination. "I am sorry for what I said four years ago. I don't even remember that conversation." She seemed to wince at his admission. Miles grew even more frustrated with himself but continued on. She needed to understand. "I can only assume I was unbelievably tired or distracted or overwhelmed, though that is no excuse for having been so unfeeling. And though I cannot place that conversation, I have a horrible suspicion it occurred shortly before you left Epsworth."

"The night before," Elise answered in a pained whisper.

Miles closed his eyes against the guilt that swept over him at her admission. "Is it the reason you left?" Miles asked, unable to look at her as he did.

"It was the reason I couldn't stay."

There was a difference there, though Miles couldn't exactly pinpoint it. Something had driven her from Epsworth. If Miles's suspicions were correct, she was on the cusp of fleeing Tafford.

I am in trouble. Elise had told him she'd said those words years ago—in the Epsworth library, he suddenly realized. Precisely what she'd said only moments earlier in the library. Was there perhaps a connection? Had she come to him at Epsworth because she was being threatened? Had she fled out of fear for her safety, convinced Miles would not help her?

"We are going to fix this, Elise. Whoever is writing these letters will be found, and you and Anne will be safe. I assure you I will not rest until that happens."

She appeared doubtful.

"I need you to trust me," Miles said, praying that she did.

"I want to," Elise answered. "But I don't know how."

"Give me a chance to prove myself to you. You've trusted me with these letters. Now you can see if I truly will help you."

"Will you?" Elise asked bluntly.

"I solemnly swear to you that I will."

Elise nodded, a movement of acceptance, if not confidence. "Thank you, Miles."

"I'll arrange for a groom or footman to accompany you when you walk over to visit Mama Jones," he said. "And it would be wise to have one or the other with you whenever you are outside."

She sighed, the sound of it conveying relief rather than frustration. "I will worry less if Anne and I are not alone."

He would worry less as well. "Will you meet me in the library tomorrow afternoon after you have had lunch?"

Elise nodded.

Miles held out his hand. "Allow me to walk you to your bedchamber door."

The tiniest of smiles spread fleetingly across her face. Elise laid her hand in his.

He used his free hand to pick up the letters he'd abandoned on the sofa. "May I keep these?"

"Yes." She sounded relieved to have them out of her possession. "And any others that come?"

"I will take those as well, if you wish."

It seemed but a minute later that they reached her bedchamber. Elise twisted the knob and opened the door but turned back at the last moment to look at him. "Strangely enough, I think I will sleep better tonight than I have in some time," Elise said.

"I hope so."

She offered only an enigmatic smile before slipping silently into her room and closing the door.

* * *

Miles didn't used to smell so nice. Why that thought continually ran through her mind, Elise couldn't say. They sat next to each other in the library, and Miles silently sorted a stack of papers while Elise tried to ignore the fact that he smelled rather wonderful. She couldn't identify the scent, only that it was vaguely spicy and the slightest bit sweet.

He straightened a stack of papers. "Collins, the runner, was thorough; I'll give him that."

Elise remembered very little about the Bow Street Runner who had investigated the murders, beyond the fact that he'd had only a few strands of hair combed ineffectually across his very bare head and that he had constantly worn an expression that put her firmly in mind of her father's basset hound. And he'd asked a great many questions she hadn't wanted to answer.

Miles was creating stack after stack, spreading the piles across the desk.

"Is there a method to your madness here?" she asked.

"Believe it or not, there is." He half laughed as he spoke. "Each stack represents a suspect."

"There were this many?" He'd created at least two dozen piles already.

"*Everyone* was a suspect. Very nearly anyway. Some were eliminated quickly."

She was relieved to know the field had been narrowed somewhat. "Like you?"

"Actually, no. I was not exonerated very easily."

"But how could they believe you would murder your own father or mine or—" The words lumped in her throat.

"Or try to kill you?" Miles finished for her.

She nodded.

"I wouldn't be the first son to murder his own father. Sadly, it was not my sterling character that proved my innocence but the fact that my valet, several of the footmen, and the housekeeper were all able to vouch for my whereabouts that night."

"That must have been horrible." How could anyone suspect Miles?

"The fact that Langley was also a suspect eased the sting a little. His character is far more impeccable than my own. He too had witnesses to confirm his alibi."

"I don't remember any of this." Entire segments of her life seemed completely absent from her memory. She didn't like the feeling at all.

"You had been through a harrowing ordeal, Elise." Miles laid his hand on top of hers, where it rested on the desk.

Her heart flipped about in her chest. It was the oddest reaction to have to Miles, and yet it happened more and more often. He would look at her or touch her, even as lightly as he did then, and she would find herself turned about inside.

"You did not hold up well when the runner first questioned you," Miles said. "We decided it would be best if you were left out of most of the rest of the investigation. He asked you questions only when he had to. He was none too pleased at first. But I managed to convince him that you had been through quite enough already without being hounded day and night."

"You were my greatest advocate," Elise said, feeling quite unaccountably nostalgic. "You always were."

A certain sadness slipped into Miles's smile. "*Nearly* always, it seems."

"But you are helping me now," Elise insisted, unsure why his self-castigation bothered her so much.

"An opportunity for which I am infinitely grateful." He wrapped his fingers around her hand beneath his and raised it to his lips, placing a light kiss on her fingers. Suddenly, there was that look again, the one that made deciphering words difficult.

"Now, should we see what we have here?" He motioned to the piles of paper on the desk.

Elise nodded mechanically, very few lucid thoughts running through her brain other than the continuing awareness that Miles didn't affect her in quite the same way he had when they were younger.

Miles laid her hand back on the desk, releasing his hold to sort through his piles. She pulled the hand he'd held into her lap, clasping it with her other hand as the sensation of his fingers on hers lingered. She had the strangest urge to lay her head on his shoulder as he continued organizing his paperwork, an inexplicable reaction to a man she wasn't entirely sure she could even trust.

"Obviously, we cannot go through all of these this afternoon," Miles said. "There are simply too many. We can begin at least."

Elise couldn't even nod. Miles no longer looked at her, so her lack of reaction didn't register with him. He didn't know she was staring at him. He had changed in the last four years. She had, of course, noticed it before, but the impact was somehow greater in that moment. He was taller, his face more defined. His hair was, thankfully, still red, even if it wasn't quite so bright as it had once been. She'd always adored his red hair. His eyes were the chocolate brown she remembered.

Beside her, Miles took a long, deep breath. It had ever been a quirk of his to push out a breath longer than normal when he was working, as if slowly expelling all the air from his lungs was relaxing. The sound summoned an unbidden memory, and she was lost for a moment in the past.

A slow, deep breath. Miles had tensed. Elise had felt it. His arm around her had been rigid, his grip on the reins unusually tight. The thick mud and rain had kept them at a slow pace, so slow each step of the horse had been jarring. Elise had felt every movement vibrate in her aching body. The pain had been the worst in her shoulder, but everything had seemed to hurt.

She leaned against Miles, needing his strength. In her mind, she could still hear each gunshot: One the moment the carriage had stopped. One that had killed Papa. Another for Mr. Linwood. One for her as she'd tried to stagger away. She'd very nearly escaped.

And that laugh. She would never forget it. There was no humor in the sound but something like triumph, like maniacal glee. Gunshots and laughter bounced around in her brain until she couldn't bear it any longer.

Elise pressed herself into Miles's damp coat. The noises wouldn't stop. Flashing images, moments from the nightmare she'd lived swam endlessly in her mind.

"I am sorry, Elise," Miles whispered, his arm pulling her more firmly to him. "I am so sorry that this happened, that I wasn't there. I might have—"

"He would have killed you." Elise was certain of it.

"Perhaps not," Miles argued, a near panic in his tone. "It might have made a difference."

She held more tightly to him. "He killed everyone."

"He didn't kill you."

Elise couldn't stop the sob that rose to her throat. "I wish he had."

"Don't say that, Elise." Miles sounded as though his own emotions were barely in check. "Please don't even think that."

"It would be better to be dead." Elise allowed her anguish to spill over. "I don't want to remember any of this. I just want it to be over. To be gone. Done."

Miles pulled the horse to a stop. "Please, Elise." Emotion thickened his words. "Don't say that. You are all I have."

She wept, but crying didn't lessen the pain. She'd lost her papa. She'd lost Mr. Linwood. She'd rather have died one hundred times over than endure what she had.

She felt Miles press a kiss to her rain-soaked forehead. She leaned against him. He held her as he always had. Miles would help. Somehow, he would find a way to help.

"Elise?"

She jumped back to the present.

"You are crying," Miles said.

Crying? Elise wiped at her eyes. Tears were indeed spilling from her eyes. The pain she had felt at fifteen was raw and new again, as if that moment had only just happened.

"What is it?" Miles asked, his voice filled with concern.

"There are so many memories attached to all of this." Elise shook her head. She couldn't form the words to explain how heavy she felt, how broken.

"We'll save this for another day." He motioned to the piles of papers. "In fact, *I'll* sort through them and see what I can find. Then, when you are feeling more equal to the task, we'll go over it together."

"Thank you, Miles," she whispered, forcing steady breaths. He'd known precisely what she needed. How like the Miles she'd once known. "Thank you."

Chapter Twenty-One

MILES SAT IN THE LIBRARY, horrified at reading about and reliving the terror of the night his father had been killed. The inquiry papers were detailed, almost too much for his peace of mind. The runner had assumed, as had Miles, that with an aim as good as the killer's had been—Miles's father had been shot directly through his heart, Mr. Furlong in the center of his forehead—Elise's wound, several inches from her heart, had been intentionally nonfatal. But Miles kept returning to the first of the anonymous letters Elise had received at Tafford.

So will my aim. The shooter admitted that his aim had been off. Her survival, it appeared, had been nothing more than an accident. The realization sat like ice water on Miles's heart. Elise was not supposed to have lived.

She had never said much about that night. Her brief testimony, which the runner had written down, gave no indication of why she might not have presented a clear target. It had been dark and possibly raining. But so had it been when the killer had shot his other three victims. Had she been running? Struggling to get away? Had the murderer been injured or held back somehow?

Miles was reluctant to ask her. Her trust in him was still very fragile, and this was not a topic she seemed at all equal to discussing. Simply sitting in the same room as these papers had nearly broken her.

Another question rose in his mind. Four shots were fired that night. Elise hadn't spoken of the killer reloading. Either she'd been too distraught to mention that, or the killer had carried more than two loaded weapons. Surely if he'd stopped to reload, Miles's father, perhaps even Mr. Furlong, if he had not already been dead at that point, could have taken the opportunity to overpower their assailant.

To have access to multiple weapons, the killer would have had to be quite well off or a hardened enough criminal to have stolen them. The accuracy of his shooting indicated not only experience but also superior weaponry. The runner had suggested the shooter had used Mantons. No other pistol was as precise. But Mantons were single-shot, which meant the murderer must have carried four of them.

Miles's own father had owned a set of Mantons. They, like everything else, had been sold. Elise's father's weapons had also gone at auction—another set of Mantons. If only they'd had those weapons with them that night instead of locked in their homes.

The runner had questioned Mr. Cane about the existence of an heir to the Furlong estate had Elise not survived the attack. A review of Mr. Furlong's will and family tree revealed his estate would have simply reverted to the crown. There was no would-be heir willing to kill for his inheritance. Even if one had existed, it wouldn't have explained why the murderer had killed Father as well.

Scribbled in the margins of the runner's notes was a question that now haunted Miles, for he had a feeling the answer held the key to the entire mystery.

Which victim was the primary target?

The crime seemed very much intentional. This was no robbery gone horribly wrong; it was a murder from the instant the killer rode up to the carriage. Why else would he have been so heavily armed? Why else would he have committed his heinous crime with no intention of robbing them of their valuables? But which of them had the murderer been after, and why?

Too many questions, too few answers.

Miles stepped away from his desk. He'd grown restless, a feeling of oppressive confinement growing with each passing moment. After four years of physically grueling labor in the West Indies, he grew restless quickly, especially when his mind was heavy.

He ventured out to the back meadow. Elise was there chasing Anne around, a footman stationed nearby. The sound of the little girl's odd laughter echoed around them. Elise seemed happy and at ease. Even with threats looming over her head, there was something inarguably light in her countenance. Miles thought that perhaps he had managed to lift one of Elise's burdens at last.

Anne spotted him. She ran to where he stood. She pointed alternately at herself and him, then threw her arms in the air.

"Up!" Only after she repeated the word three times did he finally understand it, though he wasn't sure what she meant by it.

Anne, arms still held high above her head, turned in a circle, eyes closed in apparent joy, smiling brightly and giggling.

"Upon my soul," Miles whispered, watching her impromptu dance, "you *are* your mother's daughter."

Elise used to dance in the Epsworth meadow and smile just like that.

"She wants you to spin her, Miles." Elise broke into his recollections, a little out of breath.

Her cheeks were pink from exertion, her eyes bright. Her thick black curls had begun escaping their careful knot. Here was Elise as he remembered her. Miles felt an undeniable squeezing of his heart at the sight. He was getting her back.

"I have been obliging her for a full quarter hour," Elise continued, catching her breath. "I believe it is your turn. You did start this, after all—spinning her in the air as you did at the picnic. It is all she wishes to do anymore. Poor Mrs. Ash is near to leaving us, I am afraid."

Us. That sounded so perfectly right coming from her. Elise's *us* incorporated not only herself and Anne but him as well.

He turned to Anne, who had ceased her dancing and was concentrating on his face. "You want to spin?" He spoke slowly and a bit loudly, as Elise did when speaking to Anne.

The sweet little girl grinned. Yes, she was definitely her mother's daughter. Her eyes were a different color, but otherwise, she was Elise's copy at that age—the age she'd lost her own mother. This girl had already lost her father. Why was it tragedy seemed to dog Elise's heels?

Miles reached for Anne, hands easily wrapping around her tiny frame. He lifted her high into the air and spun around. Anne laughed almost uproariously. From somewhere beyond the spinning edge of his vision, Miles heard Elise's laughter.

He set Anne on her feet, then pretended to be too dizzy to stand. The absurd display set Anne laughing harder, and soon, she too was enacting her own farce. In a moment's time, all three of them were laughing too hard to speak, almost too hard to breathe.

"Do you remember doing this when we were tiny?" Elise leaned against him as she continued to laugh. "Spinning and spinning until we couldn't stand any longer?"

Miles wrapped one arm around her; with the other, he held fast to Anne's hand. She also leaned against him, though she only came up to his thigh. And in that moment, Miles felt whole in a way he hadn't since he'd lost Elise. It was as if a part of him had been missing and was finally found once more.

"I was so disappointed when I reached Eton," he said. "Not a soul in the entire school was nearly as much fun as you were."

"They were *boys*," Elise answered as if the reason were obvious.

Miles laughed again. "I believe that is precisely what you wrote to me at the time."

Elise stepped away from him but slipped her hand in his as she did. She turned her face up to the sun, smiling with her eyes closed. "What is it about a meadow, Miles, that makes one's heart sing?"

Oh, Elise! Miles felt like shouting in triumph. This was his Elise! Miles was mesmerized by the look of contentment on her face. Her sweetness and *joie de vivre* had colored so much of his first nineteen years.

Elise's eyes twinkled suddenly, and Miles knew from years of experience that a bit of mischief had just entered her thoughts. "Do you know what Anne and I discovered by your tree?" she asked mysteriously, playfully.

Lands, it was like seeing Elise as she'd been before the murders. How long would the transformation last? How long before she came crashing back to reality again, before she clamped down her emotions and put up the wall between herself and the world? Miles hoped a very long time.

Anne was following their conversation with her eyes. How many of their words could she hear or understand? Likely not many.

He hunched down in front of her. "Do you know a secret about the tree?"

Her smile remained, but he could see she didn't understand.

"A secret?" he tried again. "By the tree?"

"Like this, Miles." Elise crossed her fingers in an *x* over her lips. "It means a secret or something she doesn't want to tell you."

Miles made the sign.

She made the gesture back, the same mischievous look in her eyes that lit her mother's. Then she pointed in the direction of the tree.

He turned back to Elise. "What is this grand secret the two of you have unearthed?"

"There are fallen leaves tucked under an exposed root," she said. "I've never seen such a vivid shade of gold. They must have fallen in the autumn months and months ago and, yet, are still vibrant. As near as I've been able to make out, Anne is convinced it is a magic tree."

Precisely what Elise would have believed at that age.

"Will you teach me how to talk to her?" he asked. "I can make out her words with some effort, and she understands me once in a while. But I don't know her gestures. I can't supplement what I say with the signs you use."

"You really want to learn?" Elise asked, looking at him intently.

"I really do."

She seemed to study him a moment longer. "Why?"

"Why? So I can talk to her. So she can talk to me if she wishes." He touched Anne's darling little face, equally enamored and heartbroken at the look of earnestness that always accompanied her efforts to understand him. He sensed she longed for a connection as much as he did. "I want to know what she thinks and feels. I want her to be able to talk with me."

"No one else has ever wanted to learn to talk to her." Confusion etched into Elise's gaze.

The conversation had become too serious. Miles wanted the lighthearted moment back. "And, I'd wager, no one else has ever had a magic tree."

That earned him a slight smile. "Perhaps not."

"Then you'll teach me?" Miles pressed his advantage while Elise was at least smiling.

She shrugged. "I guess I do owe you for the dresses that continue pouring into my room."

"Those were—"

Elise pressed her fingers to his lips and cut off his justification. Miles's pulse quite suddenly jumped to life. She'd shushed him precisely that way hundreds of times in their childhood. But now the feel of her fingers on his lips sent a shiver through his body.

"I am only teasing, Miles." She lowered her hand from his face and laid her head on his shoulder. "I think every home should have a meadow."

He'd barely managed to refrain from kissing her fingertips when she'd pressed them to his lips. And, heaven help him, the temptation to kiss her—and not on the fingertips—only grew as they stood there. He absolutely could not do *that*.

"It isn't a terribly complete language," Elise said from his shoulder.

"Language?" Miles's brain had simply stopped working. What in heaven's name was wrong with him?

"Anne's gestures," Elise explained. "We create them as we need them. She *can* hear. If a person is patient and speaks slowly, she can make sense of many things. She doesn't need a gesture for every word. And honestly, until we came here, she didn't try very hard to communicate with anyone other than Mama Jones and me."

Anne leaned more heavily against Miles's leg. Her eyes looked sleepy, her posture weary. *Is it nap time, perhaps?*

"She is a very intelligent girl." The hint of defensiveness in Elise's words spoke of past insults.

"I am certain she is." Miles turned his attention back to Elise.

She watched him very closely. Miles couldn't look away. Lands, she'd grown into a beautiful woman. He'd noticed it before but always as an afterthought. Until that moment, he'd seen only the remnants of the girl overshadowing the woman she had become. There was a hint of flowers about her, so light one had to be close to even detect it.

"Elise," he heard himself say, his voice oddly thick.

Someone nearby cleared his throat.

Chapter Twenty-Two

"Mr. Haddington, Mrs. Haddington, and Miss Haddington have come to call, m' lord," a footman said, treating Miles with the utmost deference. Elise still found the idea of her partner in mischief all those years ago now bearing a title of such prestige rather odd. "Mrs. Langley has requested that you and Mrs. Jones join them in the sitting room."

"Thank you. We will be there momentarily."

The footman made short work of returning to the house.

"Does it feel terribly odd to you, Miles, that everyone scrapes and bows to you?" She shook her head in amused disbelief. "Every time they 'my lord' you, I can't help remembering the day your father unceremoniously tossed you into the pond at Epsworth and you emerged looking like a drowned rat. Hardly what one expects of a future marquess."

He chuckled. Anne, who couldn't possibly have followed their conversation, laughed right along with them, her gaze firmly on Miles, a look of hero worship in her eyes.

"I can't imagine there was ever a marquess whose childhood exploits would have stood up to examination," Miles said. "Could you imagine if our first address in Lords was required to be a confession of all our youthful misadventures?"

"The entire kingdom would turn out for that." She could easily picture dukes and earls quite solemnly reading off a list of stolen pastries, incomplete assignments from their tutors, and Latin lessons they'd spent staring out the windows.

"We'd best make our way to the sitting room like the civilized members of Society we are supposed to be," Miles said.

"Do we have to?" She didn't care to face "civilized members of Society" knowing she'd sunk so far below them. "I'd much rather stay out here with you and Anne. We were having such a lovely time."

"Yes, we were." He took her hand. "But then, we always did know how to have fun together."

She set both her hands around his. Even with the new flutterings in her heart, the familiarity of his touch was welcome and soothing.

"But, yes, Elise, we do have to go greet our visitors." He didn't seem much more excited at the prospect than she was.

"Perhaps they'll keep their visit short," she said.

"Would you mind if Anne came with us to the sitting room? Only for a moment, of course." He kept his hand in hers, his other hand gently wrapping around Anne's. "She is such a sweet girl, so adorable. I want the Haddingtons to meet her so they can see just how lovely she is."

Elise could have cried. All anyone in Stanton had ever seen in Anne was a poor, overly quiet girl hardly worth noticing. "She is easily overset by people she doesn't know," Elise warned.

"She'll have the two of us." Miles looked down at Anne with absolute adoration. "But I have no doubt she will charm them as effortlessly as she did me."

Bless him, he cared for Anne so much he'd entirely forgotten there'd been nothing "effortless" about his earliest acquaintance with her.

She'll have the two of us. Elise had seen Anne through many of life's difficulties. With Miles on her side as well, Anne could certainly face a room of strangers.

"I suppose a quick courtesy would be fine," Elise said. "I only hope they'll be patient with her. She doesn't really speak, after all. Not in the way most people are accustomed to."

"Miss Haddington will be gracious, I'm certain of that. As for her parents, I will not allow them to be unkind."

Elise smiled at the fierceness of his tone. She slipped her arm through his and pulled up close to his side. "You are nearly as frightening as Beth when you make a decree."

"There is no one as frightening as Beth."

Elise knelt in front of Anne and offered a quick explanation of where they were going and whom they were likely to see. Anne didn't appear to comprehend it all, and confusion tugged at her features, but Elise squeezed her hand reassuringly. "I'll be with you, dear," she promised.

Anne glanced up at Miles, a question so clear in her eyes that anyone seeing it would understand on an instant.

Miles took Anne's other hand. "I'll be with you also, sweetie."

As easy as that, Anne nodded her agreement.

The three of them walked together toward the house as naturally as anything. She could almost imagine herself at Epsworth or Furlong House, as if nothing had changed. Though the ball had been something of a disaster for her, she didn't feel as intimidated as she had expected when she approached the sitting room. For perhaps the first time since arriving at Tafford, it felt almost like home. Almost.

Mr. Langley and Mr. Haddington rose as Miles, Elise, and Anne entered the sitting room. Would that ever stop feeling strange? Gentlemen didn't rise for an impoverished woman of the lower classes. Her station didn't warrant the social nicety, but in treating her as an equal, Miles had set the example his neighbors followed. He'd managed to bend that rule for her and grant her badly beaten pride at least a temporary reprieve.

Her gaze lingered on him as the realization sank in more fully. He didn't have to treat her as kindly as he did, and he certainly didn't owe her the efforts he made on her behalf. But how grateful she was to him for his kindness.

"Good afternoon," Miles greeted them all. "I am pleased that you chose to visit."

Mrs. Haddington beamed. "We hadn't come by since the ball and were longing for the company of our nearest neighbors."

Miles released Elise's hand. With both of his hands laid gently on Anne's back, he nudged her slightly in front of him. "This lovely young lady is Miss Jones, our most distinguished house guest."

Though Anne most certainly didn't understand everything that was happening, all of the adults in the sitting room smiled at her adoringly. How odd that must have been for her. Until the last few weeks, Anne had lived her life entirely unnoticed. Miles hunched down next to Anne and pointed to each of the new arrivals in turn, telling her their names but not making a point of her deafness. For her part, Anne simply watched Miles, eyes wide with fascination and tenderness. How quickly he had woven the same spell around her daughter as he had around Elise as a girl.

He stood once more and turned to a maid just on the other side of the doorway. "Would you accompany Miss Jones to the nursery?"

She dipped a curtsy. "Yes, my lord."

Anne looked up at Elise, a question in her eyes. Elise gave her a reassuring smile, then subtly made the sign they had developed to mean nursery. Anne nodded her understanding and allowed the nurse to take her hand and lead her away. How much Anne had changed these past weeks. She'd once been afraid of anyone other than Elise and Mama Jones. But in Miles's home, she had found safety and refuge and a reason to trust. More surprising even than that, Elise had begun, in small ways, to feel the same.

"Come sit with us, Mrs. Jones," Mrs. Haddington said, waving Elise over.

So much for safety and refuge. If not for Beth sitting with the other ladies and Miles's nodding reassuringly, Elise would have formulated some excuse or other and followed Anne out of the room. Still, she was no coward.

Elise took a seat amongst the other ladies. Miles sat not far off with the gentlemen.

"Your daughter is so beautiful," Miss Haddington said. "Her curly hair is absolutely adorable."

For a moment, Elise wasn't sure what to say. "Thank you," she managed.

"Actually," Beth said, "she is the very image of Mrs. Jones when she was a child. I confess I always envied her thick curls."

"How old is she?" Mrs. Haddington asked.

"She is three years old."

"Three?" Mrs. Haddington's gaze turned pointedly ponderous. "How soon will she turn four?"

An odd question, admittedly. But Elise knew it would be rude not to answer. And she would rather not draw more attention to Anne. "Not for a few more months."

"How many more months?" Mrs. Haddington pressed.

"Quite a few more." And that was all Elise meant to say on that matter.

Thankfully, Miss Haddington seized control of the conversation once more and directed it away from her mother's line of questioning. "Your daughter clearly has Lord Grenton wrapped around her finger." There was nothing but friendliness in Miss Haddington's tone, something Elise thoroughly appreciated.

"Yes. He has been very kind during our stay here."

Beth took a small sip of tea. "My brother has always adored little children. He is more at ease with them than most nursemaids, I daresay."

Mrs. Haddington nodded her approval. "That is a very fine quality for any gentleman to have. A rare one as well." She gave her daughter a knowing look.

So many things became clear in that instant. Elise had seen for herself at the ball how many young ladies and their mothers were particularly interested in Miles. It seemed the Haddingtons had more than a passing curiosity. They were in full pursuit.

"We have so enjoyed getting to know you and your brother better," Mrs. Haddington said to Beth. Her look of deeply forged friendship didn't quite match the brevity of their acquaintance. Mrs. Haddington was firming her footing with the people she knew mattered to her end goal.

Elise watched Miss Haddington, wondering if her mind was as firmly fixed as her mother's. She had certainly seemed quite at ease with Miles. The day of the picnic, they had chatted amicably, even made each other laugh. Miles had found Elise during the ball based on Miss Haddington's instructions. He seemed on easy terms with both of Miss Haddington's parents.

And Miss Haddington is an acceptable match for a marquess. She was not recently dredged up from the ditches.

Though Miss Haddington fit the mold of what Miles ought to have been looking for in a wife, and despite the fact that Elise really did like the lady, she found herself grimacing at the idea. Perhaps it was her own selfishness. Miles was her very best friend; he always had been. When he married, she would be relegated to the periphery of his life. Having only just been reunited with him, she wasn't sure she was ready to lose him again.

She couldn't allow herself to entirely trust him, yet she was already mourning the day when he was no longer part of her life. It was little wonder she was so confused.

"Beth, dear," Mr. Langley spoke into the momentary lull in the ladies' conversation. "Did you know that Mr. Haddington knew your father?"

"I didn't." Beth was clearly pleased.

"We belonged to the same club," Mr. Haddington said. "And we shared a few interests. We often spent an evening debating the merits of a new invention or investment opportunity and whether or not it was likely to catch on or prove profitable. We didn't always see eye to eye, but Mr. Linwood and Mr. Furlong and I always got on well. Fine gentlemen. Sharp."

A prick of pain pierced Elise at the mention of her father. She'd never met Mr. Haddington until the ball, but he had been a somewhat close acquaintance of her father's. It shouldn't have surprised her to hear her father had a world outside of the one that had encompassed their home and her very narrow experience as a child, yet somehow it did.

"I was sad to hear of their passing," Mr. Haddington continued. "Everyone was shocked. It was so unexpected and so very tragic. They were murdered, I understand."

Elise kept her hands primly folded on her lap, trying to push the words from her mind. Miles had shielded her from these conversations during those first weeks after her father's death. She'd not been forced to talk about or listen to discussions of the details of that night. Very few things about leaving her home had been a relief, but that part was. Away from Epsworth, she needed not say a word about that night she knew she would never forget.

"The word about the club was it was a robbery gone terribly wrong," Mr. Haddington said. "No one was entirely certain of the exact details. The number of shots fired was a point of great debate for many weeks. Some believed it was a quickly accomplished thing, while others were just as certain the scene was gory in the extreme."

Elise closed her mind to his ramblings. She couldn't imagine why anyone would wish to know more about a person's violent death. Was it not enough to realize that two murders meant the loss of a father, a friend, a neighbor? Could he not respect the fact that he was speaking of two very real, very good people who deserved some degree of dignity rather than a passage from a sordid novel or sensationalized stage play?

He had known Mr. Linwood and Father, after all. He even claimed to have liked and respected them. Was he not at all bothered by the thought of how violent an end they had met? From the sounds of it, speculation had been bandied about their club amongst the rest of their acquaintances.

She rose to her feet, trying to appear less shaky than she felt. "If you will excuse me," she said. "I need to make certain Anne has gone down for her nap."

She offered an abbreviated curtsy and moved swiftly from the room. Mr. Haddington would likely continue his rather callous discussion of death and suffering, but she wanted no part of it. She didn't need to hear the details; she had lived them.

Chapter Twenty-Three

ANNE'S AFTERNOON IN THE MEADOW had worn her to a thread. She was asleep already when Elise arrived. Mrs. Ash had retired to her bedchamber, leaving Elise alone in the quiet solitude of the empty nursery.

Elise took several long breaths. Abandoning the sordid discussion in the sitting room had been the wise thing to do, but clearing her mind of it would take time.

"Is Anne asleep?" Miles spoke in the very same moment he stepped into the nursery.

"She is." Elise hadn't expected him. "I am sorry if my leaving was rude. I simply couldn't bear it any longer."

"I know. And I swear to you had Mr. Haddington taken even a single breath, I would have seized the opportunity to turn the topic of discussion, but he never once stopped." Miles looked more closely at her. The concern on his face was nearly her undoing.

She kept her emotions under control but only just. "I don't understand how he could speak of their deaths so casually. He said he knew them, that they were close acquaintances. But he acted as though they weren't people deserving of even a small degree of mourning. It was so . . . callous."

Miles clasped her hands in his. "I know, and I'm sorry. I truly am."

Elise let her shoulders slump with the weight she felt. "I suppose it's too much to hope that he'll never bring the subject up again."

Miles's look of doubt was noticeably apologetic. "He seemed too fascinated to abandon it. And seeing as the Haddingtons live just up the road, I don't think we can avoid them." Miles shrugged. "We could always build a very tall wall and place archers atop it. That might keep away the morbidly curious."

She leaned her head against his chest. "I suppose I will simply have to teach myself to not listen when people discuss what happened. It will certainly come up again."

Miles put his arms around her. The pain of the past half hour or so melted away. She had missed the teasing, playful side of him during their years of separation, but she had longed for this deeply compassionate side of him even more.

"Forgive the interruption, my lord." Humphrey stood just inside the doorway to the nursery. "The Haddingtons are leaving, and Mrs. Langley wished me to convey to you that she will see to the proper farewells on your behalf."

"Very good." Miles turned a bit toward the butler, his arms slipping slowly away from Elise.

"And a letter has arrived for Mrs. Jones," Humphrey added, holding out the missive for her to take.

Elise stepped to where he stood and took the letter. "Thank you."

"My pleasure, Mrs. Jones." He offered a bow and a barely concealed smile before quietly leaving the nursery.

Miles's initial description of the very formal butler had proven remarkably accurate: more of a puppy than a bloodhound.

"I do believe you have won over my butler, Elise." Miles chuckled. "And I noticed Mrs. Humphrey served bread pudding again last night."

"They are very kind people." She sighed, trying to ignore the sinking feeling the letter in her hand caused.

"Is that another one?"

She knew what he meant. "It is. I am tempted to simply hand it to you unopened." She watched his reaction to her casual suggestion. He didn't seem the least bothered at being burdened with her latest difficulty. She longed for a reprieve from the letters, so rather than trying to be stronger than she felt, she gave it to him, still sealed.

"Do you want to know what it says?" he asked.

"*Want* to know? Not really. But I probably ought to."

"Then I suggest we take this to the library, where all of the others are," Miles said. He slipped the letter into the pocket of his coat, then took Elise's hand once more. She felt instantly better.

He walked with her in just that way, keeping their short conversation to light topics. She could almost pretend there was nothing wrong in all the world. But a moment later, they settled into the armchairs on either side of the library's fireplace, and he pulled the letter out of his pocket.

Elise held her breath as he opened the seal. What would this message be? More threats? Another mention of Anne? She clutched her hands together in her lap and waited.

"It is blank." Miles flipped the page over in obvious confusion.

"Blank?" Elise came to his side and looked over his shoulder. Except for the address on the front—her name and Tafford, Derbyshire—the parchment was empty. "What do you suppose that means?"

"I have no idea." Miles continued studying the page.

"I don't like this." She paced, tension surging through her body. "Every other letter has contained a message, some of them very precise." She shook her head. "He wouldn't now send an empty letter without a purpose."

"I agree," Miles said. "There is certainly a reason, but I am at a loss to say what that might be." He sat there, hand rubbing his mouth even as his brows pulled in.

"I feel ill at ease enough not knowing who is writing, but not understanding what his message is either only magnifies the feeling of helplessness." She pressed her hand to her heart, trying to will it to calm down. Panic would do her no good. She needed to think clearly.

"The investigation papers haven't yielded any clear clues," Miles said. "I haven't narrowed down the identity of the murderer at all."

She looked back at him. "And after Mr. Haddington's discussion today, I can't help thinking the possibilities are even more numerous than we expected."

"What do you mean?"

She dreaded voicing the worry that had entered her thoughts as Miles's neighbor had spoken. "He knew our fathers, though neither of us had ever met him. How many others are there who fit that description—people who were part of their lives who we would never think to suspect because we aren't even aware they exist?"

Dread filled his face as her words sank in. "It did seem like a very personal attack, not at all random. But if their circle of acquaintances was broader than we are aware of—"

"Then we may never solve this riddle. Not ever."

His eyes met hers, and on the instant, his expression softened. He rose from his chair and crossed to her, his gaze never leaving her face. Her cheeks warmed at his approach.

"You look worn out, Elise." Empathy touched his tone. He slid the letter into his pocket once more. "Has this day been too much for you? You said you have been sleeping better."

She'd said so in passing after breakfast the morning before. He remembered that? Elise could tell her blush remained. "I confess I didn't sleep well at all last night. And yes, today has been more trying than I'd expected."

Miles cupped her face with his hands. Her heart pounded again. How did he do that with a simple touch?

He pressed a kiss to her forehead, just as he'd often done when they were children—it was the most sentimental of his gestures. He would hold her hand for virtually no reason, but a kiss on the forehead was reserved for the more difficult moments, those times when she needed him more than any other.

The now-familiar scent of him hung in the air around them. Elise's pulse pounded in her head, her mind whirling. Each breath filled her with an exquisite ache, and in that moment, she knew. She knew.

Despite everything that had happened and her lingering uncertainties, she had fallen in love with him.

* * *

Miles stepped into the sitting room after dinner that night to find Beth in there alone. He was disappointed that Elise wasn't there, but she'd looked exhausted. And no wonder after the day she'd had. He hoped she was resting.

Beth joined him at the window. "You must realize, Miles, how inappropriate it is for you to hold Elise's hand the way you do."

The unexpected remark caught Miles so off guard he did not manage so much as a single word in response.

"A gentleman is seldom seen holding his *wife's* hand," Beth continued. "To do so is a declaration that some relationship exists between himself and the lady."

"'Some relationship' *does* exist between Elise and me," Miles answered, recollecting himself enough to answer her. "She is my dearest and oldest friend."

"That is not enough. The gesture will be misconstrued."

"It will not." Where had this attack come from?

"It already has been, especially considering you have been seen doing far more than holding her hand."

"I sincerely hope you intend to explain that remark." Miles bit back a sudden flare of temper. Of what misconduct could anyone truthfully accuse him?

"Just today you were apparently seen in the meadow embracing, her hands all over your face."

"All over—" he spluttered. "I will have you know they were not *all over* my face. She was shushing me like she always did when we were children."

"But you are not children any longer, Miles," Beth said, obviously frustrated. "She cannot press her fingers to your lips or hold your hand or allow your embraces—and do not deny you have embraced her; one of the maids saw her in your arms in the nursery this morning. In doing so, you risk having Elise labeled as fast."

"Fast?" How utterly ridiculous.

"I am only saying the two of you had best watch yourselves lest you inadvertently compromise her reputation," Beth said. "And it wouldn't do yours a great deal of good either. You are newly ascended to your title, Miles, and virtually unknown in Society. The reputation you gain now will have long-term implications. You do not want your reputation to be that of a bounder."

The realization that Beth might be at least partially correct slowly began to overshadow the absurdity of the situation.

"One is certainly permitted a closeness to a childhood friend," he insisted.

"If this were Epsworth or Furlong House, I would not quibble with you," Beth said. "Those were *our* people. They knew you and Elise all your lives. They understood your connection, knew that the two of you had grown up closer even than two siblings."

"I embrace *you*, Beth. Doing so with a sister is not exceptional. And you said yourself Elise and I are as close as siblings."

"It is not the same, and you know it." Beth gave him a reprimanding look.

"I'm supposed to treat her like a stranger, then?"

"I am only saying, unless you are prepared to marry her, you had best have a care for her reputation."

Marry her? His childhood friend? A gentleman had quite different feelings for the lady he married than that of friendship. "If I promise to be more proper, will you stop worrying yourself into a pelter?"

"I have reason to worry, Miles." If anything, Beth's expression grew more concerned.

"Don't tell me you suspect me of anything—"

She shook her head. "It is not *my* suspicions that should concern you."

Suddenly, she had his entire attention. "Someone *does* suspect me of something untoward."

Beth hesitated a moment. "Not necessarily, Miles," she finally
answered. "But there is a great deal of curiosity. Elise was married at
fifteen. She was only sixteen when Anne was born. That is unusual enough
to raise eyebrows. Now she is living in a bachelor's home. Only the fact
that Langley and I are here makes the arrangement the least bit acceptable.
But coupled with her history, your obvious closeness will most likely not
be interpreted in a favorable light."

Miles stared unseeingly out the window. Was Beth being overly
dramatic, or were her warnings warranted?

"Just today, Mrs. Haddington questioned Elise quite pointedly about
Anne's age," Beth added. "And though I cannot be certain she did so as
a means of discovering just how young Elise was when her daughter was
born, it felt very much that way. Elise's position in Society is infinitely
more fragile than yours. You must be careful, Miles."

He couldn't imagine interacting with Elise as if she were simply a
nameless face among the young ladies of the *ton*. How ridiculous they
would be, carrying on inane discussions. Yet, if questions were being raised
about Elise's reputation, he had to be more cautious.

"I can see I have upset you." Beth sounded genuinely contrite. "I
am simply worried. For you *both*. I would not wish you labeled a rake,
for you are certainly not one. And Elise is the sweetest girl I have ever
known—in all fairness, I must admit she is hardly a *girl* any longer. I
could not bear to see her endure more heartache than she has already or
see either of you forced into a marriage not of your choosing."

Long after Beth quit the sitting room, Miles remained. Her words
of warning would not leave him. He was, perhaps, a little more familiar
with Elise than a gentleman generally was with a genteel lady. But there
was nothing untoward in their behavior. Besides, he continually reminded
himself, they were friends of very long standing. *Childhood* playmates.
Practically brother and sister.

*A brother does not wish to kiss his sister. Nor does he find himself suffering
a growing attraction to her.* He had very much wished to kiss Elise on more
than one occasion—twice that day alone. First in the meadow, when she'd
stood so close to him, her fingers pressed to his lips, her mouth turned
up in a teasing smile. Then the urge had assailed him again as he'd stood
beside her in the library. Those same lips had shifted into a more adult
version of the pout she'd often worn in childhood. It might have been
labeled cute if it hadn't accompanied a look of very real concern.

That thought brought Miles back to his other topic of reflection: the letter that still resided in his coat pocket. Why had there been no message? Certainly the as-yet-unknown man had not run out of threats and insults.

A letter without a single word of communication was actually more unnerving than the more pointed missives had been. He certainly thought on it more than any of the others. Miles imagined it worried Elise more as well.

Could that have been the point? After an unbroken stream of intimidations, the murderer chose to leave his latest threat up to its recipient's imagination, a recipient who knew firsthand the atrocities of which he was capable.

Chapter Twenty-Four

ELISE FUMBLED OVER MORE THAN one note when Miles stepped into the music room the next afternoon. How she hoped he didn't realize the nature of her swirling emotions. Her unrequited feelings would sound the death knell to their friendship, a friendship she was only just beginning to reclaim.

"Good afternoon, Miles," she greeted, grateful to hear she'd kept her emotions out of her voice.

"Good afternoon, Elise." His smile melted her. "I didn't mean to interrupt."

"I would appreciate an interruption, actually." Elise sighed. "My fingers do not wish to cooperate, it seems. I can't manage to play any of the tunes I once did."

"Perhaps you are simply out of practice." He came and stood beside the pianoforte.

"Four years out of practice." She'd severely mourned the loss of her music when she'd left Epsworth.

"Was there no one who would allow you access to an instrument?"

No one notices a woman of the lower classes. Jim's voice echoed in her head as clearly as if he stood there whispering in her ear. How hard they'd worked to perfect her disguise. She'd found safety in anonymity . . . and such profound loneliness. Elise had lived as an outsider, her neighbors never truly accepting her. Those few she encountered whose equal she was in birth if not in situation spared her not a glance.

She'd longed for a pianoforte, for the freedom to play without risking so very much. She'd often lain awake at night trying to remember the words of her favorite books, knowing she would never have them again or be able to read in public without raising suspicions. And she'd worried for Anne. Her circumstances would rob the girl of so much.

Elise pulled herself together, forcing such maudlin reflections from her mind. Perhaps a lighthearted reply would cover the sudden tension in the room. "I fear I was kept from an instrument quite cruelly, like a heroine in a Minerva Press novel."

When had his smile become devastating? For perhaps the hundredth time, she wished she had been near him as he'd grown into the man he'd become. There were too many holes in his history, things she didn't know about him.

"If only Tafford had a dungeon," Miles said. "You could be the wilting heroine. Humphrey could be the mysterious butler. I, of course, would be the dashing hero." He gave a self-deprecating shake of his head. "And we already have a villain."

A villain. Yes, they certainly had that. In a flash, the teasing mood of their conversation vanished. There had been no letter yet that day, but there was sure to be one. Would it be blank again? Would there be a threat? A warning?

"I am convinced within myself that the last letter was blank simply to worry me that much more." Her thoughts grew ever more heavy and pensive.

She reached for Miles's hand, feeling more at ease the moment her fingers slipped inside his. She forcibly ignored the little flip of her heart that accompanied it. If she didn't keep *those* emotions clamped down, Miles would see her feelings in her face, and she would lose him. Again.

"I concur with your assessment. I believe he wanted to cause you more concern." Miles squeezed her fingers quickly, then pulled his hand from hers and crossed to the window. He clasped his hands behind his back.

"I am anxious to see if today's letter is also blank," Miles said from his position halfway across the room.

"No letter has arrived," Elise said. "I hope today proves a respite."

"So do I."

Miles kept his gaze on the window. Elise kept her gaze on him. Something had changed, but she couldn't identify it.

"How is Anne today?" Miles asked after the silence between them had stretched to uncomfortable lengths. "Is she still insisting on being spun about?"

"Of course," Elise replied, a tiny smile creeping up again.

"So am I to expect Mrs. Ash's resignation at any moment?"

He was teasing her again, a very good sign. Elise smiled more brightly. "It may be on your desk even now."

Miles looked back at her and smiled mischievously. "Should we check and see?"

Elise nodded, relieved. Friendly revelry was far more familiar footing for the two of them. "And if it isn't there," Elise continued with the joke as she crossed to where he stood, "we can always go to the nursery to retrieve it. Save her the trouble, you see."

Elise took his hand again, grinning.

"She has, no doubt, drafted her letter in tremendous detail, delineating her many abuses and her injuries sustained from profound bouts of dizziness." Miles pulled his hand from hers again. He had never once done that, not in all their lives. And he'd just done so twice. Miles had held her hand whenever either of them wished for it, pulling away only out of necessity.

He kept his distance as they walked to the library. Even his conversation seemed oddly disconnected, as if they were acquaintances speaking at a fete or musicale. Elise didn't dare reach for his hand again. Having her gesture pushed aside once had been easily explained away. A second was proving more difficult. Should she be denied a third time, the rejection would sink like a dart into her heart.

"No letter of resignation," Miles said when they'd reached their destination. He had been quite careful to leave the door slightly ajar. She felt rather like an acquaintance with whom one wished not to be seen as overly familiar.

"I'll sneak around the nursery later to see if I can find it," Elise said with forced joviality.

Miles nodded, distracted. He clearly wished for her to leave. Perhaps that had been the reason for the open door, a subtle hint that her stay in the room was temporary.

"I will see you tonight at dinner, then." Elise made her way to the open door.

"Yes," he said. "Until dinner." The inclination of his head was not precisely formal, but neither was it at all personal.

Something had indeed changed, but she was at a loss to determine exactly what.

* * *

He simply had something on his mind, Elise told herself repeatedly as they passed through dinner. Miles was acting more his normal self. He, Beth, and Mr. Langley were conversing as easily as always.

The gentlemen did not remain for port after the meal but went directly to the sitting room with Beth and Elise.

"Mrs. Jones," Humphrey said almost immediately upon their arrival in the sitting room. "Another letter."

"Thank you," she managed to say, taking the letter from the butler.

She reached blindly behind her for Miles's hand. Her fingers found his and, to her relief, he held them. Her need for his reassurance had only grown in the time she'd been at Tafford. No longer was she Ella Jones, who needed no one and kept a tight hold on every feeling. She couldn't prevent herself from reaching for him now.

Beth and Mr. Langley were in the room, so very little could be accomplished immediately. Miles pulled Elise off to one side on the pretense of showing her a book on a side table. Beth, Elise noticed, watched them rather more closely than usual.

"May I?" Miles dropped her hand to take the letter.

Elise waited, wishing Miles would reach for her again. She needed the connection. She was painfully tense, her head beginning to throb anew. She wouldn't show the others how worried she was, but the effort was taking its toll.

"I am watching," Miles said, his eyes scanning the letter in his hand.

What? Miles was watching her? What did that mean?

"That is all he writes," Miles explained. "'I am watching.'"

Elise glanced around the room, half expecting to see a shadow lurking in the corner or a face in the window. "I don't like the idea of him watching me."

"I doubt he is watching at this precise moment," Miles insisted, his brow creased with concern.

"Knowing he is watching *ever* is enough," Elise said. *Especially having no idea who he is.*

"I have been going over the papers." Miles lowered his voice further. "Perhaps tomorrow we can discuss what I have deduced."

Elise nodded. Fisting her hands wasn't relieving her tension. She needed help. She needed support, someone who could share this burden with her, for she very much suspected she was not strong enough to do so alone.

She sighed and leaned her head against Miles's shoulder. Would this never end?

Miles's hands took hold of her shoulders. He would hold her now, wrap his arms around her, and tell her everything would be fine. A sudden memory surfaced of Miles at no more than seven, perhaps eight years old, with his arm around her while she cried. She had been crying for her mother, only a week dead.

She needed that again. But instead of pulling her close, Miles put her a bit away from him.

"Miles?" she whispered in bewilderment. First he would not hold her hand; now he pushed her away?

"This is a more appropriate distance, Elise."

"More app—" Elise shook her head. "You've never before—"

"Circumstances are not what they once were," Miles explained.

Circumstances? Elise was keenly aware of her circumstances.

"We must have a care for our standing in Society, our positions."

Standing in Society? Whatever did he mean by—

"Oh." Elise took the tiniest step backward.

Their positions. He was now a marquess. She was an impoverished widow of an infantryman, poor and unimportant. No. Things were not as they once were.

"Oh." The truth sank ever deeper. "You are right, of course. I wasn't thinking."

Miles glanced past her to where Beth and Mr. Langley sat, then shifted his eyes to the window. He wouldn't even look at her.

The pounding in her head intensified. She pressed her lips together forcefully. With a few hard swallows and quick breaths, she managed to keep back the sudden sob that rose in her throat.

This was his home, the home of a peer, and she was a guest there, one most of Society would point out barely warranted *that* distinction. Their circumstances had indeed changed. If Miles felt those changes ought not to be overlooked, she would abide by his wishes. She would do her best to pretend this new distance between them didn't sting. She'd done so countless times in Stanton when she'd been looked down on by people who would once have treated her with respect. She'd pushed away every hurt, every prick so she could carry on despite the bleeding in her heart.

"Elise—"

She was certain he meant to explain, to offer detailed reasons for his objection to her gestures of affection. Elise knew she couldn't endure that. Her composure would surely break. "I understand," she quickly replied, the words physically painful to utter. "Really. I understand."

"It just wouldn't be appropriate."

"I know." Good heavens, she was about to cry. She could feel it. She had already allowed herself to become far too vulnerable. Her defenses had been lowered, allowing her to depend on him again. With a single sentence, he had reminded her why she'd worked so hard the last four years to never allow that to happen. "Thank you for your help with my letter. Now, if you will excuse me, I would like to go practice my pianoforte." She offered a curtsy and left the room. She managed to maintain her entirely unruffled exterior up until the moment she reached the empty music room.

A tear broke against the wood floor before she could stop it. If she lost control now, she would crumble entirely.

Even the gestures of their lifelong friendship were no longer acceptable now that he was a marquess. But, she knew, it went further than that. She was not Beth's or Mr. Langley's equal either. Elise had been harboring foolish delusions of reentering the world she'd fled.

There'll be no goin' back to yer world, Jim had warned her the day he'd offered his hand in marriage. She'd thought then that she understood. The full truth of Jim's statement had not entirely sunk in until now. She couldn't go back.

She sat at the pianoforte but didn't play a single note. She silently struggled to keep the pain in her heart at bay. But a breaking heart, she was discovering, was harder to ignore than many of the other emotions she'd fought in the years she'd been in Stanton.

Elise dragged herself to her bed and lay down. She promised herself she would be fine in the morning. She would regain her iron-fisted grip on her feelings. She would protect herself again. She needed only this one night to come to terms with her heartache.

Chapter Twenty-Five

"She has started calling me 'Lord Grenton,'" Miles said to Mama Jones, pacing around her small room, something he did more often lately. "How utterly ridiculous is that?"

"Ella calls you Miles when she speaks of you here."

"And what does she say when she speaks of me? Do her comments fall more along the lines of 'That Miles, I certainly don't despise him,' or 'Miles is the worst person I have ever known in all my life?' Because, in all honesty, I am no longer sure which opinion she holds of me."

"You can find out for yourself," Mama Jones said, a look of mischief in her blue eyes. "She'll be here in a minute."

"Why do I have a nagging suspicion that you arranged this?"

"She was back to her usual blank faces and hollow voice when she was here yesterday," Mama Jones said, unaffected by Miles's accusation of meddling. "Somethin's got her hiding again. I can feel in m' bones it has to do with you. So I told her to come later than she usually does. Said my old bones needed rest and a great deal of nonsense like that."

"I think you could teach Wellington a thing or two about strategy, Mama Jones." Miles chuckled, shaking his head.

"Take a look out the window, Miles Linwood," Mama Jones instructed with a laughing smile. "She'll be comin' down the walk any minute."

Miles complied. With the growing feeling that Mama Jones had the world's most amazing sense of timing, he spotted Elise, with Anne at her side and a footman not far behind, walking toward the house.

"You are correct, as always," he said, watching Elise's approach.

"I know full well how hard it can sometimes be caring about her when she works so hard to keep a person at a distance," Mama Jones said. "But it's not coldheartedness or even true anger that makes her push people away. She's lonely and afraid and doesn't know what else to do to protect herself and her sweet little one."

Miles met Mama Jones's eyes. "If I cared less, I might be able to shrug and walk away. But I could never do that. And I never will."

She nodded as though she'd known the answer all along. "Then brace yourself, Miles Linwood. She's likely to fight you over whatever it is that's sent her running this time."

He turned back to the window. She'd very nearly reached the cottage. Watching her approach, he could see that she was indeed very closed off again, her expression empty and unreadable. What had gone so wrong? She was curtsying and referring to him by his title and, he was absolutely certain, avoiding him as well.

This was the girl with whom he'd slipped out at night searching for will-o'-the-wisps and watching for falling stars. She alone knew he had been paralyzingly afraid of water for a large part of his childhood. Only to him had she confessed, at the tender age of five, that she was beginning to forget her mother.

Grow up, Elise. Grow up and solve your own problems. His own voice echoed in the recesses of his memory, harsh and uncaring . . . and weary.

It was Elise's voice that followed, small and frightened. *I need your help. Please, Miles. I am in a great deal of trouble.*

The memory remained vague and incomplete. Still, he could actually see her standing beside his father's desk in the Epsworth library. Tears rolled down her face, her terribly young face.

"Oh heavens, what did I do?" Miles closed his eyes tightly against a wave of guilt.

"Come in, Ella," Mama Jones called out, recalling Miles to the present. He hadn't even been aware of Elise's knock.

"Mama Jones." Elise greeted her mother-in-law with that tone of eerie solemnity she'd acquired during her years away, apparently not even noticing him at the window.

Anne caught sight of him quickly, however. She moved toward him, arms outstretched. Elise held her back.

"I have tried to explain to her that you cannot be forever spinning her about, but she doesn't seem to fully understand." Elise's tone was apologetic and unnecessarily humble, as if she were begging the pardon of the Prince Regent himself. She lowered her eyes, her posture that of a servant before her employer, of a tenant before a landowner.

"We need to talk, Elise."

Her eyes darted up again, confusion and apprehension in her gaze, quickly replaced by an empty expression. "Of course, my lord." His title was beginning to sound far too comfortable to her. *That* would have to stop.

"Blast it, Elise," Miles muttered in frustration. "Must you keep *my lord*ing me?"

A barely noticeable quiver shook her chin before her lips clamped closed and her entire frame seemed to tense. Elise's eyes dropped once again to her hands clasped in front of her. She was retreating again.

"Mama Jones, will you watch Anne for a moment, please?" He glanced quickly at the older woman rocking and watching them. "I need to speak with Elise."

"Take her for a walk, Miles Linwood. Talk till you're blue in the face."

"It might come to that," Miles acknowledged. Then, consigning all of Beth's advice to Hades, he took Elise's hand and marched her from the cottage.

Elise attempted to pull free of his clasp, but he didn't allow her to. Mama Jones had a small garden behind her cottage, and he tugged Elise to the low retaining wall at the far corner of it. He brushed off a light coating of dirt, then laid out his handkerchief for her to sit on.

Elise sat. Miles actually breathed a sigh of relief when she stopped trying to pull free.

"You said you would not hold my hand anymore," Elise said, her voice barely louder than a whisper. Miles couldn't determine her feelings on the subject. Was she as disappointed by the necessary distance as he had been? Did she care?

"Yes, well . . . don't tell Beth," Miles answered, squeezing her fingers. Her hand felt so right inside his, he could hardly imagine never holding it again.

"Beth?"

"She reminded me that we really ought to be more circumspect in our attention to one another." Miles sighed. He probably ought to be sitting a little farther away from Elise and certainly shouldn't still be clasping her hand. There was comfort in Elise's presence that he had sorely missed in the two days since he'd enforced a distance between them. She had, in those same two days, pulled away from him emotionally as much as physically.

"Beth said that?"

"She pointed out that we are no longer children."

"And you are now a marquess," Elise added in a matter-of-fact tone.

"Which puts me in mind of something else about which I wanted to talk with you." He faced her square-on and made no effort to hide his exasperation. "At what point, Elise, did I become *Lord Grenton* to you? You have been calling me that lately, and it makes no sense. I have always been *Miles*. And you've been *my lord*ing me half to death. I am apt to go loose in the brain box if you keep it up."

"But you *are* Lord Grenton." Elise seemed to grow even more tense. "I am only being proper."

"*Proper*? Elise, you are my oldest friend. There is—"

"You said yourself," she interrupted. "Circumstances have changed. Our relative positions in Society dictate a certain formality. Like you said." She hopped off the low wall. "I understand, Miles. I know our positions are not equal as they once were." Elise walked a little away from him, her back to him. "I am learning to accept it, but having to continually discuss it is . . . is—" She took a shaky breath. "Oh, I don't know how to explain." She waved her hands in frustration. "I know we are no longer social equals, and I assure you I will not embarrass you. Only, please, do not force a detailed discussion on the topic. I can only bear so much without—"

"No longer social equals?" Miles cut across her in confused astonishment. Then, in a sudden flash of understanding, the past two days made sense: the curtsies, the *my lord*s, the posture of servitude that had returned to her demeanor. Elise believed he had brought an end to their closeness out of a feeling of superiority or aristocratic arrogance.

"I am the impoverished widow of a man Society is not even aware ever existed." She quickly covered the break in her voice with an increase in solemnity. "You are the Marquess of Grenton. Even a simpleton would recognize the discrepancy."

"Elise—"

"I am sorry for any embarrassment I have caused you," she went on, apparently unaware he had attempted to cut off her self-deprecating apology. "I am finding it difficult to think of you as anything other than Miles. But I will try." Emotion broke her words. "I do not wish for you to be ashamed of me."

"I have never in all my life been ashamed of you, Elise Furlong. *Jones*," Miles added when he realized his oversight. He turned Elise around so she faced him. With all the authority a marquess ought to possess, he continued. "You are a kind and giving person. You may have ordered me about mercilessly throughout our childhood, but you also displayed a level of compassion I have not seen in another human being." Miles cupped her face in his hands, determined to be understood. "We were born equals. We are equals yet. And I am proud to call you my friend."

"Truly?"

Miles dropped his hands to her shoulders and closed his eyes against the pain her doubt continually caused him. Every step forward was followed by a step backward.

"Good heavens, Miles," Elise said abruptly. "The look on your face just now was precisely the one your father wore when he came to Furlong House to tell me his pointer had killed my little kitten." Sadness crept into her eyes. Either she was not making the effort to force it back, or she was simply unable to do so.

"Actually, it is the look of a man who is beginning to realize how badly he hurt his dearest friend."

She was silent then. Miles could sense her defenses rising again.

"I should have helped you when you came to me, Elise." Miles still hadn't let go of her shoulders. "I was distracted, overwhelmed. I would have—"

Elise stepped back from him, tense and standoffish once more.

"If you had come back, given me another chance—" Miles ran his hand through his hair and pushed on through his frustration. "Why didn't you? Why didn't you ask again instead of running away?"

"I was fifteen, Miles. Fifteen. I *had* already asked, a dozen times at least." Her back was ramrod straight, her fists clenched beside her. But Miles knew instinctively it wasn't anger that gave her such a formidable stance. This was how she looked when she was holding back something: a word, an emotion. She was fortifying her wall, which, Miles realized, meant she felt more than she let on. "I was little more than a child, and I was terrified. When I came to you that final time, I was desperate. I was in no position to make a rational decision, but a decision had to be made. There was no one who would help me. I did the only thing I could think of."

"You were in that much trouble? That much danger?" Miles asked. "Enough to leave?"

"Leaving seemed like the only option."

"Did leaving solve your problem?"

"No. Jim did." A look bordering on reverence crossed her features. "By the time he found me, I was hungry and very, very ill. I was too weak and too poor to do anything to save myself, and I was alone. I was so utterly alone."

Guilt and regret crashed over him in alternating waves. He had failed her. He ought to have been there. She should never have been in that situation to begin with.

"But Jim found me, and he helped me."

Gratitude warred with jealousy in Miles's chest. "Helping you was always my job."

"Yes, but you weren't there."

How those words stung.

"I don't wish to talk about this, Miles," she said quickly and turned away. "I cannot expect Mama Jones to watch Anne any longer."

"Elise," he called after her before she had gone more than a few steps.

She stopped and turned back to look at him.

"What was the problem you were running from?"

"It doesn't matter now, Miles," Elise insisted. She'd shut him out again. "Jim took care of me and hid me away until the danger had passed. And in his home, I learned to take care of myself."

Chapter Twenty-Six

"You have to promise me, Ella, that you'll take care of Mama."

"I will." Elise swiped at the tears trickling down her face. They'd put this off as long as possible. "And you'll be careful? Very, very careful?" Emotion nearly choked her as she spoke.

Jim chuckled. "The most careful soldier in the regiment."

"Don't tease, Jim," Elise pleaded. "I can't bear it. I have this horrible feeling you're not coming back."

Jim sobered instantly. "I feel it too," he said. "Here." He tapped his finger against his chest. "M' father was the same way, sensed his end coming."

"Then you have to stay." Elise was crying in earnest, something she never did anymore. "I need you. Mama Jones needs you."

"Mama understands." Jim put his arm around her shoulders. "She will care for you, and you'll care for her. Neither of you will be alone."

"And you?" Elise whispered through her tears.

Jim leaned in and whispered in her ear. "I'll watch over you from above until your Miles comes for you."

Elise's shoulders drooped with the weight of loss. How she missed Jim. She hadn't known him long but had mourned his loss deeply. Mama Jones had held up better in the days and weeks that followed word of his passing than Elise had. Too much pain in too short a time had torn at her tender heart. If only she could thank him one more time, tell him again what his kindness had meant to her.

Theirs had not been a love story in the romantic sense, but she had loved him in a very profound way. He had restored her faith in humanity. He had saved her life. Above all, he had been kind and gentle at a time when she had been nearly convinced such traits no longer existed in the world.

Until your Miles comes for you. He had firmly believed Miles would search her out. But time had relentlessly marched on without Miles appearing. Jim's regiment had fought in a battle within forty-eight hours of arriving on the Continent. Jim had not survived. At eighteen, he'd become another casualty of war quickly forgotten by a country that had long since grown numb to the reports of death and suffering. At fifteen, she had become a widow. Anne had been born later that year.

"Ma."

Her wandering thoughts had distracted her from the game she was playing with Anne. The blocks sat unstacked in front of her.

Elise pasted a smile on her face, hoping Anne wouldn't see past the façade, though she knew it slipped more each day.

Anne held out one arm, hand fisted around a crumpled sheet of paper.

"What is it?" Elise asked.

Anne sat on Elise's lap, turned a bit so she could see Elise's face.

"Have you drawn me a picture?" She hoped Anne would someday learn to understand sentences. As it was, Elise labored through single words, trying to convey her meaning.

Anne tapped the paper, watching Elise expectantly. She took the paper from Anne's hand and turned it over to examine it.

"Oh, Anne," she whispered so her daughter wouldn't hear the frustration in her voice. Anne had somehow found the sketch Elise had done of Miles years earlier. Now it was crumpled and smudged.

Elise gently smoothed the paper against one leg, Anne sitting on the other. She felt Anne tug on her sleeve. "Just a moment," Elise replied.

Anne's hand forcibly turned Elise's head toward her.

"Just a moment."

But the girl was not satisfied with that answer. She pointed to the paper, then tapped one index finger on the tip of the other, then tugged at her hair. She repeated the same series of gestures several times.

What is she trying to say now? Elise wondered, still attempting to straighten the sketch as she tried to decipher Anne's words.

"The paper?" she asked, pointing to it.

Anne shook her head no.

"The drawing *on* the paper?" She indicated the sketch of Miles. At times, Elise felt like she was living one long, drawn-out guessing game.

Anne repeated the finger-tapping gesture, which Elise recognized. It had long ago been made the symbol for the color red, owing to a badly cut finger at the time Anne was beginning to learn her colors.

"Red," Elise acknowledged, returning the gesture.

Anne tugged at her hair.

"Red hair?" Elise guessed. *Red hair* could refer to one of two people: Beth or Miles.

Anne, it seemed, wished to know if the person in the drawing she had found was the person with the red hair.

"Yes, Anne. This is Miles. Red hair." She mimicked Anne's earlier gestures.

But Anne looked unsatisfied.

"Perhaps if it were less crumpled, you would see the resemblance more easily," Elise said.

"Or perhaps if I were *more* rumpled."

"Good heavens, Miles!" Elise very nearly jumped.

"You must realize that talking about someone only increases the chances of that person appearing unannounced."

He smiled like a little boy who had managed to sneak a toad into his governess's bed. She half expected him to produce a set of nine pins and challenge her to a game. How could a grown man look so much like a carefree little boy? And how was it that even a boyish grin made her insides tumble around?

He sat on the floor next to her. "That is a very good likeness." He motioned to the sketch still in her hands. "Though I don't remember posing for it."

Elise felt her face turn pink. She'd rendered the sketch from memory at a time when she had been desperately lonely. Somehow having him see it made her feel horribly opened up, as if he would be able to read in the lines of the sketch every heartache she'd endured.

Anne came unexpectedly to the rescue. She climbed over Elise's lap to Miles. She looked up at him, a contented smile on her face. She tapped her fingertips together again.

"What did that one mean?" Miles asked.

"'Red.' Anne is fascinated by your hair."

"Most young ladies are horrified by it. Red hair is not considered very handsome, you realize."

That was the general consensus. But Elise had always liked it. When they were tiny, his hair had been fiery, almost startling. Time had darkened it.

His attention was fully on Anne. He puffed out his cheeks. Anne tentatively pressed her palms to his face, pushing against the air in his cheeks. When nothing changed, she pressed harder. Miles let the air out in a whoosh, blowing Anne's curls up and away from her face.

She giggled, her sweet little mouth grinning wider than it ever did when Miles wasn't nearby. He laughed, wrapping his arms around Anne's tiny frame.

"She has your smile," he said. "Although you never would have sat this long simply looking at me."

"I don't know why she does that," Elise admitted. It had baffled her for weeks.

Anne pressed her hands to either side of Miles's face, pushing and pulling and distorting his features.

He puffed out his cheeks once more, but she immediately shook her head. "No," she said. "No."

Miles obliged, returning his face to its usual state. A pout pushed out Anne's lips.

"That is another look I remember well," Miles said, his words made difficult by Anne's continued attention.

"Are you saying I used to pout?"

"Adorably," he answered.

Elise attempted to force her heart to stop its sudden flipping about. That traitorous organ did not seem to care one jot that it was opening her up to even more pain.

Anne's hands continued their efforts. She glanced at the sketch still in Elise's hand. She looked back at Miles and then at the sketch once more.

"I believe she is comparing you to the drawing."

"That is unfair," Miles said. "I believe I was quite a bit younger in that sketch. And that was before I spent four years under the sun in the West Indies. I do not believe I would stand up favorably in such a comparison."

Miles was even more handsome than he'd been as a youth, whether or not he realized it.

Anne's gaze became intense again, that staring sort of look that always made Elise feel the need to apologize to Miles. Anne dropped her hands, turned her head to one side, and looked at him. Her brows furrowed. She touched Miles's face with one hand, gently, as one might touch a very soft fabric.

Anne gestured *red*, then *hair*.

"I *do* have red hair," Miles answered Anne.

Anne pointed at the paper in Elise's hand, then back at Miles.

He nodded. "That is a drawing of me."

Then Anne wrapped her arms around Miles's neck and laid her head on his shoulder.

"I do believe I have made a conquest." Miles held her tightly and rocked her back and forth.

Please don't break her heart. The thought remained silent but no less fervent than if she'd begged aloud.

"I originally came in to see if you two ladies would be interested in a little surprise," Miles said, resting his cheek against the top of Anne's head.

"A surprise?" Elise fought back the urge to lean against Miles the way Anne was. Had she looked as perfectly contented with Miles during her younger years as Anne did at that moment? She forced those recollections back.

He spoke with an air of mystery. "Something arrived this morning, and I have been anxiously waiting to show it to you. Would you like to see it?" he asked.

She did indeed wish to join in his surprise. She needed that joy again. "Yes, please." She rose to her feet and laid the sketch on one of the small nursery tables.

"Excellent." Miles shifted Anne to one arm and held his free hand out to Elise.

"Won't Beth object?"

Miles sighed and returned his arm to supporting Anne. "Probably," he answered. "And she would be right. I have no desire to tarnish your reputation."

Elise nodded. She'd had time to think over Beth's concern and saw the wisdom in it, though she missed that very personal connection with Miles. "Humphrey might not simply roll his eyes at our antics as Thomason always did."

"Thomason was a king among butlers," Miles said. "Now, are you ready for your surprise?"

"Ready? I have been ready ever since you told me there was one. You are the one who is dithering."

"Dithering?" Miles feigned offense, obviously not surprised at her teasing. "We shall simply see who arrives there first, then, shan't we?"

"That sounds almost like a challenge." Elise half laughed.

He was acting so like he had as a child. And as if the nursery truly were a magical fairy kingdom, Elise's heaviness was easing.

"A race, Elise." He grinned mischievously. "Beginning now."

With that declaration, he sped across the nursery, Anne giggling as they flew through the doorway.

"Miles!" Elise called after him.

She hesitated only a moment before hitching her skirts up a trifle and following in his wake. She looked both directions at the doorway. Miles was at the end of the corridor. When their eyes met, he smiled and disappeared around the corner.

"I don't know where you're going." Elise laughed out loud and followed. They'd once chased each other through the corridors of Epsworth for a full thirty minutes before Beth's very proper governess had brought their adventure to a halt. Elise had never liked Miss James after that.

Down a second corridor and up a flight of stairs Miles led her, speeding ahead, then waiting enough for her to see where he was headed. He abruptly stopped at a door and leaned against the frame. Anne laughed, clutching Miles's neck for dear life.

Elise laid her hand on Anne's back. "Now she will wish to be run all over Tafford as opposed to simply being spun." Elise's words broke as she attempted to catch her breath.

"You used to love running through the corridors."

What a perfect childhood they'd had. She felt a measure of freedom to have relived it, even for just that brief moment. She'd nearly forgotten how wonderful it was to feel happy.

She had the most overwhelming desire to wrap her arms around Miles as tightly as Anne was. Her heart thumped at the thought. To be held by Miles . . .

Elise clasped her hands together to prevent herself from reaching out for him. After a steadying breath, she nodded.

Chapter Twenty-Seven

ELISE WASN'T EXACTLY SMILING, BUT a spark of such honest happiness had entered her eyes that Miles couldn't look away. He'd decided after spending much of the previous night evaluating the tense and uncomfortable conversation he'd had with Elise about Jim—*St. James*, as Miles found himself thinking of the apparently perfect young man—that he needed to at least attempt to recapture some of the laughter that had once been a part of his connection to her. In their pursuit, he had been more than adequately repaid for his effort.

He smiled at Anne, who was still giggling in his arms. "We won the race."

He could see she didn't understand his words, but she didn't seem bothered by it. He bounced her in his arms, and she smiled almost coyly.

"I lost our race," Elise said. "But am I permitted to see this great surprise of yours?"

Miles opened the door to a large room. It was an unused bedchamber in an odd corner of the house. There was no furniture, but a set of heavy, dust-laden drapes hung on the window. He'd opened them earlier so there was no need for candles. The items he'd had brought from the Furlong House attics had arrived, and rather than tuck them into another attic, he'd placed them in this room, where Elise could see them again.

They stepped inside.

"My mother."

Miles had wondered what Elise would notice first. He'd settled on the paintings of her parents and had, it seemed, been spot on the mark.

"And Papa," she added.

"When the estate was auctioned, I held back a few things I thought might be meaningful to you," Miles explained. "These portraits had far more sentimental value than monetary."

Elise had already crossed to where the large paintings of her parents leaned against the wall. "I thought they'd been sold," Elise whispered.

There was something physically painful about watching her kneel in front of the portraits, her gaze intense and unwavering. If sheer need could bring a painting to life, Elise's gaze would have done just that.

And Anne, Miles discovered, was watching him with much the same intensity. Though he hadn't seen it before, there was a deep and unspoken need in her gaze.

She wore somber colors, the same homespun cloth from which Elise's clothes had been made. Her dark hair hung loose as Elise's always had. He wanted Anne to be as light and carefree as Elise had always been.

Miles spotted a doll lying in an open crate. *Heloise.* Elise had carried Heloise all around the grounds of their homes for years. Somehow, the poor doll had managed to survive.

He carried Anne to the crate and lifted Heloise out. Miles showed it to Anne, holding it close enough for her to take it. But she only looked, apparently confused.

"A doll," Miles said when Anne looked at him.

She looked back at Heloise and gingerly touched the doll's clothes, then its hair. She pulled her hand back quickly. The look she gave Miles next begged for reassurance.

Has she never played with a doll before? Miles glanced at Elise, who had discovered a short stack of books near the portraits and was thumbing through them. How poverty-stricken had they been since she'd left Epsworth? Had she not been able to afford even a doll for her daughter?

Grateful he'd thought to have a couple of chairs brought up to the room for when Elise undertook the task of sorting through her inheritance, as paltry as it was, Miles lowered himself into a straight-backed chair and settled Anne on his lap. He kept one arm around her. With his free hand, Miles held up the doll, wiggling and bouncing it in a way he hoped made the doll appear to be walking or dancing or anything that would appeal to Anne.

She looked up at him, still uncertain.

I can't believe I am about to do this, Miles thought. He held the doll against his chest and hugged it with his empty arm, all the while smiling brightly at Anne. He even went so far as to kiss the doll on its cheek.

Anne smiled at him.

So Miles pressed the doll's face to Anne's cheek, then to his own. He repeated the gesture several times. All at once, Anne took hold of Heloise and hugged the doll to her.

"Very good," Miles whispered. He wrapped his arms around Anne as she studied her new friend.

"Oh, Miles."

He looked away from Anne toward Elise. She sounded very near tears, and his heart thudded at the sound. She seldom showed her emotions, but they were raw in her voice now.

"Our music box," she said. "You saved it."

"You danced your first minuet to that music box," Miles said.

He had taught her the minuet using "their" music box, which had actually belonged to Elise's mother but had become a regular part of their time together.

"I remember." Elise opened the lid.

A composition of Bach's filled the room. Anne continued playing with Heloise, unaware of the soft music. Slowly, Miles was coming to understand the sweet girl better, to know what volume she required, what speed of words.

Elise stared at the box as it continued playing the very familiar and poignant tune. "You were going to dance the minuet with me at the Christmas assembly."

Miles lifted Anne from his lap, rose, and set her back on the chair. She looked questioningly up at him. He placed a kiss on her forehead, the familiarity of that gesture hitting him with tremendous force. How often had he done precisely that with Elise? He had, in fact, kissed her forehead after promising to dance with her at her very first assembly.

He stopped just in front of Elise and extended his hand. "Dance with me."

"Now?" She looked up at him, her eyes mirroring Anne's from only a moment before.

"You promised me a minuet," Miles reminded her. There was no teasing left in his tone or in her expression.

"I'm not sure I remember how."

"You do," he insisted. "Dance with me, my dearest Elise."

Her eyes boring into his, Elise laid her fingers on his upturned palm. He closed his fingers around hers and felt warmth spread through him. Slowly, she rose to her feet.

"Papa was going to buy me my first ball gown," Elise said, pain in her eyes.

Neither of them moved as the music continued to play. A sudden thought flashed through Miles's brain.

"I nearly forgot," he said. Still holding her hand, he turned back to the open crate. "I had convinced your father to allow me to choose something for you." Miles dug through the small crate until he found the narrow box he'd been looking for. "It was to have been an early Christmas present."

"And you kept it all this time?"

Miles placed the box in her hand. She only looked at it, unmoving.

Finally, Elise untied the green ribbon, faded and dusty with age, and lifted the lid. He heard a sharp intake of breath and prayed it was a positive reaction. Elise pulled from the box a fan made of ivory so thin and delicately carved it resembled lace. She gently opened each section, lightly fingering the carvings as she did.

"Every young lady needs a fan," Miles said in explanation of his reasoning at the time of the purchase, which, in light of the crippling poverty she'd endured, seemed ridiculously frivolous. "I was certain the moment I saw it that you would love it. I couldn't pass it by."

Elise laid the fan back in its box, refitting the lid. Her head was lowered over her task, and Miles couldn't see her expression. Was she disappointed? The thought knotted his stomach. He watched, discouraged, as she laid the box on a closed crate just behind her.

"Elise—"

Elise set her hand gently on the side of his face, cutting off his apology. She leaned forward and kissed his cheek. "Thank you," she whispered and didn't pull away.

Elise wrapped her arms around him. Miles returned the gesture. He wasn't sure what he'd done to finally break through Elise's wall, but he was grateful just the same. Indeed, in that moment, he never wanted to let go again.

The music box was winding down, the notes coming more slowly.

"The fan is beautiful, Miles," Elise said from within his embrace. "And to have my parents' portraits . . ." He felt her lean more heavily against him.

"Your mother's pearls are here also," Miles said when Elise didn't say anything more. "As well as her betrothal ring. I am afraid I had to sell the rest of the jewelry and the other paintings from the portrait gallery." Miles held her tighter, the guilt of those decisions washing over him anew. "There were so many debts. I simply couldn't—"

Elise's fingers were suddenly pressed to his lips. "Do not worry over it, Miles."

"You ought to have been left with more," he insisted when she shifted her fingers enough to allow him to speak.

"You saved what was most important."

No. I didn't save you. The silent words pierced his brain. He hadn't saved Elise. She'd said so herself. *Jim* had saved her.

"Truly, Miles." The slightest hint of a chuckle slid into her voice. "Where would we be without Heloise?"

He realized Elise was watching Anne. His gaze shifted to her as well. Anne gestured to the doll, attempting to make the doll's hands return the words.

"I would like to get her another doll," Miles said, still keeping Elise in his arms. He'd needed her there the past four years. She fit there, belonged there even more than she had in their youth. "I don't believe there is one in the nursery." Not if Anne's confusion over what to do with Heloise was any indication.

"Perhaps for her birthday?" Elise laid her head on his shoulder.

"Need I wait so long?" Miles had hoped to send to Derby for one that very day.

"Two months is not so very long."

"A little girl ought to have an entire collection of dolls," Miles said. "Enough for imaginary teas and lessons—"

"Under a tree in a meadow," Elise finished for him. "How many of those very activities did I force upon you?" She laughed as she said it.

"All of them. Hundreds of times." Miles had attended more teas as a boy than he had as a grown man. "And I plan to have precisely those things forced upon me by Anne, but she cannot possibly do so with only Heloise to join us."

"All these years, I wanted her to have a doll." Elise sighed. "I never could."

"Let me do this, Elise. It would mean a great deal to me." He couldn't explain precisely *why*, beyond a desperate desire for Elise and Anne to be happy.

"You are very good to her, Miles." Elise looked up into his eyes. "To *us*."

She had the bluest eyes. A deep, dark blue, like the sky just after sunset. And her hair had begun to escape its knot, no doubt from their race through the halls of Tafford. Miles brushed a nearly black curl from her face, his hand lingering on her cheek.

"The music has stopped," Elise whispered, her eyes locked with his.

"We never had our dance." He was whispering as well.

A flicker of a smile lit Elise's eyes. "You seem almost disappointed."

"I am, in fact. Do you waltz, Elise?"

"Waltz? No." Heavens, she was adorable when she blushed—she always had been, he remembered.

"You must learn to waltz, my dear." Miles continued caressing her cheek, finding the gesture almost addictive. It was not one left over from their younger years.

"My lord." A footman stood in the doorway, bearing a tray laden with tea things.

"I'd forgotten I asked for tea to be sent up," Miles said. He stepped away from Elise to direct the setting down of the tea. "Please place it here on this end table."

The footman brought the tray in, a maid directly behind him with linens. As they worked to set out the tea, a second footman entered.

"A letter for Mrs. Jones," he said.

Elise stiffened noticeably. Miles indicated the footman should give the letter to her. She accepted it with a "Thank you."

The tea was set out. Both footmen and the maid slipped out, leaving Miles, Elise, and Anne alone in the room once more. Elise stood at the window, glancing down at the grounds. She held her letter, unopened, in her hand.

"Another of his letters, no doubt," Miles said.

"Yes. Can he not even allow me one day's respite?" An enormous amount of frustration filled her tone. The lighthearted, smiling Elise he had seen only moments before had disappeared entirely.

"Would you like me to open the letter?"

She shook her head. "I will this time." Her lips pressed tightly together as she broke the seal. "Do not underestimate me," she read.

Miles had no intention of taking these threats lightly. "I have made progress with the inquiry," he said. He'd avoided the topic of late, not wishing to give her false hope. His progress had, in all actuality, been minimal. "My solicitor and Mr. Cane will be arriving in a few more days,"

Miles said. "They are bringing our fathers' financial papers. I found a note amongst my father's things shortly after his death that indicated he had some idea of how to turn around his and your father's financial situation."

"Pay off their debts?"

"Presumably. I would like to find out what my father's *idea* was."

She looked intrigued. "And this, you think, is related to the murders?"

"At this point, it is the only possibility I can think of."

Chapter Twenty-Eight

Elise rushed into the library a few mornings later only to find Miles in conference with Mr. Cane and one other man. They looked up at her indecorous entrance, surprise on all three of their faces.

"Forgive me," she quickly muttered, taking a step back toward the door.

"Elise." Miles stopped her. "This is Mr. Hanson, my solicitor. Mr. Hanson, this is Mrs. Elise Jones. Elise, you, of course, are already acquainted with Mr. Cane."

Elise nodded toward Mr. Cane. He wore his usual sober expression.

"If you will excuse us for a moment," Miles said to the solicitors before turning to face Elise.

He guided her across the library with his hand on her back. That simple touch had her pulse racing through her. Every day only proved to her more that she truly had lost her heart to her childhood friend.

Elise's eyes darted to the solicitors for a moment. "I do apologize for my embarrassing entrance. I had forgotten about your meeting. At least I look presentable, even if I don't act it."

He took a moment to survey her. His gaze stopped at her heavily worn boots. A look of surprised confusion crossed his face but was immediately replaced by a look of embarrassed frustration. "I didn't even think of ordering you slippers and new walking boots." He shook his head. "Why did you not tell me?"

Elise lowered her eyes in a wave of embarrassment. "I was humbled enough to need the dresses. I couldn't ask you for more."

Miles touched her face. Elise very nearly melted.

"Please don't hesitate to ask me for anything, Elise. Not ever."

"I very nearly did say something before the ball," she admitted. "I was so embarrassed attending such a fine evening without the proper gloves and in my old boots."

"You looked beautiful," he insisted. "You could be wearing regimental boots and still be lovely."

Heat rushed to her cheeks. "You are becoming a flatterer, Miles Linwood."

"And you are beginning to sound like Mama Jones." He chuckled softly. "Now"—Miles threaded her arm through his—"what was it you rushed in here to talk to me about?"

Ah, yes. Her rather unladylike entrance into the library moments earlier. "Your solicitor, no doubt, thinks me a perfect hoyden."

"Hanson thinks nothing of the sort," Miles said reassuringly. "Mr. Cane, on the other hand, has known us both from childhood and, no doubt, knows us for the unruly savages that we are."

"That is terribly comforting, Miles." Still, she smiled.

"I try to be a voice of reassurance." Miles squeezed her arm. "In what other matters might I be of assistance?"

"I wanted to show you this." She held up the letter she'd only just received. "It arrived a few moments ago."

Miles released her arm and took the letter. He unfolded it. In a very low whisper, he read it aloud. "I am closer than you know."

A chill rippled through her.

"You aren't leaving the house unaccompanied?"

Elise shook her head. "Not ever."

Miles sighed. "I fear there is little else we can do."

Mr. Cane and Mr. Hanson had returned to the piles of paper scattered across the library desk and a large round table moved in for their use. "Have you discovered anything?" she asked.

"Not very much. Of course, neither man knows the actual reason for my search, only that I am attempting to sort through and organize my various accounts and holdings, along with yours."

"I know this is hardly a lady's area of expertise, but might I be permitted to stay? I don't like being left out of matters that so closely concern me."

"Of course." Tension pulled at his expression. Because of her request? Or the memories attached to their fathers?

"Mrs. Jones will be joining us," Miles announced as he directed Elise back to where the two solicitors waited for him. Mr. Hanson merely nodded. Mr. Cane studied her a moment, then shook his head and shrugged as if resigning himself to her participation.

Miles sat behind his desk and eyed Mr. Hanson and Mr. Cane. Elise enjoyed watching him. Somewhere along the way, he had acquired an inarguable air of authority. The two solicitors seemed to notice it as well and instantly began telling him what he was apparently wishing to hear.

"These were monumentally bad investments." Mr. Hanson tapped one stack of papers and shook his head. "An entire series of them. From what I can see, Mr. Furlong made the same investments."

"He did," Mr. Cane acknowledged. "I drafted most of the contracts on their behalf. It was unfortunate they did not prove lucrative."

"They were shaky from the beginning," Mr. Hanson said, a hint of reprimand in his tone.

"I served as legal counsel for my clients, not as a financial advisor." Mr. Cane took obvious offense at the insult he perceived in the comment. "I suggested both men consult a reputable banker before embarking on any investment schemes. I know the limits of my expertise, Mr. Hanson."

Poor Mr. Cane. He really had worked very hard on Papa's behalf and must have felt a bit guilty, or at least regretful, when Papa's finances had begun to turn. Though, as he had pointed out, Mr. Cane could hardly be held liable. If the tension in his jaw was any indication, he was not enjoying this meeting.

"Did they?" Miles asked. "Consult a banker, that is?"

"It does not appear they did," Mr. Hanson answered. "At least, I found no correspondence that would indicate they did."

"I would like to look into these investments." Miles spoke with his air of aristocratic authority. "I was far too inexperienced and had far too much to see to at the time of my father's death to truly understand the situation."

"I am certain you'll not be able to regain any of the financial losses from these investments," Mr. Hanson warned.

"I am not interested in financial redress. I would simply like a better understanding of where he went wrong. I would rather not repeat the mistakes of the past."

Mr. Cane nodded, though the offense in his eyes didn't dissipate. Having one's professional aptitude called into question, no matter that Mr. Hanson hadn't directly done so, could not be a pleasant experience.

Elise's eyes met Miles's. A blush spread across her face.

"Would you like me to create a summary of the late Mr. Furlong's investments?" Mr. Cane asked.

"Yes." Miles nodded. "They are, as near as I remember, almost identical. So there may be some redundancy. But with both of you gathering this information, we are less likely to overlook something and, thus, less likely to see the Grenton accounts or Mrs. Jones's drained in similar fashion."

"Very good, Lord Grenton," Mr. Hanson answered.

Mr. Cane appeared less pleased at the assignment. No doubt he felt this was some sort of trial, his professional abilities being tested.

"Do you think this will tell us anything?" Elise asked as Miles escorted her to the door, the solicitors gathering up papers behind them.

"I have no idea." He sounded pained at the admission. "But at the very least, it might put to rest questions that have plagued me since my father's death."

Elise had never known her father or Mr. Linwood to be anything less than sound in their judgment. If they had been advised to consult a financial expert, they would have. She was certain of it. Why hadn't they? "I still cannot fathom Papa being so irresponsible."

"Nor my father," Miles said. "It is that inconsistency which has piqued my curiosity."

Elise had expected to hear something more substantial, something significant enough to give her more hope. Instead, she only felt more tense, more uneasy.

"You are frustrated," Miles said. When they were young, he'd had the uncanny ability to tell what she was feeling with a single glance. He was doing it again.

"I suppose I was hoping we would sit down and you would give them one of those stern looks you seem to have perfected and they would—"

"Tremble and weep, perhaps?"

Elise shook her head and laughed lightly. "No. I had hoped for something more helpful, I suppose, than what was done today."

"They have only just begun," Miles said. "Perhaps they will come up with something yet."

Miles put his arm around her shoulders as they continued walking. The natural thing to do next was lean her head against him.

"Now, on to matters of even greater importance." Miles was teasing again.

Elise was glad for it. She'd had too much worry lately.

"I have been pondering Beth's feet," Miles said.

"Beth's feet?"

"Oh, yes." He sounded almost serious. "I believe they are not much larger than your own. And I am confident I can persuade her to loan you a pair of slippers until we can have a pair or two delivered from Sheffield."

"Miles, you don't—"

"Do not say I don't have to," Miles interrupted. "I *wish* to. And I am a marquess, you know. I can do anything I want."

He sounded so theatrically pompous, Elise couldn't help laughing. "Are all peers so toplofty?"

"Oh yes. I've only met a few, but I'm convinced the lot of us are unbearable when we're assembled at Lords." Miles squeezed her shoulders again. "I shall have to introduce you to a few of the more entertaining amongst our ranks."

"Not in these boots, you won't." She was only half kidding.

"Very well. I'll wear my own boots, though they aren't half so dainty." Miles's eyes softened, sending Elise's heart flying to her throat, beating hard in her neck. "I hope this means you will allow me to buy you slippers?"

"Did I ever have a choice?"

He rested his hand on top of hers, where it lay on his arm. "No choice whatsoever."

All Elise could do was lean against him. No words were possible when he looked at her in just that way. Was this what love did to a person? Or did the impact lessen with time? Perhaps, she decided, a person simply learned to function despite the fluttering inside.

"I believe we will find Beth in the sitting room," Miles said.

"We don't need to bother Beth." To go begging shoes was nearly too much for Elise's already battered pride.

"Nonsense. I have a sinking suspicion your footwear has bothered you far more than you are letting on." He was precisely correct and seemed to know it. "Come now. We'll simply pester Beth like we used to until she finally goes along with anything we ask."

"And we wondered why she stopped spending time with us."

"Unfathomable," Miles replied, an ironic laugh in his tone.

Outside the doorway of the sitting room, Elise had second thoughts. She stopped, pulling Miles to a stop along with her. Mortification slipped over her. How would she keep her chin up if she had to beg for shoes? "Do we really have to ask Beth about the slippers, Miles?"

"You don't wish for slippers to match your new dresses?" He looked doubtful.

"I just . . ." She pulled back, needing space to think. "It's terribly humiliating having to beg for shoes, especially from someone I grew up with. It's hard enough accepting charity from you, Miles, without—"

"Charity?" Miles laid his hands on her shoulders. "Have I ever indicated that I saw you as some sort of philanthropic endeavor? That you were a charity case?"

"I *feel* like one."

His hands shifted to either side of her face, gently nudging her gaze upward to meet his. "My dearest Elise," he said quietly. "We have shared everything all our lives. Why should that change now?"

"What, Miles, do I have to offer you in return?" She felt a sting at the back of her throat.

"You two." Beth sighed from directly beside them.

Elise darted her eyes in the direction of the voice. Beth looked frustrated.

"Well, at least come inside the sitting room rather than enacting this display in the corridor." Beth turned and walked back through the doors of the sitting room. Miles and Elise followed, a proper distance between them now. "Obviously, my warnings had little impact."

"I think you are overreacting, Beth."

"I can tell you with certainty that I am not." She turned to face Miles. Elise took up an unobtrusive position not far from the door. "Mrs. Ash has been working quite hard to squelch the rumors your recent behavior has created."

"Rumors?" Miles sounded wary.

"Apparently, you two were seen in an extremely friendly embrace not many days past," Beth said.

Elise felt her cheeks redden. She knew precisely the embrace Beth meant: in the room where Miles had stored her family's belongings, with the music box playing. At least three servants had witnessed that, though she hadn't regretted it until that moment. Of course it would spark rumors below stairs.

"*This* coming on the heels of the realization that Anne was born a little early," Beth added.

The heat that had flooded Elise's face moments before turned suddenly icy. She was beginning to understand the nature of these rumors. *Please, not that.*

"Everyone has noticed the resemblance between Anne and Elise," Beth continued. "That resemblance has only served to emphasize the one difference between mother and child: their eyes."

A feeling of dread crept through Elise. Her breaths grew harder to take. Her head throbbed once more.

"They are brown instead of blue," Miles acknowledged. "How, pray tell, is that significant?"

"*Your* eyes are brown, Miles. Very nearly the exact shade of Anne's." Beth sighed. "I, of course, realize the speculation is absurd, but the staff here does not know either of you as I do. They have conjectured that Anne was not, indeed, born early but was, in fact, conceived prior to Elise's marriage. Prior to her leaving Epsworth. Prior to her leaving *you*." Beth gave Miles a pointed look. "Some have speculated that you, Miles Linwood, Marquess of Grenton, are Anne's true father and not Mr. Jim Jones. If you and Elise continue with your affections as you have, these rumors will simply grow more credible in the eyes of those who hear them."

They were labeling Miles a cad? A rake, even? And she herself was seen as a scarlet woman. Or, at best, a deceived and abandoned schoolroom girl. And what stigma was this attaching to Anne? Her diminished hearing created enough of a barrier between her and the rest of the world without whispers of illegitimacy adding to it.

"This is ludicrous," Miles declared. "To think I would . . . would—"

"I know, Miles," Beth assured him. "And, as I said, Mrs. Ash has done what she can to counter the damage. But if you two don't exercise a bit of circumspection, the only solution left to you will be marrying each other. I do not want either of you forced into a marriage of convenience. You deserve to choose the relationships you have and keep."

"I'm sorry, Miles." Dread swept over Elise at the enormity of the implications. Her presence in his home was causing him difficulties she'd not anticipated, and she felt powerless to stop it. "I am so sorry they are saying this about you. It is so terribly unfair. I'll think of a way to make it right."

Chapter Twenty-Nine

ELISE HAD, FOR ALL INTENTS and purposes, moved in with Mama Jones. For the past three days, she'd broken her fast in her room, then, after Anne had finished her morning lessons with Mrs. Ash, walked with her daughter to Mama Jones's cottage, not returning until after the dinner hour.

Miles understood. Beth's warnings had unnerved him as well. Neither he nor Elise needed scandal or rumors attached to their names. He certainly did not wish for speculation to taint Anne. After hearing the love in Elise's voice when she spoke of her late husband, Miles couldn't condemn her to a marriage that was any less loving. He cared about her, loved her even, but as a friend, a brother, a lifelong companion.

"It is, perhaps, best to put a little distance between you," Langley said from atop his mount. They'd ridden out that morning and had spied Elise making her daily pilgrimage. "I do not think it would be wise for her to become too dependent on you."

"You think I would fail her?"

"On the contrary." Langley kept his horse to an easy canter. "Watching you since her return, I think you would go to the ends of the earth for her."

"I would."

"And I think she is beginning to trust that you will. What happens to your Elise when it is time for her to be on her own once more?"

"On her own?" Was she leaving? Had Langley heard something to that effect?

"She cannot live here indefinitely, Grenton. For one thing, Beth and I really do need to return to Lancashire, and without our chaperonage, her presence here would be ruinous for you both."

"But where would she go?" Miles's eyes blindly surveyed the land around them. Elise had no one. She had no home. Thanks to a few well-made investments, she had an income, but it was not much.

"I would guess she will return to living with her mother-in-law," Langley said. "She is probably beginning that transition already."

Miles thought of the poverty in which he'd found Elise. She'd begged scraps from a heartless shopkeeper. She could not go back to that. He could not allow it.

She would be living with Mama Jones on Tafford land. He could see that she was taken care of, that she never went hungry. She would have new dresses and slippers and picture books for Anne.

But the thought wasn't comforting. His misgivings, in fact, only increased. The Lord of the Manor bringing offerings to a tenant cottage would only give rise to more rumors. She would be seen as a kept woman. But to have her so close and be unable to help her, unable to see her daily as he'd become accustomed to—frequent visits would create the same problems as gifts—would be unbearable.

"Beth has suggested that Elise come to Lancashire with us," Langley said, recalling Miles to the present. "My mother, as you know, has remarried, so the dower house at Gilford is vacant. Elise and Anne, along with Mrs. Jones, could live there with no difficulties for as long as they wish. And, of course, there would be no hint of scandal or impropriety connected with that arrangement."

"But Lancashire is so far away," Miles objected immediately.

"Part of the benefit, Grenton."

"I could visit." He was really only thinking out loud, trying to reconcile himself to being so far from Elise.

"It would be best if you didn't. Not often anyway. And, then, only to the main house."

"I will not travel all that way and not see Elise. It would be preposterous."

"Seeing your sister would not be reward enough for rough roads and nights at inns with questionable reputations?" Why did Langley seem like he was laughing?

"You might think me an unnatural brother for saying so, but no, it would not be," Miles replied curtly. "Elise is a sister too. Except, she's *more* than that. I'm not certain I can explain it beyond her being a very close friend. We have shared our entire lives, Langley. We were never without one another, and losing her four years ago was like losing part of myself. In a very real way, she is my other half. The one person on this earth I could not imagine living my life without. I—"

"Miles." Langley using his Christian name was enough to stop his unplanned confession in an instant. "What you have described is not a *friend*. That is the way a man thinks of his wife."

Miles pulled his mount to a stop, too shocked to do anything but stare.

"Beth and I will be here only another week," Langley said. "We will extend the invitation for Elise to return to Gilford with us. I think you had best reconcile yourself to her departure before that time. If she believes leaving will cause you pain, she's likely to stay. But doing so would be a terrible mistake."

"I don't want her to leave," Miles quietly confessed.

"I know," Langley said. "But as her 'very close friend,' you need to not hinder her attempts to do what's best for herself and her daughter. You need to let her go."

* * *

Miles tossed his cravat onto his bed, his mind in turmoil. *That is the way a man thinks of his wife.* But it was Elise he'd been speaking of. Elise, who had run wild with him all over Epsworth. Elise, who had pushed him out of a tree, whose nursery he'd sneaked into more times than he could recall, the two of them sleeping in her bedchamber when they were very small children.

"Just where I expected to find him." His father's words rushed over him in a wave so strong Miles could actually see in his mind his father standing in the doorway of Elise's bedchamber in the Furlong House nursery.

In his memory, Miles had awoken only a moment earlier. He, at only nine, had cut across the meadow the night before to see Elise. She hadn't come by in the four days since Miles had broken his wrist. He'd been convinced she was still crying over pushing him from their tree. So he'd shown her that his wrist was healing well, though the inches-thick bandage and wood splint hadn't reassured her.

He'd sneaked into her bedchamber dozens of times before, and as always, they'd fallen asleep there, that time in the middle of reading a book. Miles had pretended to still be asleep when he'd heard his father's voice. His mind had whirled frantically, searching for an excuse that would appease his father.

But Father hadn't been angry. He'd seemed almost amused.

"And you'll allow him to sneak back home, as always?" Mr. Furlong chuckled in response, both men keeping their voices low.

"Of course. No harm done. I daresay Elise has been beside herself worrying over his injury."

"None of us could convince her Miles wasn't on his deathbed," Mr. Furlong answered. "But she was too afraid he was angry with her to go see for herself."

"What an odd pair they are," Father said. "So perfectly matched."

"So long as we are not finding this situation ten years from now," Mr. Furlong said.

"Miles leaves for Eton this year," Father told him. "Their connection will change. They will both grow up."

"I am already dreading the day I find out my little girl has her first beau. Or worse yet, her first kiss."

Looking back, Miles realized Mr. Furlong had sounded very much like a father who felt his child was growing up too quickly, though Elise had only been five years old at the time.

"You realize, of course," Father had answered, "Miles will likely be both."

"I know." Mr. Furlong had answered with something of a sigh. "It is a very good thing I like the boy."

Miles stopped unbuttoning his waistcoat, frozen by the impact of that memory. Their fathers had expected a romantic relationship to develop between Elise and himself? And all based on their childhood antics?

They had predicted Miles would be Elise's first beau. *That*, as far as Miles knew, had been Jim Jones. And her first kiss as well. His feelings on that subject were far too jumbled to make the slightest sense of them.

Miles let out a frustrated breath and finished removing his waistcoat. He supposed he ought to have allowed his valet to help, but four years without a personal servant had made doing things for himself a habit. His waistcoat joined the discarded cravat.

He crossed to the empty fireplace—the evening was warm enough to forgo even a low-burning fire—and leaned his arm against the high mantelpiece.

How he wished their troubles had an easy solution. A great many gentlemen married ladies to solve financial woes or to hastily patch up a compromised reputation. And a great many people would likely argue that Miles was insufferably bacon-brained not to simply disregard Elise's feelings on the matter and rob her of the chance to someday marry the gentleman of her heart and her choice. No. There was nothing at all easy about their situation.

Would Elise take Beth and Langley up on their offer of the dower house at Gilford? Doing so might be safer, both in terms of her reputation and the threat that hung over her head. But then again, the murderer might simply follow her there. Then who would protect her?

If Elise chose to go, Miles would need to tell Langley about the letters. He would have to impress upon his brother-in-law the importance of looking out for Elise, of protecting her. He'd have to tell him that Anne was in need of dolls and books and dresses and that Elise, though she would never ask, was in need of so much herself.

Langley was generous and the best of men, but he didn't understand Elise the way Miles did. He wouldn't know how to offer her what she needed without hurting her pride. He wouldn't know that beneath her poise of solemn reserve was a mountain of emotions kept hidden from the world. He certainly wouldn't be able to recognize when she needed a shoulder to cry on or a hand to hold.

It simply wouldn't be the same. She would be so far away again. He'd spent four years separated from her. How many more would he have to endure?

He thought of the look of disapproving accusation Elise had received from the innkeeper in Stanton and the fleeting look of humiliation he'd seen in Elise's eyes when Beth had warned them of similar conjectures among the staff. Distance would solve that difficulty. Could he give her that? Could he deprive himself of his dearest friend in order to save her from the whispers and speculation, in order to ensure she had every opportunity for happiness? He could and would. For Elise, he would do anything.

Long after he'd extinguished his candle, Miles lay awake on his bed, staring up into the darkness. Heavens, he was going to miss her. His entire house would be empty with Beth and Langley's departure. He alone would be left to walk the abandoned corridors and sit in the deafening silence.

I have to do what is right for Elise. I cannot disappoint her again.

But letting her go would hurt.

His bedchamber door creaked open a bit. At the sound of little footsteps, Miles sat up on his bed. Anne hurried up to the bedside.

"Sweetheart." He reached down and lifted her up onto the blankets. "What are you doing in here, love? You should be asleep."

He could only just make out her face in the moonlight spilling in through his windows. Her eyes were wide, her mouth pulled tight. She clutched his arm in her tiny hands.

"What happened?" He spoke loudly and slowly, knowing she probably couldn't see his mouth clearly enough to help her make sense of his words.

Anne threw herself against him, holding him almost desperately. A nightmare, perhaps?

"Were you scared?" he asked.

She clutched him with such strength, as if terrified to let go.

Poor thing. "I'll take you back to your room, dear." He began slipping to the edge of the bed.

She only clung tighter, shaking her head firmly. He could remember being small and frightened of dreams. It wouldn't hurt anything to let her remain until she fell asleep again.

He settled in once more and sat with her in his arms. He hadn't realized Anne even knew where his bedroom was. She'd come quite a distance for one so small. She had her mother's tenacity.

Memory after memory accompanied that thought. Elise had been quite a force to be reckoned with, even as a little girl. When she set her mind to something, nothing stopped her.

Miles held tighter to his precious armful. She was so young. If months or years passed before he saw her again, would she even remember him? How quickly she'd claimed her very own place in his heart. Losing her would leave a void.

His tumultuous thoughts led to a restless sleep. People he'd known slipped in and out of his dreams: His father watching over them. The child Elise had been changing to Anne. Mr. Furlong and Mr. Cane. Miles's mother and Elise's. Associates he'd had in the West Indies. Beth. Langley. So many people.

"Miles!"

He jolted awake at the sound of Elise's panicked voice. She was rushing toward him from his open door.

"I can't find Anne!" She seemed to spot her daughter in the next moment, asleep on Miles's chest. "Oh, merciful heavens."

Elise dropped to her knees beside his bed, a panicked desperation still heavy in her posture. Whatever had brought her rushing in, it was not as simple as a mother who was unsure about which room her daughter had wandered to.

"What's happened, Elise?" He sat up, careful not to wake Anne.

"I awoke and"—she took a shaky breath—"this was on my pillow."

Without lifting her head from its position buried against his blanket, Elise held up a folded piece of parchment, the handwriting on the front horribly familiar. Miles muttered a curse, staring.

"On my pillow, Miles! He was in my room. In there while I was sleeping. Standing right there. Watching me!"

Miles set Anne on his pillow, then slid out of his bed. Elise climbed up on the instant, crawling to where her daughter slept. She pulled Anne into her arms, stroking the girl's hair.

Miles lit the bedside candle and unfolded the paper. "Ladybird, Ladybird, fly away home," he read aloud.

Elise watched him with fear-filled eyes. "It's a nursery rhyme. You remember it. 'Ladybird, Ladybird, fly away home. Your house is on fire and your children are gone.'"

He did remember. "'All except one and—'" His heart dropped to his toes as the next line of the poem came to him. "'And her name is Anne.'"

Tears welled in Elise's eyes. "I ran to the nursery, and she wasn't there."

"She came in here," he said. "She seemed scared. I couldn't manage to ask a question she could understand, but I assumed she'd had a nightmare."

Elise turned an unearthly shade of pale. "What if it wasn't a nightmare? What if she was afraid because she saw someone who frightened her? Someone in her room?"

Saints above!

"Stay here." He would rouse the staff. He trusted them. Langley. Anyone available to search.

"He might still be in the house," she said. "We'd be safest if we're not alone."

Even in her distress, Elise was thinking more clearly than he was. Miles lifted Anne into his arms, then grabbed Elise's hand. They rushed down the corridor. The jarring movement woke Anne, who looked about in confusion. Neither Miles nor Elise paused to explain.

He pounded on the door of Beth and Langley's bedchamber. Anne rubbed at her sleepy eyes. Elise trembled beside him. Fear sat deep in her shaky breaths.

He pounded again. What was taking so long?

The door opened. "Yes?" Langley asked, only a slight crease in his brow indicating the situation was at all unusual.

"I need your help."

"What is going on?" Beth's voice came from inside the bedchamber.

Miles jumped directly into the explanation, not wanting to waste a moment. "Someone has been sending Elise extremely threatening letters—the man who murdered her father and mine, we suspect."

Langley's eyes grew wide.

"This one"—Miles held up the letter Elise had relinquished to him—"she found a moment ago on her pillow."

"Laws," Langley muttered. Miles was taken aback at the sound of the usually very proper Langley issuing a decidedly lower class bit of cant. "What does the note say?"

"The Ladybird nursery rhyme," Elise whispered. She still shook, though her voice was steadier than it had been in his bedchamber. "The one that mentions a child named Anne."

"Beth," Langley called over his shoulder. "Tug the bell pull. Several times. We need as much of the staff roused as possible." He looked back at Miles expectantly.

Miles pulled Elise up to his side, holding her and Anne as near to him as he could manage. In his mind, he could see a menacing silhouette looming over Elise as she'd slept, the same one creeping into Anne's nursery. They might have been killed, murdered in their beds!

Chapter Thirty

"ANYTHING YOU CAN TELL US, Mrs. Jones," Squire Beaumont pressed. "Anything at all to help us form an idea of the man we are attempting to find."

"It was long ago." Elise fidgeted. Not long *enough* ago. "It was very dark, and he wore a mask."

"You must remember something about him," Squire Beaumont insisted, scratching at his hairline. "How tall was he?"

"Taller than my father. But not as tall as Mr. Linwood."

"I knew neither man." Squire Beaumont looked to Miles and Mr. Langley with a helpless expression.

"That would make him somewhere between my height and Mr. Langley's," Miles explained.

"What about hair color?" Squire Beaumont asked.

She felt like she was gasping for air. None of these memories were welcome. And sitting heavy on her mind and heart was the knowledge that this man had been inches from her only the night before. He might have actually touched her.

"I don't know . . . darker hair. Brown or black."

"Eyes?"

"I couldn't see his eyes well. He wore a mask. They were shadowed."

"If you had to guess?"

Elise swallowed. She forced out several quick breaths. "I would . . . guess . . . brown. Dark."

"He used pistols, correct?"

Elise nodded. She paced away from the gentlemen, who were watching her too closely. Would the questions never end? Would she never be free of this burden she'd carried for four years?

"What do you remember about the pistols?"

"They killed three men," Elise snapped. "I remember *that*."

Complete silence descended on the room behind her.

"I'm sorry," she whispered and dropped onto the window seat.

The pain in her head pulsated with each heartbeat. Her neck and shoulders hurt from the tension she'd carried with her since the night before. Anne had insisted she'd fled to Miles's room over a nightmare, but Elise couldn't be entirely calm. The letter was too pointed to be misunderstood. Anne was being threatened.

She leaned her head against the window, trying to stay calm. If she could remember something crucial, they might have some idea what to do next.

"I really saw only one of them in detail," she said. "It had a handle of dark wood. And there were ivory flowers inlaid in the handle. They looked like . . . not daisies, precisely." She could still see that gun in her mind, never having been able to forget, no matter how she'd tried.

"Crocus, perhaps?" Miles asked.

Crocus? "Yes. I think it might have been."

Miles muttered what sounded like a curse.

"Grenton?" Mr. Langley asked, obviously curious.

"I am absolutely certain those were my father's Mantons," Miles said. "Ivory inlay in a crocus pattern. They were custom made."

"Your father was killed with his own pistols?" Mr. Langley sounded shocked.

"We've estimated the murderer carried four," Miles said. "At least one of those pistols, it would seem, belonged to my father—his duelers."

"And the others?" Squire Beaumont asked.

Elise didn't look back at the gentlemen. She clenched and unclenched her fingers, trying to keep herself calm.

"Part of me suspects both of Mr. Linwood's weapons were used and that the remaining two pistols were Mr. Furlong's," Mr. Langley answered.

"My thoughts as well," Miles said. "Which means this bounder had access to both homes and knowledge of where the pistols were kept."

"And the ability to return them after the crime," Mr. Langley added. "Both sets were auctioned when the estates were settled."

"He showed Mr. Linwood the pistol before he shot him," Elise said. "He made certain he saw it."

That sobered the mood further.

The squire shook his head in obvious disgust. "What kind of hideous villain would kill a man with his own weapon and actually pause long enough to make that fact known to his victim?"

"The kind who would send letters threatening to kill the recipient rather than simply doing it," Mr. Langley said. "It seems to me he enjoys tormenting his victims."

"Or," Miles added, "is simply so proud of how easily he avoids detection that he makes a game of it."

A breeze outside rustled the heavily leafed branches of the oak tree growing along the banks of the River Trent. The scene was so deceptively calm and peaceful. Elise wrapped her arms around her waist.

"You believe he will follow through with his threats?" Squire Beaumont asked. "Or does he simply mean to cause her endless misery?"

"I believe we must proceed under the assumption he will make good on his threats," Miles said. "Including those aimed at Anne."

"And he would stoop to hurting a child?" Squire Beaumont sounded nervous.

"There is nothing he would not stoop to," Elise answered without looking away from the tree. "I do not think this is a man with a conscience, with any basic human compassion. And I would further wager he is quite expert at hiding underneath everyone's noses."

"Do you believe the neighborhood is in danger?"

"It is a possibility we would be well advised to prepare against." Miles really did sound like a marquess when he chose to.

"The men and gentlemen in the area will, of course, be warned," Squire Beaumont assured the room at large.

"Squire Beaumont?" Elise rose from the seat and turned to face him. She fought against a sudden trembling in her legs.

"Yes, Mrs. Jones?"

Her nerve nearly failed her. Her pounding heartbeat echoed through her from head to toe. She must give him the added warning. How could she live with herself if she did not and something unthinkable happened? "Please warn the men to . . . to be particularly protective of their daughters and their wives."

"You think this man poses a threat to women in particular?" Squire Beaumont paled considerably.

"He is capable of terrible things," Elise said. Her stomach tied in painful knots. The eyes of all three gentleman were on her, questions obvious on their faces. "Now, if I am no longer needed, I would like to go visit Anne. I want to make certain this has not unduly upset her."

No one objected. As calmly as she could force herself to move, Elise slid from the library. In her mind, she could hear that long-ago laughter that had accompanied cold-blooded murders and the haunting refrain of a children's rhyme. *Ladybird, Ladybird, fly away home.*

* * *

"Miles Linwood." Only Mama Jones called him by his full name in that matter-of-fact tone she seemed to have perfected.

"Mama Jones." He rose from his seat in the library, where he had remained after Squire Beaumont and Langley had both taken their leave. He offered her a bow, something that always made her shake her head at him, as if he had completely taken leave of his senses.

"I need to talk to you."

"Of course." He would very much like to talk to her as well. "Please have a seat."

"That I will." She hobbled across the room, leaning on her cane. Her life had obviously been difficult. She was young yet to be as physically worn down as she was. Miles had learned early in their acquaintance that she did not appreciate him offering his arm to assist her. She considered accepting it to be "getting above herself."

Mama Jones slowly lowered herself into a high-backed armchair near the fire, sighing as she settled in more comfortably. Miles chose the chair opposite her. Mama Jones set the bag she'd come with on her lap.

"Heard there was trouble here last night." Mama Jones jumped into the heart of the matter as she always did.

"Lands, *was* there!" Miles sighed. He leaned against the back of his chair, rubbing his forehead with his fingers. "We were lucky, Mama Jones." He shook his head, his worry over the previous night's events still heavy. "We were very lucky."

"The man who tried to kill her before my Jim found her," Mama Jones said, "he is here?"

"He is. Somewhere."

"And he has been threatening m' Ella and Anne?"

"He has."

"And last night he was in Ella's room?"

"Yes."

"She escaped unharmed?" Mama Jones looked more intently at him.
"She did."

"Are you certain?"

"She appeared perfectly well."

Mama Jones's lips pursed, her eyes drifting away for a moment. A look of determination crossed her cragged features, and she began rummaging through her bag. She pulled from it the awkward wooden box that usually resided on her mantel.

"M' Jim told me some things." Mama Jones lifted the box's lid. "An' I can't tell you directly. I gave m' word, I did, not to tell a soul."

"About Elise?" Even as he asked, Miles knew the answer was yes.

"You need to know." She nodded slowly. "Though I can't say it right out, you're bright. You'll see it for yourself."

Mama Jones handed him the sketch Elise had done of Jim Jones.

"Keep it till you understand what I'm showin' you for," Mama Jones instructed.

Miles knew she treasured the drawing, probably the only likeness she had of her son. "I promise to treat it with utmost care."

"I know you will," Mama Jones said. "But look at it. See if you can understand. I worry for Ella." She slowly rose.

At the door, she stopped and looked up at Miles. "Jim knew he would not come home from the war." A tear hung in the corner of her eye. "But he promised Ella he'd look after her, from above, you know? Promised to until you came and found her."

"Until *I* came?"

"She spoke of you often enough. 'Twere apparent to Jim and to me that she loved you and missed you fiercely. Jim was certain you hadn't forgotten her."

Miles joined her in the doorway. "I never forgot. I simply couldn't find her."

"She did not wish to be found," Mama Jones answered. "Though I think she wanted you to."

"To find her?"

"Aye. She was confused and very frightened." Mama Jones patted Miles's cheek. "Study the picture. You need to know what tore her away from you and what Ella is afraid of now."

Mama Jones left the library, and Miles settled back at his desk, staring into the eyes of a man he had been trying for weeks not to dislike. Jim

Jones was revered by all who knew him. He was the shining knight Miles had failed to be, the sainted war hero.

"Be fair," Miles muttered to himself. He pushed out a puff of air before settling back in and taking another look.

Jim Jones had been a boy. He had died the youth Miles saw on the paper before him. He'd left behind a wife, a child he would never even see.

"I have been envying him that? A life cut tragically short?" Miles shook his head at his own folly. Had his pride not permitted even a glimmer of gratitude? This boy had saved Elise. She'd said herself that Jim had saved her life.

Miles treasured little Anne. He had introduced her to the idea of having "tea" with Heloise and the new doll he had bought for her, whose name he hadn't yet deciphered. Anne had come alive as she'd learned to play. She was loving and sweet.

Her smile, like so much of the rest of her, was the exact copy of Elise's. Miles melted at the sight of it. That same smile had convinced him to go along with any number of schemes when he was a boy.

He glanced back at the sketch once more. Anne's resemblance to her mother was obvious. But in what ways did she look like her father?

Then Miles saw what he was certain Mama Jones had been hoping he would: Jim Jones's light eyes.

He thought back on every couple he knew, thought of their children. He could not think of a single couple who were both blue eyed and had produced a dark-eyed child. It likely *could* happen but was rare enough that Miles had never known it to occur. Miles's brown eyes were the reason some had begun to speculate on his role in Elise's life. A brown-eyed girl with a blue-eyed mother almost certainly meant there had been a dark-eyed father.

He stared at the sketch of Jim Jones, focused on the obviously light eyes. He knew in an instant this was what Mama Jones wished him to see, the only way she could think of to tell him this important piece of Elise's puzzle without breaking her word to her son.

Jim Jones was not Anne's father.

Chapter Thirty-One

MILES PACED THE LENGTH OF the library.

Two months. Elise had said Anne's birthday was in two more months. That meant she was born in August. Elise had married Jim in mid-January. Babies born at seven months simply did not survive.

But if Anne had actually been born after the usual amount of time, Elise would have to have been with child before leaving Epsworth, just as the servants had speculated.

I am in a great deal of trouble. Suddenly, Elise's declaration the night before she'd fled took on new meaning. A woman unwed and increasing was indeed in a great deal of trouble.

Miles rubbed his face with his hands. No wonder she'd been so frightened.

Leaving seemed like the only option. Elise had told him so only days earlier. *I was hungry and very, very ill. I was too weak and too poor to do anything to save myself.*

Miles's throat grew tight as he recalled her words. *Weak and poor. Hungry and ill.* Expecting a child and entirely alone in the world.

But then Jim found me. And he saved me.

"God bless you, Jim Jones," Miles whispered into the empty room. The young man had given Elise the protection of his name, had saved Anne from the shame of illegitimacy, had saved them both from starvation or worse.

But who, Miles silently demanded, was the rake who'd created the situation in the first place? He could think of no one in whom Elise had shown an interest all those years ago. There'd been no one he could recall who had shown any interest in her.

She'd been fifteen years old, for heaven's sake! So fragile after witnessing and barely surviving an unspeakable crime. What kind of monster would take advantage of that?

But the answer settled into his mind, leaving him instantly ill.

The murderer.

Elise had said just that day that she believed him a threat to women specifically. She had also said she believed the unidentified man had dark eyes. Anne's eyes were dark.

Miles sank onto a chair. "Oh, merciful heavens."

She'd been only a child when this had happened. *Fifteen* years old. She had been so young and innocent and untouched by the world. He could see in his memory Elise dancing in the meadow only the day before their fathers' deaths, giggling at the thought of an assembly.

He dropped his face into his hands. She'd been entirely unprotected. *He* had been hiding at home, avoiding the dinner party because it would have been uncomfortable. He hadn't been there to protect her, and he'd failed her again only a few weeks later.

"Miles?"

To hear Elise's voice at that moment startled Miles to the point of actually jumping.

"Mama Jones said you wanted to see me."

He looked up at Elise, but all he could see was the fifteen-year-old girl she'd been, the joy that had radiated from her. He realized quite suddenly that a light had gone out in her eyes the night of the attack. He hadn't seen it since. Not in the days immediately afterward, not in the weeks since she'd come to Tafford.

"Are you unwell?" Elise asked, crossing the room to where he sat in the same seat he'd occupied during Mama Jones's visit. "Truly, you seem very upset about something."

"Oh, Elise." It was all he could get out. Miles closed his eyes and hung his head. He had failed her so monumentally. How much she'd endured, and entirely alone.

"Miles?"

Miles couldn't bring himself to look up at her. He knew he would see that lurking sadness in her eyes and couldn't bear the added guilt.

"Are you upset with me?"

That was the last thing he wanted her to think. "No, Elise."

"Will you tell me what is wrong?" Concern etched her voice. "I believe I am a good listener."

Miles let out a frustrated breath and forced himself to look into her face. "We don't talk as easily as we once did."

"I wish we did."

Miles took gentle hold of her hand. She didn't pull away. "What can I do to show you I am trustworthy?" Obviously, she hadn't thought him so four years ago.

Elise glanced quickly at the door, which she had apparently closed when she'd entered. Was she thinking of leaving already? But she didn't.

"I am sorry the staff has been saying so many things about you," Elise said. "You don't deserve to be treated that way."

"They have been saying unflattering things about you too." The rumors had implied that she had been brazen, fallen. "Do you not feel you also deserve better treatment than that?"

A flicker of pain passed through her eyes in the moment before she dropped her gaze. "I do wish they wouldn't talk about me. The people in Stanton did that also."

They had probably pieced together the evidence that cast doubt on Anne's parentage.

Elise moved a little away from him, slipping her hand out of his. "I didn't do anything wrong." She wasn't looking at him, but Miles felt as if she were pleading with him. "But they treated me as if I had. Looked down on me and"—Elise looked at him once more, an almost desperate look in her eyes—"I didn't do anything to deserve their condemnation."

"I know, Elise." Miles rose and crossed to where she stood.

"No. You don't understand. They thought that . . . But, I didn't . . . None of it was my fault, Miles. I—"

"Elise." He tried to stop her increasingly frantic words. Her ability to remain frighteningly calm had been slipping lately. Would she break down again?

"*I* didn't do anything. I wasn't—"

Miles pressed his fingers to her lips, the way she always hushed him. Her pleading eyes locked with his own.

He shifted his hand to her cheek. "I know, Elise."

"No, you don't," she said, her voice breaking with emotion. "There's something I didn't tell you. I never told anyone except Jim."

Miles could feel her trembling. She began lowering her head once more.

"Elise. Do not look away from me now. I need you to hear what I'm saying." Miles looked directly into her eyes, holding either side of her face. "I *know*. Jim told Mama Jones. And she told me enough for me to piece together what happened."

Elise paled drastically. "It wasn't my fault," she said almost without making any noise.

"I never for one moment thought that it was. I only wish you'd told me *before* you were desperate."

"Oh, Miles." Tears flowed freely. "I kept hoping I was wrong. I waited until I was absolutely certain. Once I knew, I tried to tell you. Again and again I tried."

"But I pushed you away." The bits of memory were falling into place, forming a picture of his past that he felt utterly ashamed of.

"You were so very busy, and every time I started to tell you, you insisted you didn't have time to listen to my troubles. Eventually, you didn't want to listen to me at all." She brushed a tear away with the heel of her hand. "Those were the worst days of my life."

He pulled her into his arms. There would never be words enough to apologize for those thoughtless moments.

From inside his embrace, she continued her explanation. "I was too afraid to tell anyone else. Even young as I was, I understood how Society views an unmarried lady in that state, no matter how the situation was created. You were the only one I was certain wouldn't condemn me."

"And I wouldn't even listen." He rubbed her back as he held her, wishing he could somehow return to that awful time and make this right.

"If I had been older or less fragile in the wake of all that happened, I might have made a better choice than running away," she said. "At some point in the last four years, I realized I could have talked with Beth. She and I were not as close as you and I were, but she would have helped. She could have found a place for me to go, away from prying eyes. But problems are always easiest to solve in hindsight."

She sighed and leaned more heavily against him. Miles kissed her hair, then rested his cheek on the top of her head. "How did Jim find you? It honestly seems almost miraculous."

"I have always considered it the greatest miracle of my life."

He adjusted his position enough to look into her face. "Would you tell me? If it's not too difficult to talk about, of course."

"Do you truly want to hear it?" Her doubt was understandable. He had on more than one occasion been more than a touch gruff about Jim and his rumored perfection. But knowing what he did now, he'd replaced his jealousy with an unspeakable gratitude.

"I truly do," he assured her.

She nodded. Miles led her over to the window seat and sat. She took the space beside him and slipped her hand into his.

"I rode the mail coach as far as Cheshire before I ran out of money," she said. "So I hid in a small tool shed behind an inn."

He felt sick thinking of his dear, sweet Elise huddled in a shed all alone.

"That was my home for ten days. Ten miserable, terrible days. I kept hidden and quiet, sneaking out only to try to find food. Jim came upon me in the alley behind the bakery when I was searching through crates for any bits of flour or dough that might have been there. He didn't say anything for a long moment but simply looked at me as though he were reading all the details of my life." She wrapped her fingers more firmly around Miles's, her eyes focused off in the distance. "He bought a half-penny bun from the baker and gave it to me. He said I didn't need to say anything or tell him anything; he simply could feel that I needed help. There was something about him that I still can't even explain. But I knew in that moment that I didn't have to be afraid of him. We sat on a bench, and he told me he could see that I was in trouble and would help in any way he could."

Elise slipped her hand free and wrapped her arm around Miles's. Miles leaned into the corner of the window seat, settling in as comfortably as he could so she wouldn't feel the need to leave. He had waited four long years to understand what had happened to her.

"I told him everything. I know that seems foolish, considering we'd known each other but a few minutes, but he was the nearest thing to an actual angel I think I've ever come across. He was good in a way that filled every part of him. I never worried, never doubted." She laid her head on his shoulder. "I needed that. I needed the reassurance of someone I trusted from the very beginning. He really was a miracle."

A miracle, indeed.

"Leaving Epsworth was likely not the wisest decision," Elise said, "but it was the only solution I could think of at the time. And I cannot for a moment regret that it brought Jim into my life. He gave me hope at a time when I had none. And I like to think that knowing I was with his mother eased some of his worries."

"What do you think Jim would say knowing that you and I have found each other again?"

"He would say, 'I told you so.'" A smile was evident in her voice, a sound that did Miles's heart a great deal of good. "And then he would laugh the way he always did. He was the happiest person I've ever known."

"I think I would have liked him." Miles was surprised by the realization but grateful to know he'd begun to let go of his envy of the poor young man.

"I know you would have."

They sat in the window seat for a long while, neither feeling the need to speak or leave. The secrets that had long separated them were giving way. The walls were crumbling at last. He knew enough now to understand why she had struggled so much over the past weeks to trust him again. He hoped that her willingness to tell him about Jim was a sign that some of her wounds were beginning to heal.

Chapter Thirty-Two

THINGS WERE DIFFERENT WITH ELISE after their discussion in the library. She smiled more, though the hint of sadness didn't entirely leave her eyes. Miles could tell she was no longer hiding from him. Only time would entirely bridge the chasm between them, but they were closer now.

Her newfound ease in his company extended to others as well. The Haddingtons, along with another family in the neighborhood, dropped by for an afternoon visit two days later. While Elise had rather looked like a frightened rabbit during the Haddingtons' last visit, she was entirely composed during this one.

She chatted quite amicably, wearing a serene smile, but she likely wasn't nearly as self-assured as she appeared. Miles watched her with no small degree of pride. Elise was a wonder.

"We heard the squire was here," Mr. Haddington said. "Something about a break-in or a murder or something." His curiosity could not have been more apparent.

Elise met Miles's gaze. Though no one would detect the wariness in her expression, Miles could see it. Mr. Haddington's morbid fascination with their fathers' deaths had bothered her considerably. This line of questioning certainly would as well.

"Yes, there appeared to have been an intruder in Tafford a few nights ago," Miles explained, keeping his tone matter-of-fact. "And though we cannot be certain, we do suspect it may have been the same person who took the lives of my father and Mrs. Jones's several years ago."

A few of the ladies expressed their immediate concern. Mr. Haddington was the only gentleman present other than Miles. He clearly already knew the details and simply watched eagerly for more information.

"Until we are certain there is no immediate danger," Miles continued, "the neighborhood is advised to be cautious."

"How terrifying," Miss Saunders said.

The Saunders' estate sat on the other side of the Haddingtons'. The Saunders were generally considered quite a social family, though they'd hesitated to visit Tafford, apparently feeling overawed at the thought of a marquess. That would take some getting used to. Miles was not at all accustomed to being intimidating.

"I must say, Mrs. Jones, you do not seem overly frightened," Mrs. Haddington observed. "Does the thought of a murderer on the loose not worry you?"

Elise didn't so much as flinch. "I have lived four years with the knowledge that there was a murderer on the loose. As much as the realization worries you after only a few days, I assure you it worries me a great deal more."

Miles felt like applauding. Here was the Elise he remembered: the perfect combination of grace and plucky tenacity.

"And what is being done about this threat?" Mrs. Haddington demanded the answer of Elise as though she were somehow personally responsible.

There was no doubt Mrs. Haddington had decided not to like her. Miles had his suspicions as to why. Not a single visit passed without the woman practically tossing her daughter at him. He couldn't even pass them on horseback without being stopped and peppered with questions about how lovely Miss Haddington looked or how fine a horsewoman she was. Miles liked Miss Haddington well enough, but he had no interest in that direction.

"What is being done?" Elise repeated the question aimed at her. "I believe that would be a question best asked of the squire."

"How is your sweet little girl?" Miss Haddington jumped in before her mother could pose any more questions. "She was such a darling in the short moments she visited with us before."

Relief showed in Elise's eyes as she gladly took up the new topic of discussion. "She is well; thank you. I am afraid she is far too shy of strangers yet to make her curtsies to a group as large as this one."

"Yes, understandably so," Miss Haddington said.

"She is four years old, did you say?" Mrs. Haddington pressed.

Elise's smile turned just a touch icy as she answered. "She is *three* years old."

"And has the most darling curls," Miss Haddington said, turning to Miss Saunders. "Am I the only one who always longed for elegant curls as a girl?"

Miss Saunders laughed happily. "I think every little girl with straight hair wished for curls."

"And every girl with curls longed to be rid of them," Elise added.

A weight lifted from Miles's shoulders as the ladies embarked on a conversation that steered clear of murders and thinly veiled questions about Anne's age. This wasn't the easiest of visits, but Elise was surviving it nicely.

However, by the time the last visitor left, Elise looked exhausted. "I do not know how ladies of the *ton* survive their at-homes in Town. We had not a half-dozen people here, and I am ready to lock myself in a room somewhere and refuse to see anyone for days."

Miles walked with her toward the back sitting room. "That is actually what the men of the *ton* generally do. Only we lock ourselves in our clubs."

She grinned up at him. "You are all cowards, then?"

"Yellow through and through."

She stepped through the door ahead of him. "I had a feeling Mr. Haddington would be particularly interested in the news that a murderer was in our midst. He seems rather too fond of that kind of thing."

Miles had noticed that as well. "I have had a few conversations with him, but our fathers' deaths are the only ones he's brought up. Either he hasn't been privy to any other morbid tales, or he's particularly interested in this one."

Contemplation sat heavy on Elise's brow. "That is something of a worrisome thought, isn't it?"

"It has swarmed in my mind a great deal lately," he said. "He knew our fathers and is exceptionally interested in being told what we know about their murders."

Elise stood quite still, watching Miles but with the aura of one whose thoughts weren't entirely in the moment. "I have found myself wondering if he is asking these questions in order to know if he has adequately covered his tracks. Do you think that is overly suspicious of me? Perhaps I am assuming too much."

Miles stepped farther into the room, resisting the urge to pace. "If you are assuming too much, then so am I. Those same suspicions have entered my mind."

"I worried after the murders that the killer might have been someone I knew. Every person who passed by after that night, anyone who offered a 'good day' or even looked at me made me wonder." She rubbed at her arms as if a sudden chill had taken hold. "I don't like the idea any better now than I did then."

He set his hands on her arms. "Considering the weight of worry you are carrying about, you were in fine form this afternoon. Even Mrs. Haddington's attempts to upend you were fruitless."

Elise smiled a little. "I have been afraid of my own shadow long enough. It is time I found my backbone again."

"Well, I for one am happy to see this side of you again." Miles stroked her cheek as he spoke.

The sudden appearance of a blush broke her pallor. Miles held her face in his hands, his eyes drawn to hers. Something in her expression lightened, almost as if she'd smiled without moving her mouth. It wasn't enough. Miles wanted to see a sparkle in her eyes again; he wanted to hear her spontaneous laughter. He wanted to keep her in his arms.

He wanted, in that moment, to kiss her. His gaze dropped to her mouth. He traced the outline of her lips with his thumb. Like a magnet to metal, he felt drawn to her, leaning closer. His heart pounded. She didn't pull away.

The sensation of his lips pressed lightly to hers stole his breath away. Miles held her face more fervently, kissing her with more feeling. When Elise's arms wrapped around him, Miles was lost. She kissed him in return.

One kiss proved insufficient. But recalling they were the only people in the room and the household was already suspicious of their relationship, Miles forced himself to pull away from her very tempting mouth.

Where had this come from? He'd never kissed her like that before. He tried to summon the words to apologize for his ungentlemanly behavior, but she spoke before he did.

"The last time you did that, Miles Linwood, I pushed you out of a tree."

Miles suddenly burst out laughing, the tension of the moment entirely dissipating. "Is that why you pushed me?"

"Don't you remember?"

"I can't say that I do." He let his arms fall and stepped back, still confused at what had brought on that kiss.

"You were cross with me over something," Elise said, her cheeks still pink. "You threatened to kiss me if I didn't stop pestering you—that was quite an effective method of torture at the time."

He chuckled. "There is nothing a nine-year-old boy dislikes quite as much as a kiss. I probably assumed you would dislike it as well."

"And I kept right on pricking at you," she continued. "So you made good on your threat."

"And then you pushed me out of the tree?" This conversation was on far more familiar footing.

"Of course." Laughter danced in her eyes. At least she didn't seem offended by his kiss. He hadn't dealt a blow to their friendship with his inexplicable actions. "And you promised afterward never to kiss me again. Admittedly, that was one of the reasons I cried afterward."

"You wanted me to kiss you?" For just a moment, he was tempted to kiss her again. Sanity won out in the end.

"I had decided not long before that day that you were going to give me my first kiss," Elise admitted, the blush only intensifying.

"And I actually did." Miles smiled.

"You actually did." She sighed. "Was there anything in our childhoods we didn't share? It seems every moment was a connection of some kind between us."

"Very few people have been so lucky," he said.

"And we were lucky enough to find each other again. I had honestly reconciled myself to that never happening."

Though he'd held out hope, Miles had realized over the past four years how unlikely a reunion was.

"I should go," she said. "Someone is liable to come in, and I'll ruin your reputation entirely."

"Elise," he called after her as she reached the door. She turned back to look at him. "Did I tell you how lovely you look today?"

"You didn't."

"Well then, you look more than lovely, my dearest Elise. You look beautiful. I think that is my favorite of your dresses."

"It's mine as well." Her smile brightened in the moment before she slipped from the room.

Only after she left did he let the full implication of what had happened hit him. He'd kissed her, though he wasn't sure why. And she'd kissed him, something he was even less sure of. A gentleman didn't generally go about kissing his closest friend. But, then, most gentlemen weren't the closest of friends with an unwed lady.

He didn't think he was in love with her. Indeed, the moment the thought occurred to him, he shook his head at the absurdity of it. This was Elise, after all. His dear friend, his childhood playmate. He likely shouldn't have kissed her. She didn't seem overly bothered by it, so he needn't be either.

Nothing had changed. He told himself that more than once. It was a simple kiss, a moment of whim. They'd laughed about it afterward. That his heart still pounded a bit was nothing so extraordinary.

It had been a rather amazing kiss. For a moment, he was lost once more in the recollection of it. He pulled himself together quickly. Elise was his friend. He would do well to remember that and not do anything in the future to risk losing someone so precious.

* * *

Elise sat in the formal garden behind Tafford, trying to clamp down the all-encompassing grin she could feel just below the surface. Miles had kissed her, and it hadn't been a brief peck on the cheek either. Her stomach tied in joyous knots at the memory. Her four-year-old self had set her heart on Miles kissing her. How little she'd understood that the experience would shift her entire foundation.

Her heart would never be entirely whole again without him. How long she'd loved him, Elise couldn't say. Perhaps she always had a little. She'd been fighting down the realization for weeks. She could still feel his arms around her, his lips pressed to hers. She would never forget that feeling and would most likely blush every time she saw him.

Beth turned the path and smiled when she saw Elise sitting there. "May I join you?"

"Of course." Elise clamped down an immediate surge of worry. If Beth had somehow learned about that more-than-friendly kiss, she would ring such a peal over Elise's head.

"I don't know if you have heard," Beth said, "but Langley and I will be leaving for Lancashire shortly."

"I hadn't, but I cannot say I am surprised."

"Our departure will necessitate a change in your situation," Beth said. "Without me here lending propriety to your residency, you simply cannot remain."

Elise hadn't thought of that but couldn't deny Beth was entirely correct.

"And though I hate to bring your reunion with Miles to an end, I do need to return to my own home." Beth's words were free of reprimand. She understood, at least in part, how much Miles meant to Elise.

"Mama Jones would allow Anne and me to live with her," Elise said, hoping to set Beth's mind at ease. "That is not so far away from Tafford."

Beth didn't look happy with the solution. "It might very well be *too* close." After the death of Elise's mother, Beth had often taken on a maternal role. She did so once again. "Miles would come visit you often if you lived that nearby. You can imagine how that would look to the neighborhood."

"They might think he had an interest in me." Elise tried to keep the hope out of her voice. She wanted to believe he did, in fact, have an interest in her.

"They most certainly would," Beth said. "But I would wager they won't assume that 'interest' is an entirely honorable one. I am sure you don't wish to add fuel to the fire of speculation already rampant in the area."

She didn't at all wish to harm Miles's standing with his new neighbors. But if he did have a romantic interest in her—she didn't doubt for a moment his intentions, whatever their exact form, were entirely honorable—she certainly wanted to give that a chance to blossom. She rose from the bench and let her feet wander even as her thoughts did. Beth walked at her side.

"I am not sure what to do," Elise admitted.

"There are really only two things that can be done," Beth said. "You two either have to marry, an idea of which Miles has already disabused me—you two have always been such a unique combination of friends and near-siblings that I imagine it is hard to think of anything beyond that."

"It would be odd, yes." She managed the very calm reply despite the ache Beth's admission brought to her heart. "What is the other solution?" They turned a corner on the garden path.

"Langley's mother is recently remarried, and the dower house on our estate sits empty. We both would love to have you and Anne and Mama Jones, of course, come live there. You would have a home of your own, your own little garden, but you would be near enough to us for regular visits."

The offer was both unexpected and wonderfully generous. But Lancashire was so very far away. "That is very kind of you. I don't know how Miles will feel about this."

"Langley already discussed it with him, and Miles thinks it a fine arrangement."

"He does?" Surprise prevented her from saying more than that for a moment. Surely Miles didn't wish her to be so far away. "How long ago did Mr. Langley make the suggestion?"

"Several days ago, actually," Beth said. "The two of them have already begun making arrangements to move your belongings should you decide to go."

Then Miles had been planning for her to leave when he had kissed her. Perhaps their moment together had changed his mind. The alternative wasn't one she cared to explore—that he'd kissed her the way he had fully expecting her to be gone in another week or so. Surely he'd felt more of a connection than that.

"How soon do I need to decide?" Elise asked.

"We hope to leave at the end of the week," Beth said. "But, as I said, Miles and Langley have worked out the details so the arrangements could be made very quickly. You needn't decide right away."

She was grateful for time to make a choice but was bothered by Miles's apparent ease at letting her go. "Miles really does think this is for the best?"

"He does," Beth said. "I know he will miss you. He will miss you terribly. But he recognizes the implications of your continuing to live so nearby. The distance will protect your reputation and his, not to mention Anne's."

The reasoning was solid and, much to Elise's relief, not dismissive. Sending her away out of concern was far preferable to not caring enough to want her there.

Not caring. She nearly laughed at the ridiculousness of that thought. Miles might not have been desperately in love with her, but he most certainly cared about her. She was allowing her very confused heart to speak louder than her mind.

Not many steps ahead of her and Beth were two people Elise recognized immediately. Miss Haddington and Miles. They were walking beside each other, her arm through his. Though their conversation could not be overheard, their expressions were inarguably friendly.

"I would wager Mrs. Haddington is somewhere nearby feeling quite pleased with herself," Beth said.

Yes, but was *Mr.* Haddington nearby? Elise had no proof that he was the man who had killed her father, but she couldn't shake the suspicion. The thought of him in close proximity unsettled her. But she didn't wish to show her unease to Beth. She would never be able to explain it.

She managed something of a smile. "Mrs. Haddington's ambitions are rather obvious."

"And perhaps more successful than I'd at first suspected." Beth eyed her brother with open curiosity. "They do seem to enjoy each other's company."

They did. But, then, Miles was a very friendly person. Anyone would enjoy his company.

"She would be a very appropriate match for a marquess," Elise said.

"Does it not seem odd that Miles, who spent his entire childhood jumping from one foolhardy scheme to another, is now a respected Peer of the Realm?" Beth asked.

"Your father would have laughed uproariously at the very idea." Elise could easily picture that exact scene.

Their path crossed with Miss Haddington and Miles's. Elise held tightly to her composure, not willing to let so much as a drop of envy show when she looked at Miss Haddington.

"Good afternoon," their visitor greeted. "I see you had the same idea we did. It is, after all, a fine day for a walk."

"And I do have a rather impressive garden," Miles added with his usual laughing tone.

Elise watched him as the four of them engaged in a very commonplace conversation. His gaze didn't linger on her any longer than anyone else. He spoke to Miss Haddington in the same friendly tone with which he spoke to Elise.

This was the first time they'd seen each other since he'd kissed her so deeply and, it had seemed to her, passionately. But nothing in his look, posture, or tone had changed in the least. She didn't think he was quite so skilled at hiding his thoughts. She had certainly always been good at deciphering his feelings.

The kiss they'd shared had solidified her conviction that her heart belonged to Miles. He hadn't, it seemed, undergone quite the same transformation. He was still entirely comfortable with her, still unfailingly friendly. But there was nothing beyond.

She and Beth continued on the path toward the house while Miles and Miss Haddington walked farther into the garden. Elise only allowed herself to look back once. Though she liked Miss Haddington, she didn't at all care for the sight of her on Miles's arm.

He might yet learn to love you. Hope isn't lost.

Still, she did need to see to her future. "May I give you an answer in the morning?" she asked Beth.

"Of course."

Elise would ponder it all that night and come to some conclusion, and she would do her best not to worry over Miles's heart. Her own gave her enough to fret over.

Chapter Thirty-Three

"*Why are you cross with Mr. Jefferies?*" *Elise rolled onto her side to look at Miles. He was lying on his back on the grass in their meadow, hands beneath his head, staring up at the star-filled night sky.*

Miles didn't answer but made something like a shrug.

"*Did he do something horrible, Miles?*"

"*No,*" *he said, though he seemed sorry that the answer wasn't different. "Not horrible, exactly.*"

"*But you didn't dislike him before. A person doesn't suddenly dislike someone for no reason.*"

"*He was arguing with Father,*" *Miles said, bitterness obvious in his voice. In Miles's anger, Elise heard pain as well. "He called him a fool.*"

"*Why would Mr. Jefferies say that?*"

"*I don't know, but he did say it.*" *Miles turned his head enough to look at her. "He said, 'I have offered you sound financial advice, Mr. Linwood. Only a fool would disregard it.' To which Father said, 'Then you must think me a fool.' And Mr. Jefferies said, 'I cannot think otherwise.'*"

At eleven, Elise was not very experienced in matters of adult disagreements or the conversations between a man of business and his client. But she knew Miles, and he was upset. "I think Mr. Jefferies was saying your father acted foolishly, not that he was a fool."

"*It amounts to the same thing, Elise,*" *Miles grumbled.*

"*Do you think I am a fool?*"

"*Of course not.*" *His sincerity would have been obvious to anyone hearing his words. "Indeed, there are more than a few of my school chums who would be hard-pressed to hold their own in a battle of wits against you.*"

"*And yet, Miles, you have told me countless times over the years that I have acted foolishly. For example, the time I tried to climb from my bedchamber window using only a newly grown branch of ivy.*"

"You could have killed yourself. That was remarkably foolish."

She gave him her best think-that-over look.

Slowly, a smile spread across his face.

"Point taken," he answered. "Now, if I promise to stop my grumbling, can we return to our stargazing?" His eyes had already returned to the sky.

"How long before you return to Eton, Miles?" Elise asked.

"Another week."

Elise sighed. "I suppose that will have to do."

"Have you missed me, then?" he asked.

"Terribly. I have been left here with only the companionship of our fathers, and as you know, one of them is a fool."

Miles laughed quite heartily. One arm left its position beneath his head and snaked around her shoulders, squeezing them as he continued to chuckle. "There is no one like you in all the world, Elise."

Lowering herself to the floor, Elise closed the lid of the music box with a sigh. So many memories had flowed over her in the weeks she'd once again been with Miles. Her entire life was entwined with his. She had hardly a memory that was not, in some way, connected to him.

And now she was leaving him again.

Their kiss had likely been something of a passing fancy for him. Gentlemen, her governess had once explained to her, do not, as a rule, put as much store by kissing as ladies do. That was, she'd been warned, the reason a gently-bred young lady did not kiss a gentleman with whom she did not have an understanding.

Beth's offer of the Gilford dower house was, in all reality, a godsend. Given the state of her affections, she could not remain at Tafford if she knew that Miles saw her only as little Elise Furlong, the ragamuffin with whom he'd undertaken countless acts of mischief throughout their childhoods. She would always have his friendship, but distance would keep her unrequited love from turning painful.

It wasn't as if she would never see Miles. She would be Beth's nearest neighbor, after all. And she could certainly write to him.

Mrs. Ash had agreed to go to Lancashire with Anne and her. Elise had enough to pay her a very modest salary, though Mrs. Ash insisted she would come whether she was paid or not. Mama Jones, to Elise's immense worry, had said quite emphatically that she would not uproot herself again.

"I love you, Ella. You know that. But these bones of mine are too tired and weary to be moved again."

Mama Jones couldn't be blamed. Elise knew she was more comfortable and content than she'd been in years. They both knew Miles would look after her. But Elise would miss her. She would miss them both. And Anne would lose two staunch allies.

"Have you not decided where to place any of it?"

Elise actually gasped at the sudden sound of Miles's voice.

He laughed from the doorway behind her. Elise frantically ordered her cheeks not to heat and her heart not to pound so fiercely, but neither obeyed. In the next moment, Miles sat on the floor beside her.

She hoped her glance in his direction gave away none of her feelings. "I was not expecting company."

"Am I unwelcome?" He did not look or sound as if he felt unwelcome. Elise shook her head. He was not unwelcome in the least.

Miles glanced around the room that had for several days housed all of her inheritance. "You have a very unique collection here, Elise. What do you mean to do with it all?"

"Take it with me."

He watched her more closely.

"The Langleys have offered me a home," she explained.

"The Gilford dower house," Miles said with a nod. "And you have decided to accept?"

"I have. It seems the best course of action."

Only a creasing of his brow indicated the news had at all impacted him. "As much as I will miss you, I find myself forced to admit that it is the best option." There was an intensity in his gaze that Elise found almost instantly uncomfortable. Was he displeased? Thinking through the logistics of the move? Were his thoughts on something else entirely?

"I do need to settle somewhere." Elise voiced the arguments that had finally convinced her to accept the offer. "Anne needs stability in her life, and I cannot continue living in transition either. We need our own place."

Miles nodded his agreement.

His easy acceptance of her departure brought a fresh wave of pain. Elise forced any evidence of heartbreak out of her expression.

"You realize, of course, you have to pay off your debt before you go."

"My debt?" She was not aware she owed anyone money. Was it more than her modest income would cover? How had it been acquired?

Miles must have seen her anxiety. He reached out and touched her face. *Good heavens.* He had to stop doing that. Her heart couldn't take it.

"You owe me a minuet," he explained.

A sigh of relief forced its way through the constriction in her throat.

Miles opened the lid of the music box, rose to his feet, and extended his hand to her.

A dance with Miles. It would be yet another memory of him that would both haunt and comfort her in the years to come.

How she managed the steps without faltering Elise did not know. She had to fight tears and keep her expression light, all the while aching inside. Every time the movement of the dance required that Miles release her hand, Elise had to force herself to allow him to let go. As she curtsied to conclude the dance, she very nearly sobbed out loud. Perhaps dancing with Miles hadn't been a good idea.

"I was certain you still remembered how," Miles said, his voice unusually quiet.

"Yes. It seems you were right."

"Well then."

Elise bit down on her lips, unable and unwilling to reply. If she spoke, she very much feared she would confess all and ruin one of their final moments together before she left.

"How soon do you begin your journey to Lancashire?" His voice wasn't quite steady, which she chose to see as a sign that he wasn't quite as unaffected as he seemed.

"At the end of the week."

Miles nodded. "And Mrs. Ash?"

"She will be coming with us."

"And Mama Jones," he said with obvious certainty.

"She wishes to remain here." Elise knew that her unhappiness was evident in her voice but could not have prevented it. "You must promise you will look after her, Miles. I know you have given her so much already. But I will worry myself sick if I do not know she is being looked after."

"Why does she not want to go?" Miles asked, obviously surprised.

"She is settled and happy here. The home you have given her is finer than any she's ever known. For once, she doesn't have to work her fingers to the bone. She said you promised she could stay there for the remainder of her life."

"I did," he confirmed.

"Her joints ache. She cannot work as she once did. And without me to take in mending and stitching and baking—"

"You did all of those things?" Why did he look so disturbed by that admission?

"I did what I had to in order to survive." Elise felt suddenly defensive.

She turned away from him, closing the lid of the music box, though the music had long since unwound, and placed it inside a crate full of other belongings. She heard Miles sigh behind her.

"Oh, Elise. I didn't mean to upset you. Honestly, I didn't." She felt Miles's hands rest on her shoulders. How tempted she was to lean back against him. "Will you promise me one thing, Elise?"

She nodded.

"If you continue receiving letters, promise me you will tell Langley."

"I will," she answered quietly.

For an interminable moment, they stood just as they were—his hands on her shoulders, Miles standing behind her, neither speaking a word. Elise committed to memory the smell of him, the sound of his breathing, the feel of his hands holding her.

"You will be sure to tell me how you like your new home," Miles quietly requested. "How Anne likes it."

"Of course I will." She felt like weeping. It was as close to a good-bye as she could imagine Miles coming without actually uttering the word. "And you will write to me?"

He hesitated only a moment, but it was enough to pierce her heart. "I will write."

Conversation died between them, but still, he didn't move away. His hands remained on her shoulders. Miles stood so close Elise could feel his breath rustle her hair.

"Elise," Miles said in a whisper.

What would he say next? A good-bye? A plea for her to remain?

Miles didn't say any more. After a moment, he left the room.

Chapter Thirty-Four

HE WAS A MESS. A complete and utter mess. Miles couldn't seem to decide what to do with himself. He'd walked out to the stables earlier only to turn around and return to the house. He'd sat down with the estate ledgers and never accomplished a thing.

Elise was leaving.

Intellectually, Miles understood why. The reasoning was sound, the logic irrefutable. And considering he was finding himself tempted almost beyond endurance to touch her, to kiss her, to hold her to him every time he was in her company, putting distance between them grew more and more essential.

But on a deeper level, he couldn't accept that she would soon be gone. How could he be expected to live without her? He'd endured four years of separation. Now that he had found her, he was to be deprived of her again? It was insupportable!

Miles glanced up at the sky from a window in the drawing room, where he, Beth, Langley, and, of course, Elise had gathered after dinner.

"It is a very clear night," Elise said, joining him at the window.

He kept his gaze on the sky. "It is, indeed," he said with believable neutrality.

"Miles, I need your opinion on something." Elise dropped her voice to a level that suggested a desire for privacy but also a certain urgency that immediately pulled his eyes to her. "The day is all but over, and I have yet to receive a letter."

He had wondered why she hadn't brought him the daily correspondence. He'd worried, in fact, that she felt she no longer needed his support or advice. He was glad to be wrong, though it was a bittersweet realization in light of her imminent departure.

"I would very much like to feel relieved by the change, but I find I cannot be," Elise said. "I am almost certain that he means to worry me more by not sending a threatening note."

"You are most likely correct," Miles admitted, though it gave him some pain to do so. He would much rather have been a source of reassurance and consolation.

"Surely he will eventually run out of things to write and simply give up his campaign," Elise said, though she sounded unconvinced. "He would not, I hope, continue this for the rest of my life."

"I am confident we will discover his identity before long." Miles spoke with more conviction than he felt.

"You will keep me informed of your progress?" Her eyes entreated him. "I will worry less if I know something is being done."

Again, she was requesting correspondence, quite as if they were old schoolmates leaving behind their days of education to begin separate lives. His feelings might have been in a jumble, but hers did not appear to be.

"Of course I will write to you," he promised, feeling once more as if the foundation beneath him were crumbling. "How are the preparations coming for your move?" He decided to tackle the matter head-on rather than wait for her to force it upon him.

"Anne and I have very little to our names, so there is not much preparation to be completed. Mrs. Ash has agreed to help in the kitchen as well as with Anne. I have written to Mr. Cane, asking that he send along to Gilford more particulars of my finances. I think all shall turn out well for us in the end."

"I sincerely hope so." Miles fought an almost overwhelming urge to plead with her to reconsider. How could she leave him? How could she not be as disheartened by the prospect of a separation as he was?

He had to say something, had to cover his desperation and frustration. "You leave on Friday, Langley tells me."

"Yes." Elise nodded. "Immediately following breakfast."

"The journey will require three days at the very least," Miles said, suddenly seeing an impediment. "Are you ready for such a long carriage ride? I know you are still uneasy traveling."

"Another reason to settle permanently." She far too easily sidestepped his objection. "After I reach Gilford, I need never travel far from there again."

She would never come back to Tafford? Not even to see Mama Jones? Not to see him? Miles hoped it was merely nerves that caused her to say as much.

"If there's anything I can do to help you prepare," he offered halfheartedly.

She nodded but didn't speak. Beth called her over in the next moment, and all Miles could do for the remainder of the night was watch from a distance, knowing he was days from losing her again.

* * *

"Is that ever'thing?"

"Yes, John," Mr. Langley answered. "We will be on our way momentarily."

Elise felt her heart crack painfully. She would be leaving in a moment. She had thought the prospect of getting into a closed carriage would be the most difficult part. It was not.

Miles stood beside her on the front steps of Tafford.

"Are you certain you are equal to this? You are facing three entire days."

"It is a necessary evil," Elise answered.

"I suppose it is."

She knew she could delay the inevitable no longer. "Thank you, Miles, for everything these past weeks. I have been happier here than I have been in years." Her words broke with emotion despite her desperate efforts to prevent her inner turmoil from showing.

"Oh, Elise." He pulled her into a warm hug. "Do not cry, dear. It isn't as though we will never see each other."

Elise held to him, repeating those words in her mind. He intended to see her again. He would come visit. He'd all but promised.

"Beth has already insisted I come for Christmas," Miles said.

That was more than six months away. Would she not see him until then?

"By Christmastime you will be settled in and happier still." He hadn't let go yet. "You will look back on this moment and wonder why you were even reluctant to be on your way."

"You will look after Mama Jones?" Elise needed a topic to ponder other than her own breaking heart.

"Of course." He put her a little away from him and offered a very friendly smile.

"And you will tell me if you discover anything else about the man we are attempting to identify?" she asked.

He nodded. "Just as I expect you to tell Langley and write to me if you begin receiving any of those letters again."

It was Elise's turn to nod. The murderer had not written to her all week. The only reason they had been able to concoct was that he knew she was leaving the county and, for whatever reason, did not think her a threat any longer. Even so, they were taking no chances. An armed guard sat atop the carriage with the driver.

Mrs. Ash arrived with Anne. Heloise had been given over for the doll Miles had given her. None of them knew what the doll's name was but had come to recognize Anne's sign for it. Her big brown eyes found Miles immediately. Her brow tugged low, confusion written there.

Miles opened his arms for her. She went without hesitation. He held her lovingly and watched her make several gestures. She was asking him about the horses, though he clearly didn't know that. There'd not been time enough for Miles to learn to understand her. Still, he watched her intently, fondness in his expression.

Beth stepped next to Elise. "It is time to go," she told them all.

Miles pulled Anne into a true hug. He looked almost as though he would cry. Elise's throat thickened at the sight.

"I feel like a villain in a Gothic novel," Beth said. Her eyes were on Miles and Anne. "He will miss her terribly."

"And we will miss him." Elise couldn't even begin to express how much. "But what else can be done? We need a home of our own. And staying here is not an option."

"It will all work out for the best," Beth said. "I am certain of it. And he has promised to visit for Christmas."

Elise would likely spend the next six months counting down the days until he arrived. How she hoped the roads proved passable. Such a thing was not always guaranteed in the winter.

Beth joined Mr. Langley at the waiting carriage. He handed her inside.

Miles, with Anne held in one arm, offered his hand to Elise. "I think the staff will understand a moment's familiarity," he said.

She accepted his hand. He walked her down the steps. At the door of the carriage, he released her and focused all his attention on Anne. "Have a safe journey, sweetheart," he said. "I'll see you in a few months."

She simply smiled and made her gesture for red hair, the words that had become his name to her.

Miles hugged her once more before handing her in to Mrs. Ash. He turned back to Elise.

"Good-bye, my friend," he whispered. He took her face gently in his hands and kissed her on the forehead as he had always done in the moments before they were to part. One hundred different farewells sped through her mind. How many times would she be required to say good-bye to him?

"Promise me you will come at Christmas," she said.

"I will do everything in my power to be there," he promised.

Knowing her emotions would not hold out a moment longer, Elise hastily climbed inside the coach.

She kept her gaze firmly forward as they pulled up the drive. She would not look back, she told herself. But she did.

He was gone already.

Chapter Thirty-Five

MILES KNEW HIS FEELINGS WERE written all over his face. He'd turned back toward the house before the carriage had even disappeared from view. Elise would have worried if she'd seen the agony her departure caused him. She needed support and encouragement, not misplaced guilt. Elise had found a home, a future for herself and Anne.

Anne. Saying good-bye to her had broken his heart in ways he hadn't expected. He loved that dear little girl. Young as she was, she would likely not remember him at all the next time he saw her.

By the time he reached the windows of his library, he could no longer see Langley's carriage. Anne was gone. His beloved Elise was as well.

"Good-bye, my dear," Miles whispered.

How pathetic he sounded. One would think she'd married someone else or had died rather than merely moved two counties away. It wasn't as if he'd lost her forever. He would always have her friendship, as inadequate as that felt. Perhaps in time he could convince her there was more between them than that.

He sat listening to the stillness of his house. When he'd first arrived at Tafford, the house had felt like little more than an overly large inn, a place to lay his head, nothing personal or welcoming. He'd thought the estate simply lacked the familiarity of Epsworth, that given time, it would feel like home to him.

But that wasn't it at all, he now realized. Elise had made Tafford his home because home would always be wherever she was.

"Now she's gone, and Tafford will likely never feel like home again."

Deciding he was in almost desperate need of distraction, Miles made his way to his desk. He had plenty of correspondence to catch up on. But he stopped before taking his seat. On the center of his desk sat the copy of

Robin Hood he'd given Elise on her first night at Tafford. Why hadn't she taken it with her? Surely Anne had not yet grown tired of looking at the pictures.

Miles sat in the desk chair, running his fingers down the book's spine.

What an absurdly dramatic Little John Elise had always been during their childhood games. Half the time she'd been conspiring *against* Beth's Maid Marion rather than helping rescue her from an imaginary Sheriff of Nottingham.

He flipped through the book a moment. Then, seized by a sudden desire to read the tales he'd once had almost memorized, Miles opened to the first page.

"Come listen to me, you gallants so free,
"All you that love mirth for to hear,
"And I will tell you of a bold outlaw,
"That lived in Nottinghamshire."

* * *

"Mr. Hanson, my lord."

Miles looked up from the next-to-last page of *Robin Hood* as his solicitor entered the room. "Thank you, Humphrey."

The butler bowed and left, closing the doors as he did.

"Forgive the intrusion, Lord Grenton," Mr. Hanson said, offering a bow. "I come with some information that I believe you will be interested in receiving."

Miles set aside the book. "Come. Sit." He waved Hanson to a chair beside the desk.

"I have been investigating your late father's failed business ventures, my lord."

"What have you discovered?"

"The first two of these ventures to fail were widely invested in. Many others lost money. Your father and Mr. Furlong were far from bankrupted by these disappointments but were understandably desirous to recoup their losses."

Miles nodded. He himself had lost everything and spent four years of his life halfway across the world trying to make up for it.

"The investments they made after that were not nearly so widely embraced; there were far fewer investors, and they were obviously very risky."

Mr. Cane had said as much. He had, in fact, urged Miles's father to seek expert advice before investing.

"They failed one after another. And your father began investing greater sums of capital in each successive venture, only to lose all he had invested. Based on what I have seen and read, I do not believe your father was a gambling man," Mr. Hanson said, his tone almost a question.

"He was not. There was the occasional game of whist with gentlemen in the neighborhood. But he did not indulge in true games of chance, nor did he bet on the races."

"And yet," Hanson continued, "the high-risk investing he embraced the last eighteen months of his life is precisely the sort of gamble one would expect from a hardened gamester. A gentleman like your father would be far more likely, after several losses of even minor significance, to choose investments that were *more* conservative, not *less*, in his attempt to gain back what he had lost."

"Perhaps he was feeling desperate," Miles suggested.

Hanson shook his head. "I spoke with a few well-respected members of my profession who have more experience than I in such matters—without giving names, of course—and they agree with my assessment. Your father's situation early on was far from desperate. I am confident a characteristically careful, responsible gentleman would have chosen less risk."

"What precisely are you saying?" Miles felt in his gut that Hanson had truly discovered something of significance but was unable to guess what.

"I began to suspect early on in this investigation—within the first day, in fact—that your father had been swindled."

Miles immediately tensed.

"Someone misled him or tricked him into investing in impossible schemes. So I began looking into the companies and projects in which he invested. Not a single one still exists, which, considering their failures, wasn't surprising. But I found information enough to begin piecing together a startling puzzle."

"Why do I get the feeling I ought to pour myself a brandy?"

"You may very well want one after I finish telling you what I have discovered, my lord. It is one of the most corrupt and tangled webs I have had the misfortune to stumble upon." Hanson looked angry.

"Before you go any further, tell me this. In this web you have discovered, was my father the unwitting victim or the heartless spider?"

"The victim, my lord. As was Mr. Furlong."

Miles let out a tense breath. "Tell me what you've found."

Hanson pulled out a stack of papers but did not give them to Miles or set them on the desk. "My first clue came when I traced a now-defunct canal-building project back to a single individual who could not in any way be connected with canal building. I looked into a shipping company, which, when unraveled, proved not to be a company at all but a nonexistent organization. Its bank accounts were under a single name."

"The same man connected with the canals?"

Hanson nodded. "This individual proved to be connected to every single investment your father made after the initial two, though in some instances, he had hidden his connection very well. In the end, we found bank accounts at"—he looked back at the stack of papers in his hands—"Barclays; Drummonds; Thomas Coutts & Co.; Baring Brothers & Co.; Lloyds, which is in Birmingham; and even the Royal Bank of Scotland. Deposits into these accounts coincide almost perfectly with losses sustained by your father and Mr. Furlong and several members of their club."

"They were fictionalized investments." Miles began to understand.

"Yes, Lord Grenton. Every one of them. And I have found evidence that your father did not actually authorize these investments," Hanson said. "Your father and Mr. Furlong were not the only victims."

Miles growled several curses, noticing Hanson nodding his agreement or, perhaps, his approval.

"I looked into the other gentlemen who invested in these schemes," Hanson continued. "I am sorry to say, a number of them were killed as well."

Miles's mind lurched to a halt. He couldn't quite wrap his thoughts around the startling and entirely unexpected revelation. "There were other murders? How did no one realize this?"

"They did not happen one right after the other," Hanson said. "And none of the victims were truly close friends, except for your father and Mr. Furlong. The connection wasn't at all obvious until I began looking at these fraudulent companies. Without that piece of the puzzle, the only connection is that they belonged to the same club. But considering the sheer number of members, that isn't enough to tie them together."

Members of the same club. That was how Mr. Haddington had known Father and Mr. Furlong.

"I fully believe the villain behind your father's ruination is the same man who—"

"Murdered him," Miles finished the sentence, knowing beyond a doubt that Hanson was entirely correct.

"And, as near as I can tell, Mrs. Jones is the only living witness to his crimes," Hanson added.

Which explains why he was so intent on threatening her into silence. "Who is our villain?"

Hanson held up the paper in his fist, positioning it so Miles could easily read the name written across the top of the first sheet.

Merciful heavens. Elise had no idea. If the blackguard found her, she wouldn't realize she was in danger!

Chapter Thirty-Six

"I AM SO PLEASED YOU'VE decided to come to Lancashire," Beth said. The inn's staff had already cleared their meal away.

"And I am grateful for your generosity in allowing me to," Elise said. "It is more than I could have hoped for."

"Not at all." Beth smiled reassuringly. "You will simply adore our neighbors. The area is some of the prettiest country in the entire kingdom, and the people are so dear."

Mr. Langley smiled at Beth as he sat beside her on the sofa, her hand snugly in his own. Elise looked away from such a poignant reminder of what she had left behind. In Lancashire, there would be no one to hold her hand, no one to lean on in times of trouble.

"Is there a meadow at Gilford?" Elise asked. The oddness of her question struck her an instant later, and she felt herself blush.

"No, there's not," Beth answered, giving her a puzzled look. "But there is a wonderful natural garden to the south and a formal garden to the north. And not a ten-minute walk from the house is a lovely lake."

But no meadow. She was on her way to her new home that had neither a meadow nor Miles. It would seem no more like home to her than had the cottage in Stanton. Was she destined to be little more than a guest in any house she ever lived in? No place would feel like home without Miles.

"Anne has done quite well on the journey thus far," Mr. Langley said. "I hope it has not taken too much of a toll on you."

"I am tired," she admitted.

That had been Anne's only complaint as well. She and Mrs. Ash had taken their meal in the bedchamber Mr. Langley had reserved for them and had gone directly to bed, a prospect Elise was finding ever more appealing.

"If you will excuse me, I would appreciate seeking my bed. We have a full day of travel ahead of us tomorrow."

"Of course." A look of concern immediately crossed Beth's face. Elise very much feared that Beth would forever remind her of Miles, so similar were their features.

Elise slipped from the parlor and up the stairs to her own private bedchamber. She closed the door behind her, leaning against it as she took several much-needed calming breaths.

She could do this. She had lived four years without Miles. Of course, she hadn't realized then that she loved him as she did. Living without a friend had been hard. Living without the man she loved would be torturous.

I can survive this, she silently told herself.

Elise hadn't brought a lady's maid with her. She could not afford one and needed to accustom herself once more to the necessity of doing things herself. She'd worn a very simple morning gown, knowing it would be easiest for her to remove on her own. How she'd wanted to wear the deep-blue walking gown, the one Miles had said was his favorite, the one she'd worn when he'd kissed her. She'd wanted him to remember her that way. But she could not undo the tapes or unfasten the buttons on her own.

She slipped into her white night rail and blew out her single candle. They would be departing early the next morning, and she needed to sleep. But she knew she would not rest that night. Her heart ached too acutely for sleep.

Elise lay down, pulled the coverlet over her shoulders, and forced herself to close her eyes.

Do you waltz, Elise? She could hear Miles's voice in her memory.

No, she had answered.

You must learn to waltz, my dear.

Elise flipped onto her side, that "my dear" echoing in her thoughts. She settled as comfortably as she could manage, burying her face in her pillow, forcing back the tears that pooled in her eyes. It was ridiculous to cry over a man she would see again. And he was still the Miles Linwood she had grown up with, her very dearest friend. That wasn't something to mourn.

Elise turned again, lying on her back. *You cannot do this every night for the rest of your life*, she silently chastised herself.

She closed her eyes again and tried to picture her new house, to think of the weather, the roads, *anything*. She simply couldn't concentrate.

"This will never do," she whispered, sitting up.

She would write him a letter, she suddenly decided. She would never actually post it but would write out her feelings so they would at least be expressed. Maybe then they wouldn't constantly threaten to burst out of her. Elise swung her legs over the side of the bed and stepped off.

The floor was cold against her bare feet. The room was dim, only the slightest bit of light filtering in through the closed curtains. She blindly found the writing desk and fumbled for a tinder box, knowing there was an unlit candle nearby.

The hairs on the back of her neck suddenly stood on end. Shivers of apprehension flooded over her. She held perfectly still, listening. She heard nothing beyond her own breathing and the faint noise of the taproom two floors below.

Elise shook her head, attempting to convince herself there was no need for such nervousness. She found a quill and a penknife. Her hand brushed against the inkwell, but she couldn't locate anything with which to light the candle. And her hands unaccountably shook.

Calm down, she silently told herself.

Elise picked up the quill and knife—no doubt the quill would be dull and unusable—and the inkwell. She would move the tools to the bedside table, where she'd left her candle, and lie down until she felt calm again.

Everything was fine. She was simply tired and worn down. Everything was fine.

A floorboard squeaked.

Her heart pounded. Had she imagined it?

No. There was another. Closer. Then another. Someone was moving toward her!

Elise dropped the inkwell; it fell to the ground and shattered. She could feel the ink splatter against her bare feet.

Run for the door! Run for the door!

A hand slapped over her mouth, muting the cry that rose immediately. She felt something press against her back and instinctively knew it was the barrel of a pistol. Years of maintaining her equilibrium despite the circumstances served her well in that moment. She kept her wits despite her rising panic.

"Quietly," a low voice growled, pushing her forward with the pistol. "Back stairs."

The back stairs? Servants' stairs. Elise moved as slowly as she dared with the pistol poking into her back. There was a very good chance that if she took her time, someone would run into them. Someone might ask questions, alert others. Or, she amended, this madman might simply kill whoever came across their path. He'd certainly murdered in cold blood before.

But he will be farther away from Anne.

She clutched the quill so hard she felt it split against the unyielding penknife. He rushed her down the dim stairs, not allowing her to keep her slower pace. His hand pressed painfully hard against her face, his arm pinning her against him, the gun barrel digging into her back. There was plenty of noise from the taproom, where, apparently, the staff was being kept busy. Elise saw not a soul as the man dragged her from the inn.

Think, Elise. You must think this through.

Farther from the inn, he pushed her beyond the back gate and into a small cluster of trees. He closed his fingers more tightly around her face, apparently convinced she would attempt to call out. Something about the fact that he thought her braver than she felt gave her courage.

"The games have been diverting," he whispered, his breath nauseatingly wet and warm against her face. "But I've grown weary of them. Time for one last message delivered in person."

The gun slid up her back until it was directly behind her heart. He meant to kill her, here, alone, where no one would hear and no one would find her for hours, perhaps days.

Elise refused to die that way. She let the quill drop from her hand but clutched the penknife in her fist. The man took a handful of her hair, pulling just hard enough to be painful. Elise kept her calm. She would have but one chance.

She swung her arm back with all the force she could muster and felt the knife sink in. A shout of pain and the lessening of her assailant's grip marked her only chance at surviving. She didn't hesitate. She pulled from his slackened hold and ran back through the trees. She'd dealt a minor blow, in all likelihood, and had almost no chance of escape, but she would try. Heaven help her, she would try.

Back to the inn, she told herself. *Back to the inn.*

She heard his footsteps, uneven, behind her. He groaned, and she hoped the pain would slow him down. She desperately hoped it would be enough. She needed to find another way back to the inn, since he stood between her and the way they'd come.

A shot rang out. Pain seared through her shoulder, just as it had four years earlier. Was it remembered pain or new? She stumbled but kept herself on her feet. How many more shots did he have? He'd carried four weapons before.

Elise looked ahead. Was there another gate? An entrance to the inn yard other than the one they'd taken? She saw nothing but an impenetrable hedge. Which way should she turn? Right or left? The pain grew worse with each breath, each moment.

She had to get through to the inn. Had to find someone to help her. Mr. Langley or the innkeeper. Even their coachman.

Someone grabbed her arm.

Before she could yell, another hand clasped over her mouth, this time gently but insistently as she was pulled to the ground. The pain of that jerking movement was excruciating. Whoever it was rolled her behind a smaller hedge, into the shadows. She felt something being draped over her.

Elise looked up and nearly sobbed at the blurry sight that met her eyes. Miles.

Chapter Thirty-Seven

SHE WAS TREMBLING. MILES LIFTED his hand from Elise's mouth but kept the tips of his fingers pressed to her lips. Elise nodded. She understood. Silence was essential.

They needed to be perfectly still. He moved his hand from her mouth and wrapped his arms around her beneath his greatcoat, which he had draped over her. The white of her night rail reflected too much of the moonlight—it was how he had found her. The coat would hide her better.

Footsteps sounded nearby. Miles heard labored breathing. He leaned back, pulling them both farther into the shadows. He moved strands of Elise's dark hair over her face, doing everything he could think of to make her harder to see.

"He has a gun," she whispered almost silently.

Miles nodded. He'd heard the gunshot. With one hand, he pulled a dueling pistol from the pocket of his jacket. Miles had brought three men with him from Tafford. They should be nearby. Would they be fast enough if Miles and Elise were spotted?

The now-stumbling footsteps drew closer. Elise didn't move. She didn't even seem to breathe. Did he risk making noise by shifting her behind him to further shield her? If they stayed still, they might be safer.

He held his pistol at the ready but didn't move from the shadows. They were facing a murderer, one who had thoroughly deceived a great many people and hid his inhumanity from the world.

A strange half moan, half gurgle was followed by a thud. What in heaven's name was that?

He glanced down at Elise. Had she heard it as well? She didn't look up at him but kept as still as before. She'd always shown herself brave. Never more so than in that moment.

Several pairs of footsteps then filled the eerie silence. His men?

"Lord Grenton!" Miles recognized Johnny from the stables. "He's down. It's safe now."

Relief surged through Miles. He leaned his head against the bark of the tree and told himself to breathe. The danger had passed.

"You're safe now, Elise," he said. "You're finally safe."

"I think I need help," she said.

"Elise?"

"He had a gun." She took a breath, but it stuck as she winced. "I didn't run fast enough."

Miles flung back his greatcoat but saw nothing but mud marring the front of her night rail. He turned her into his embrace, enough to see the back of her.

Blood. Dark, red, spreading blood.

He lifted Elise into his arms. She settled her head into the crook of his neck, neither clinging to him nor growing limp.

"I will have you to the inn in no time," he said.

"I just need something for the pain," she answered. Lucid thoughts. That was a very good sign. "And to know we really are safe."

Johnny stood not ten feet from them, along with Hanson and his Bow Street friend, all standing over an inert form. *Ten feet. Lud, that had been close.*

"Turn him over," Miles instructed as he approached. "I have to get her back to the inn, but I need to know we have the right man. I will not deliver her into a trap."

Elise leaned more heavily against him, her face buried in his collar. Her breaths grew less steady.

Johnny pushed the murderer over onto his back.

"That's him," Miles said, not attempting to hide his disgust. "Drag him to the inn and summon the local squire."

Miles didn't wait to see if his instructions were followed. Elise moaned in pain. She needed a doctor. He rushed to the inn, pushing open the door with his foot. The innkeeper's eyes pulled wide at the sight of them.

"Mr. and Mrs. Langley's room." Miles pulled out his marquess's voice. It worked once again.

He followed the innkeeper up the stairs. The door was ajar.

"Oh, merciful heavens, Miles!" Beth cried, rushing to the door while Langley held back. "You've found her. You've found her."

Miles only nodded, crossing to the sofa near their chamber's fireplace. Over his shoulder, he tossed instructions to the innkeeper. "Send for a doctor—the best you have."

"Yes, m' lord."

"Doctor?" Beth's voice broke. "What's happened?"

"I believe she's been shot." Miles set Elise tenderly on the sofa. He urged her to turn enough that he could tend to the wound in her back.

Beth knelt beside him. "It *is* bleeding quite a bit, but the wound seems too high to have hit her heart or lungs."

Thank heavens. To Langley, he said, "We need rags, clean water."

Langley nodded and stepped out.

"She is still breathing," Beth said.

"And listening," Elise added in a strained whisper.

The attempt at humor was welcome. Miles pressed a kiss to her temple. "We'll have you mended in no time, dearest. And I'm certain the doctor will have something to help with the pain."

Her eyes met his. "You won't leave me, will you?"

"Of course not." He reached for her hand only to find it red with blood. He took it anyway. She needed him, and he needed her.

"Is Anne safe?" she asked Beth. "I was so certain he would come back for her, all the while praying he hadn't gotten to her first."

"Anne is still asleep," Beth said. "Mrs. Ash is keeping vigil."

Elise took a breath and flinched. "I had forgotten how much this hurts."

She closed her eyes, her expression still pained. Nothing could be done until the doctor arrived. Miles pulled a blanket off the foot of the bed and draped it over her, covering her legs and bare feet. He pulled a chair over and sat directly beside her.

He held her hand between his, worried by her continued pallor. Ten feet. Another ten feet and they would have been found. Another ten feet and he would have lost her.

* * *

After a grueling half hour, the doctor managed to dig the ball out of Elise's back. Miles never wanted to see her cut open again. Not ever. With the surgery complete, Elise slept fitfully on the bed while Miles paced the room.

After dozens of circuits, Miles spied Johnny standing in the doorway.

"Yes, Johnny?"

"Mr. Hanson told me to tell ya that the man that we was chasin' is dead, m' lord. Seems he done bled to death."

Bled to death? "The doctor didn't get to him soon enough, then?" There was but one man of medicine, and Elise had been treated first.

"He were dead out there in the trees," Johnny looked ever more uncomfortable. "Before we carried him inside, he was dead. The Bow Street man said not to say nothin' till he was inside and we could be sure. And then you was busy with the doctor and Mrs. Jones. We weren't wantin' to interrupt."

"Bled to death?" Langley asked from his chair beneath the far window. "Was he shot, then?"

Miles only remembered hearing one gunshot, and that was aimed at Elise.

Johnny shook his head. "He were stabbed, real low like." Johnny motioned at his lower abdomen. "Doctor says it would've been a small knife, like one you'd cut your dinner with or sharpen a pen."

"And from that, he bled to death?" Miles tried to imagine such a small weapon doing so much damage.

"Ain't never seen that much blood, poured out all over everythin'." Johnny looked shaken. "The doctor said something about hitting in just the right place."

Miles sat on the arm of the sofa. "But who stabbed him?"

"'Tweren't no one near him when we found him," Johnny said. "The only one who'd been that close to him was—"

"*Elise.* The blood on her hand," he muttered. *That* blood wasn't her own.

"The squire says to ask you to tell him what you seen tonight." Johnny quickly assumed a more humble demeanor. "When it's convenient for you, of course, m' lord."

"Thank you, Johnny," Miles said. The hour was beyond late. "Get some sleep. You've had a long night."

"Thank you, m' lord." But he waited a moment. "It likely ain't my place to say, but if it were Mrs. Jones who took down the blackguard, well, I think that was right brave of her. Right brave." He bowed before slipping out of the room once more.

Miles's eyes met Langley's.

His brother-in-law's usual composure broke a bit. "I can't imagine what she went through tonight," Langley said. "He intended to kill her. She had to have known that. To be marched off to her death that way and still find the strength to defend herself . . ."

"Thank the heavens she had the presence of mind to arm herself with whatever she used to fight him." Worry thudded through Miles once more.

"You know her better than I do," Langley said. "How will she handle this? Knowing she killed a man?"

Even understanding she'd done so to save her life, Elise would be haunted by it. He knew she would be. Langley wouldn't understand that. Not even Beth would, not in the way he did.

"I think I'd better go with you to Gilford," Miles said.

"Or perhaps we should take Elise back to Tafford," Langley suggested.

Miles rubbed at his weary face. "We'll do whatever Elise wants. But whatever she chooses, I'm going with her."

"Of course you are. No one would expect you to do otherwise." Langley stood from his chair and stretched a bit. "I am going to check on Beth. I hope she's sleeping. We'll need her energy come morning. You and I are likely to collapse after being up all night."

But Beth stepped inside the room in the next instant, obviously not asleep. She held Anne's hand, the little girl's curls knotted up in all directions. "Anne is asking for her mother," Beth said quietly. "And also for something I can't identify. She keeps doing this." Beth slipped her hand from Anne's, then gestured, tapping the tips of her index fingers together, then tugging at her hair.

Miles knew that gesture well. Anne was asking for him. He held his arms out to her, and she rushed into his embrace. He settled into the corner of the sofa, clinging to her. Elise's fears matched his own. Anne was likely the next target. Miles didn't think he would ever let either of them out of his sight again.

"The two of you get some sleep," he told his sister and her husband. "I'll keep watch over these ladies."

He received no argument and was soon alone with his precious little Anne and Elise asleep nearby. Anne patted his cheeks with her tiny hands, then smiled contentedly.

"I love you, sweet Anne," Miles said.

She snuggled up close to him. He swung his legs around, stretching out the length of the sofa, and pulled the blanket off the back and laid it across them both. Anne adjusted her position. She finally seemed to grow comfortable.

In the low-burning lantern light, Miles looked over at Elise. He repeated in his mind again and again the reassurance the doctor had offered. Elise would be fine. She would be in some pain for a time and would have to be careful to keep the wound clean. But she would be fine.

I haven't lost her.

He should never have so casually accepted her departure from Tafford. The threat hanging over her had been real, and what had he done? Shrugged and agreed that leaving was her best option? He should have made greater provision for her safety. He should have sent extra outriders.

I should have told her I loved her and begged her to stay.

He would make the confession as soon as he was able. Perhaps not the first instant she awoke—Elise had been through quite a lot—but as soon as she was recovered enough.

Miles stroked Anne's messy curls. She'd fallen asleep against him. How far they'd come in the past weeks. Anne had watched him with wary interest, perhaps even a touch of fear, when first he'd seen her in the draper's shop in Stanton. Now she came to him so full of trust and fondness. He adored her. She felt almost like his own little girl. He kissed the top of her head. "My sweet, sweet girl," he whispered.

"She drools in her sleep." The warning came from Elise. Miles hadn't realized she was awake.

"Let us hope Anne makes an exception in this case," Miles replied. He hoped it was only the moonlight that made Elise look so pale. "Is there anything you need? The doctor left laudanum."

"I *would* like some water."

Miles maneuvered his way to his feet, with Anne still in his arms. "Will she bother you if I lay her on the bed beside you?"

"No."

He laid Anne down and placed a pillow between her and Elise. He didn't want her to accidentally bump her mother's still-fresh wound. He tucked the blankets around the sleeping girl.

"Now, water." He crossed to the bureau and filled a glass from the pitcher.

Miles helped Elise sit up. Her winces of pain pricked at him.

"Are you certain you don't want any powders or anything?"

She shook her head. "I'll be fine in time. The doctor did get the ball out, didn't he?"

"He did, though it was a messy business." Miles took her hand and kissed it. He held it between his hands, unwilling to let go. "Promise me you won't ever get shot again."

One corner of her mouth tugged upward. "I'll do my best." The smile slipped away. "What happened to him?"

Miles didn't have to ask who. He held her hand more tightly. "He's dead."

"Dead? But . . . how? What happened?"

He knew better than to lie to her. She would eventually learn the truth and would have yet another reason to not trust him. "He was stabbed."

Her eyes grew wide. "*I* stabbed him. But . . . but with a penknife. How could that . . . How could that have killed him?"

"It seems the blade severed a significant artery. He bled to death."

She took a shuddering breath. "I only wanted to get away; I didn't mean to kill him."

"You were saving your life, dear. No one can fault you for that."

"But I killed someone." She trembled. Absolutely no color remained in her face.

This was not going to be an easy thing for her to accept. Miles sat beside her on the bed and gently wrapped his arm around her, careful of her bandaged shoulder. They'd sat precisely that way dozens of times as children. It was comfortingly familiar, for her as well, he hoped.

"I was terrified we wouldn't find you in time." He hadn't truly allowed himself to think about what would have happened if he'd been but a few moments later than he had been. He rested his forehead against her temple, breathing in the familiar scent of her. *Ten feet.* They'd been ten feet from where her pursuer had fallen.

"He meant to kill me and leave me there."

She leaned more fully into Miles's embrace.

Was he comforting her at all? Relieving at least some of her burden?

"It was utter foolishness to send you and Anne out without proper protection." How could he have neglected that so much? "You ought to have had more outriders and armed guards. Better still, we ought never to have agreed to your leaving Tafford before we knew the villain's identity."

"Who was he, Miles?" There seemed to be a bit more steadiness in her voice. Miles thought her trembling had eased a bit.

"That can wait," he said. "You have suffered enough of a shock already. It can wait until morning."

"Please," Elise said, her voice breaking.

Miles sighed, stroking her hair as he debated with himself. She would eventually have to be told. The murderer's identity would, in time, become common knowledge. But was she ready?

"You are certain you want to hear this now?" he asked Elise one more time.

"Yes." She leaned more heavily against him. "I need to know. After so many years and so much pain, I need to know."

Miles took a breath, wishing he didn't have to tell her this, wishing they'd never met the man who'd ruined so many lives. "It was Mr. Cane."

Chapter Thirty-Eight

"BUT IT IS WELL PAST noon, Beth." Miles's voice carried in from the corridor. "At least let me check on her."

"You have. At least a dozen times. The poor thing is sleeping late. You would be also if you'd had a bullet dug out of your back yesterday."

Mrs. Ash's gaze met Elise's as the conversation continued just beyond the slightly opened door. Anne sat on the bed next to Elise, attempting to form a cat's cradle with a length of string. They'd been playing at string games for the entire thirty minutes since Mrs. Ash had brought Anne in to see her.

"Should we tell your visitors that we can hear them?" Mrs. Ash whispered.

"Eavesdropping is so much more fun," Elise said.

Mrs. Ash smiled broadly and returned to her knitting. Elise helped Anne adjust the string's position on her fingers.

"I am certain she is simply resting," Beth said, still out of sight in the corridor.

"I am not entirely certain," Miles answered his sister. "She was outside, *barefooted*, not at all dressed for cooler nighttime temperatures and was shot, for heaven's sake. Suppose she has taken ill or needs something and can't get it? I simply want to check on her."

"She was perfectly sound the last I peeked in the room not an hour past. She was sleeping, as she ought to be," Beth said. "Honestly, Langley, Miles was not this overwrought the time Elise had measles when she was not more than five years old, and I thought he was bad off then, hounding us all with his constant fretting. 'What if Elise needs me? What if she's asking for me?' He pestered us for days on end."

"I will have you know, she was quite ill," Miles answered.

"*Everyone* is quite ill when struck with the measles. My point is you don't need to worry so much."

"I daresay he can't help himself, dear," Mr. Langley said with something like a chuckle. "He's been fretting over her all his life. We cannot expect him to stop now."

Elise couldn't remember ever hearing Mr. Langley tease. She liked him all the better knowing that he could.

"Ma," Anne said.

Elise had been neglecting their game. She very deliberately moved one string, then another, slowly creating a Jacob's ladder, something that was decidedly trickier with one arm in a sling. Anne was fascinated, making the pain of sitting up and moving her arm well worth enduring.

Miles stepped inside in the next instant. "How are you this morning? Are you at all ill? Or unwell?"

Elise shook her head. "If anything, I'm a little hungry."

He sat on the bed beside her. "And it's no wonder. You've missed breakfast. It is very nearly luncheon." Miles watched her with such concern Elise felt almost as though she ought to be worrying over *him* rather than the other way around. The man was a mess.

"I am not so ravenous that I cannot wait until the midday meal," Elise reassured him.

"But you are well?"

"Yes." She felt herself smile, something she'd been unsure only the night before that she would ever do again. "At least, I will be."

"Oh, Elise." Miles sighed. "What a night you had."

She pressed her fingers to his lips. "Let us not talk about that. Please. I'm not ready yet."

Miles took the hand she had laid against his mouth in both of his hands and held it reverently as he kissed her fingertips.

"Ma." Anne's voice pulled their gaze toward her. She held up her string-laden hands with a look of impatient expectation.

"Do you remember this game?" Elise motioned toward Anne's string-wrapped fingers.

"I do. You foisted it on me all the time." Miles helped Anne adjust her strings until the shape was correct again.

"Foisted it on you? You can't possibly deny that cat's cradle was your favorite."

"*You* were my favorite, though you were forever landing us both in one scrape after another."

Her heart ached anew. "Last night was quite a scrape, wasn't it?"

"You are safe now, and the three of us are together again. I, for one, plan to think on nothing but that. If I let myself think for even a moment about all that happened, I'll likely pull the two of you into my arms and never let go again."

"If I didn't know better, I'd suspect you're rather fond of me." The bit of humor was forced but so very needed.

She took a shaky breath. The past hour had been emotionally treacherous. A few moments would pass in which she felt calm, then a wave of dread would follow. "I still can't believe Mr. Cane was the one who murdered our fathers and who—" She couldn't bring herself to speak of what he'd done to her. Not yet. "He came to the house. He acted so friendly and kind. We were all in so much danger and didn't know it. He might have murdered us all."

"I'm not at all sure why he didn't kill Hanson," Miles said. "Cane had to have known Hanson was investigating the murders."

"Mr. Hanson was in London most of the past weeks. Mr. Cane was in Derbyshire, keeping an eye on . . . on me." A chill shuddered through her.

Miles leaned forward and kissed her forehead, then her cheek. "I am so sorry, Elise," he whispered, his cheek gently brushing hers. "I am more sorry than I can even say."

She set her hand against his other cheek, closing her eyes and letting her fear and heartache slip from her thoughts once more. Her Miles. Her kind, dear Miles. She could face anything with him at her side. In time she might learn to reconcile the Mr. Cane she'd thought she knew with the monster he'd proven to be.

"Miles," Beth said from somewhere nearby.

He didn't pull away but raised his head just enough to look at his sister. "Do not chastise me for this, Beth." He barely maintained a civil tone. "At the moment, I couldn't possibly care less what Society deems a proper distance."

"I believe Beth only meant to tell you that Anne is making a valiant attempt to gain your attention once more," Mr. Langley said.

Anne was indeed waving her string-wrapped hands about, watching Elise and Miles expectantly.

"What is it, sweetheart?" Miles asked. He kept his arms around Elise, and she leaned into his embrace.

Anne pulled her hands abruptly apart, the strings sliding from her fingers and tying into a monstrous knot. Something about it set Anne to giggling. She laughed so long and so hard she toppled over onto her side, continuing to laugh as she lay on the blanket.

Miles's chuckle shook his frame, and Elise's with him. He slipped away from her and reached out for Anne, lifting her off the bed. She giggled all the more. Miles spun her about in the air. She squealed with delight.

Despite all she'd passed through, despite the lingering agony in body and mind, Elise felt a growing sense of contentment. Life had dealt her a great many difficult blows, but she was no longer alone.

She flipped back the blanket covering her legs and carefully lowered her feet to the cold floor. She'd spent enough time in bed. The sofa was beckoning.

No sooner had she sat down than Mr. Langley spoke up. "Beth, dear, I have a very pressing desire to walk around the inn yard."

"Why on earth—?"

"Take a walk with me, dear," Mr. Langley insisted.

Beth still looked confused, but she slipped her arm through her husband's.

"Anne should get some fresh air," Mrs. Ash said, setting her knitting aside. She took Anne from Miles's arms. "I'll leave the door a bit ajar," she told Miles.

In a mere moment, only Elise and Miles remained. He sat beside her, threading his fingers through hers. He appeared deeply bothered by something. "Are you really going to Lancashire?"

Through her surprise, Elise managed to nod.

"You cannot, Elise. Lancashire is too far away."

"But I have a home there now."

He reached out and touched her face so softly she almost couldn't feel his touch. "And what of Tafford? Were you not happy there?"

She closed her eyes as he continued his caress. She forced herself to breathe, tried to assemble her quickly scattering thoughts.

"Please don't leave me, Elise," Miles whispered. "I couldn't bear to be separated from you again. You are my dearest and oldest friend. But—"

"Miles, please." Disappointment sliced through her at the sound of his calling her only his friend.

"Could you ever come to care for me, not as childhood playmates but as something more?"

Something more. She looked directly into his beloved brown eyes, hardly daring to believe the implication she sensed in his question.

"I love you." He breathed out the words as if it were almost a relief to utter them. "Not as I did when we were children. Or while we were growing up." He cupped her face with his hands. "How could I ever love anyone but you?" he whispered. "If only you felt the same way."

"If only I felt the same way?" Shock nearly robbed her of breath. "Oh, Miles. I've been worrying over exactly the same thing."

"You have?" He looked utterly surprised.

"I was convinced you couldn't possibly come to see me as anything other than little Elise Furlong who pushed you from a tree and put a rotting fish in your bed and stole all your clothes while you were swimming in the river behind Epsworth."

"*You* were the one who did that?"

"I am certain you deserved it." Her elation was quickly turning to an all-encompassing grin.

"My dearest Elise." Miles kissed her lightly. Then again. Her heart swelled nearly to bursting. His kiss was every bit as intoxicating as she remembered. Her heart pounded, and her thoughts seemed to simply float away. The feel of his arms wrapped securely and lovingly around her filled every sense.

"Stay with me, Elise," Miles said, still so close she could feel his breath on her lips. "Come back to Tafford."

Elise leaned her head against him, listening to the thrumming of his heart. In his arms, she felt safe.

"We will make Beth and Langley return and stay a few more weeks. Langley can stand up with me and Beth with you."

"Is that your way of suggesting we get married?"

"Yes," he answered hesitantly.

"Don't you think you'd best ask me first?"

She felt Miles kiss the top of her head, felt his arms wrap more tightly around her. "Will you marry me, my dearest friend? Stay with me always. I cannot live without you."

Elise sighed.

"And is there an answer?"

She pulled away from him enough to look into his eyes. Elise touched his cheek ever so lightly. "How could I ever love anyone but you?" she whispered.

Chapter Thirty-Nine

Waiting two long months to marry Elise had been sweet, horrible torture.

He looked at her sleeping soundly beside him in his—no, *their*—traveling carriage and shook his head at his own impatience.

Beth had suggested a postponement of the wedding until Elise had had a chance to recover from the ordeal at the inn in Derbyshire. Her advice had proven sound. The physical healing came quickly, but coming to terms with that night and everything connected to it had not been easy for Elise. She was not yet entirely whole, but she was better.

Much of her fear and wariness had given way to contentment. She was more open, no longer hiding her emotions. She rode in closed carriages with only the slightest moments of uneasiness. She laughed and smiled. And she had taken London by storm. Beth, along with Miles's cousin, Lady Marion Jonquil, had insisted that Elise and Miles make their bows to Society. Elise's beauty and dignity coupled with the spark of life that had reentered her eyes and manners were irresistible.

In the course of only six weeks, Miles had made his first appearance at Lords, had been presented at Court, and had been to more routs, dinners, musicales, and balls than he could even remember. And he'd spent his days with Anne.

His and Elise's betrothal ball—could it really have been only a week ago?—had been well attended and, considering he was not generally one to enjoy a ball, had been a surprisingly enjoyable evening. But their wedding, held that very morning, had far eclipsed it. Mama Jones had even come up to Town, though she'd once sworn she'd never travel again. She and Anne were to return to Tafford the next morning.

Beside him, Elise shifted and took a deep breath. He looked down just as she opened her eyes.

She smiled at him sleepily. "Have I been sleeping long?" She sat up a little more.

"For nearly an hour, my dear." He smiled as he fingered the imprint his coat had left on her face. She looked adorably rumpled.

"Do you know, I very much like it when you call me that." Her smile came much easier now than it had in the first weeks she'd spent at Tafford. "'My dear' is certainly much nicer to hear than 'Little John,' which you used to call me with alarming regularity."

"You would have preferred 'Maid Marion,' then?"

"In all honesty, no." Elise tipped her head to one side, looking at him as if she were truly pondering it. "She spent a great deal of time waiting for you to come around. I, however, spent all that time *with* you, which is where I preferred to be."

"And do you still?" Miles ran a finger along the line of her jaw.

"Prefer being with you?"

Miles nodded.

Elise pulled her legs up under her, kneeling on the seat of the carriage, and pressed a kiss to his cheek. "Mmm-hmm," she answered as she kissed him again, on his chin this time.

That was more than any gentleman could be expected to ignore. Miles wrapped his arms around her. Elise giggled when he nuzzled her neck.

"You are not supposed to find this funny, Elise."

"I was only thinking of the looks that would have been on our fathers' faces if they had been here today," she said. "Their two mischief-making children marrying each other. They would have been shocked, I daresay."

"They would have been the least surprised of anyone," Miles insisted. "And they would have been nearly as happy as we are."

"You are presuming, then, that I am happy," she said saucily.

"I am presuming, my dear, that you are *overjoyed*," Miles corrected, unable to resist teasing her in return.

Then Elise closed her eyes, smiling the way she always had during their childhood when she'd been particularly content. "Perfectly overjoyed," she whispered. She leaned forward, resting her forehead against his collarbone, and yawned rather daintily.

"And perfectly exhausted as well," Miles said.

"Mmm-hmm," was the soft answer.

"Well." He helped her move into a more comfortable position, snuggled close to him. "We have several hours of travel ahead of us. Plenty of time for rest."

She said nothing more. Miles assumed she'd fallen asleep. He let his gaze wander to the window and the passing scenery, though he barely registered what he saw. Countless memories swam through his mind. It never ceased to amaze him how interwoven Elise was in all the major events, the minor occurrences, and the quiet, unnoted moments of his past. Now she would forever be a part of his life. He was indeed the most fortunate of men.

More than four years ago, she'd disappeared from his life, and he'd all but given up hope of ever finding her again. Part of him had been lost along with her. But he was whole again. His Elise had returned—not just physically but in every sense. They laughed together once more, smiled, loved each other.

Elise shifted beside him. He felt her hand gently turn his face toward her.

"Yes, my dear?"

She did not answer but lightly kissed him on the mouth. "I love you, Miles," she said against his lips.

"And I love you, my dearest Elise," he answered, kissing each corner of her mouth in turn. The gesture made her blush, as always. So he kissed the tip of her dainty nose, then the lid of each beloved eye before returning to her lips.

Knowing they had their entire lives ahead of them for such pleasant endeavors and remembering how very tired Elise truly was, Miles settled her back into the circle of his arms, her head resting softly against his shoulder. She slept that way as they traveled, so perfectly at home in his embrace.

She'd slept at his side countless times when as small children they were so inseparable. And she fit there still, as if his arms, his very life, were made just for her. For Elise.

About the Author

Sarah M. Eden read her first Jane Austen novel in elementary school and has been an Austen addict ever since. Fascinated by the English Regency era, Eden became a regular in that section of the reference department at her local library, where she painstakingly researched this extraordinary chapter in history. Eden is an award-winning author of short stories and was a Whitney Award finalist for her novels *Seeking Persephone, Courting Miss Lancaster*, and *Longing for Home*. Visit her at www.sarahmeden.com.